A MARJORIE McCLELLAND MYSTERY

GHOST OF A CHANCE

AMY PATRICIA MEADE

WHEELER PUBLISHING
An imprint of Thomson Gale, a part of The Thomson Corporation

THOMSON
—— ✶ ——™
GALE

Detroit • New York • San Francisco • New Haven, Conn. • Waterville, Maine • London

FIC
MEA

LIBRARY OF CONGRESS CATALOGING-IN-PUBLICATION DATA

Meade, Amy Patricia, 1972–
    Ghost of a chance / by Amy Patricia Meade.
      p. cm. — (A Marjorie McClelland mystery) (Wheeler Publishing large print cozy mystery)
      ISBN-13: 978-1-59722-670-7 (lg. print : alk. paper)
      ISBN-10: 1-59722-670-X (lg. print : alk. paper)
      1. Women novelists — Connecticut — Fiction. 2. Large type books. I. Title.
PS3613.E128G48 2008
813'.6—dc22   2007039306

Published in 2008 by arrangement with Midnight Ink, an imprint of Llewellyn Publications, Woodbury, MN 55125–2989, U.S.A.

Printed in the United States of America on permanent paper
10 9 8 7 6 5 4 3 2 1

A1200507134

NON SUM QUALIS ERAM
BONAE SUB REGNO CYNARAE

Last night, ah, yesternight, betwixt her lips
　　and mine
There fell thy shadow, Cynara! Thy breath
　　was shed
Upon my soul between the kisses and the
　　wine;
And I was desolate and sick of an old pas-
　　sion.
Yea, I was desolate and bowed my head:
I have been faithful to thee, Cynara! In my
　　fashion.

All night upon mine heart I felt her warm
　　heart beat,
Night-long within mine arms in love and
　　sleep she lay;
Surely the kisses of her bought red mouth
　　were sweet;
But I was desolate and sick of an old pas-
　　sion,

When I awoke and found the dawn was
    gray:
I have been faithful to thee, Cynara! In my
    fashion.

I have forgot much, Cynara! Gone with the
    wind,
Flung roses, roses riotously with the
    throng,
Dancing to put thy pale, lost lilies out of
    mind;
But, I was desolate and sick of an old pas-
    sion,
Yea, all the time, because the dance was
    long:
I have been faithful to thee, Cynara! In my
    fashion.

I cried for madder music and for stronger
    wine,
But when the feast is finished and the
    lamps expire,
Then falls thy shadow, Cynara, the night
    is thine;
And I am desolate and sick of an old pas-
    sion,
Yea, hungry for the lips of my desire:
I have been faithful to thee, Cynara, in my
    fashion.

                  — Ernest Dowson

ONE

"A knife? Why would you use a knife to kill someone? I'd think you'd be a bit smarter than that."

Marjorie McClelland folded her arms across her chest and sighed noisily. For a man who sold books as his livelihood, Walter Schutt had the foresight and creativity of a Brussels sprout. "Why not? It's something different. A completely spontaneous murder without a trace of premeditation. It will throw my readers completely off the track."

Mr. Schutt pursed his wizened lips in disapproval. "Too messy. I like the last one you wrote. Murder made to look like suicide. Now that was clever."

"If, by my 'last one,' you mean the Van Allen case —" Marjorie began.

He continued, unheeding. "Except that part about the girl in the dumbwaiter. That was a bit hard to swallow."

"The girl *was* in the dumbwaiter, Mr. Schutt. It actually happened — I didn't make it up. The Van Allen murder occurred right here, in Ridgebury! Don't you remember?"

"Of course I remember! I'm not gone in the head, missy. I was thinking of your audience. When you finally turn it into a true crime novel, I don't think they're going to buy that whole dumbwaiter idea."

Marjorie contemplated leaving Schutt's Book Nook, but soon remembered her reason for being there. *Medieval English Daggers and You — An Introduction,* a special order, had finally arrived after weeks of anticipation and was now clutched in the storekeeper's knobby fingers.

Marjorie fixed her gaze on the long-awaited tome. It was a widely known fact that although Mr. Schutt's primary occupation was town bookseller, his primary source of income emanated from the change, merchandise, purses, and wallets that dazed and beleaguered customers left behind in their haste to escape the elderly man's infamous tongue lashings. It was even rumored — although never proven — that Schutt had once sold a mother back her own baby after she, in a highly flustered state, had left the child sleeping in his carriage outside the shop door.

"Still, it was a halfway decent story," he wheezed on, mindless of his audience's silence. "You should try to write more of those."

Marjorie offered a silent appeal to the heavens. *One lightning bolt. One lightning bolt right here in the bookstore. No injuries. No fire. Just enough of a jolt to knock that book out of his hand . . .*

"Although I don't imagine you have a ghost of a chance of encountering a murder again. Not in a town like ours. Not with a Depression going on."

"Why not?" she asked, glad for the change of subject.

"Simple. Folks around here don't have anything worth killing for."

"Mr. Ashcroft does." Marjorie felt the color rise in her cheeks as she spoke the name.

"True," he allowed, "but I can't imagine anyone killing him. He's been courting our Sharon for a few months now and he's a likeable sort. For a foreigner."

Foreigner. The word conveyed the notion of a short, swarthy greenhorn rather than the tall, handsome, and elegantly English figure of Creighton Ashcroft. What the man saw in the Schutts' pudgy, arrogant, and

9

socially inept daughter defied explanation.

"Still, there are crimes of passion," Marjorie argued.

"Passion. Bah! I don't believe in it."

She thought of the large, intimidating, and decidedly masculine form of Mrs. Schutt. "No, you probably don't."

"That's why your books don't sell as well as they could, Miss McClelland. The average person doesn't lose their head so easily. They may lose their patience with people, but they don't envision murdering them. And your victims! Why, your victims are always these misanthropic curmudgeons with absolutely no redeeming social value. People like that simply don't exist in real life."

Marjorie narrowed her eyes and glared. "I wouldn't say that."

"No," the bookseller shook his graying head, undeterred. "I think it's high time you hung up your typewriter —"

"How does one 'hang up' a typewriter?" she interjected.

"Get down to the business of living. Settle down with that detective of yours —"

"He did ask me to marry him last night."

"And start a family. You're getting too old for this —"

"It's this shop. I age ten years every time I

walk in the door."

Schutt raised the reference book about daggers and waved it. "Wasting your time with murder and poisons and knives. What way is that to live your life? You should know better!"

"Yes, I should purchase books via mail order."

"But you'll do what you want to do. I suppose you're even running the kissing booth at the fair today —"

"Law of supply and demand dictates I should, but I'm not."

"Well, I'm not going to waste my breath. You can't argue with an idiot!"

"That's precisely why *I* wasn't arguing." Marjorie reached over the counter, snatched the book from his hand, and happily waltzed out the door.

Two

Creighton Ashcroft was a man on a mission. He strode across the freshly mowed grass of the fairgrounds, all the while anxiously fingering the dollar bill in his jacket pocket. It was a lovely late morning in June, 1935. An ideal day for the First Presbyterian Church of Ridgebury to hold its annual carnival and, Creighton decided in a rare moment of bravado, the perfect day to make his move on Marjorie McClelland.

Walking purposefully past the Ferris wheel, he made his way to a booth, above which hung the sign: *Kisses. 5 cents.* There, behind the counter, he spotted the young blonde woman counting money into a till, her back turned to him. "Good morning," he chimed. "I hope you gave your lips a rest last night because you're going to need all your strength. I've brought with me a one-dollar bill, which, if my arithmetic is correct, entitles me to twenty kisses. *Twenty.* So," he leaned his elbows on the counter and pursed his lips together, "as you Americans say, pucker up."

The girl turned around to reveal an unfamiliar face. Creighton nearly jumped out of his skin. "Who are you?"

"Susie. I'm in charge of the kissing booth."

"You're in charge of the kissing booth? What happened to Marjorie?"

"She backed out at the last minute."

"Why? Is she ill?"

"How am I supposed to know? Who do I look like, Walter Winchell?" Her eyes widened in recognition. "Say, you're that fella who lives outside of town. That big place — what's its name?"

"Kensington House."

"Yeah, you and Marjorie were in that trouble there a few months back. You're that rich guy."

Creighton had always hated that description. He ran a nervous hand through his chestnut hair. "Yes, I suppose I am."

"I never kissed a rich guy before. Are you ready for your twenty kisses?"

"No, thank you. Not that you aren't perfectly lovely," he quickly added. "But my main purpose for coming here was to see Marjorie and since . . ." his voice trailed off.

13

"Yeah, I know, I'm not Marjorie. Tell me," she challenged, "what does she have that I don't?"

"Well, nothing, I suppose. It's just —"

"You're darn right," she averred. "I'm just as good a kisser as she is. Probably better."

"I don't doubt that you are, but —" he blustered.

"Why, I bet if you were to close your eyes, you'd never know the difference."

"I don't know about that. I —" Before he could protest, Susie grabbed him by the arm, yanked him across the counter, and planted her lips on his.

Despite his initial reluctance and surprise, the experience was not entirely unpleasant. Susie was, as claimed, a competent kisser. It would be a shame not to enjoy her God-given talent to the fullest. After all, if she wanted to kiss him, who was he to deny her? He closed his eyes and joined in, but his pleasure was soon interrupted by the sound of someone clearing her throat.

He pulled away from Susie to find a radiant young woman in a gauzy, pale green dress and a floppy, wide-brimmed hat. "Marjorie!"

"Good morning, Creighton." Her emerald eyes were twinkling in amusement.

Her beau, police detective Robert Jameson, appeared beside her and placed a protective arm around her shoulders. "Hi, Creighton." He gestured to his own mouth with a tanned finger. "You have some, um, stuff right there."

Creighton pulled his handkerchief from his jacket pocket and wiped the lipstick from his face.

"I'd introduce you to Susie," Marjorie stated with a grin, "but I can see you already know each other . . . in a fairly Biblical sense."

"Why not? This is a church fair, isn't it?" He pushed the dollar bill toward Susie and whispered, aside, to keep the change. "Actually, I was looking for you, Marjorie, and figured, while I was here, I might as well do my share to help a worthy cause."

"You were looking for me?" Marjorie repeated skeptically.

"I came by to say hello, but when I saw you weren't here I was concerned you might be ill."

"I see," she teased, "so you decided to examine Susie to make sure she wasn't coming down with something as well."

"She kissed me!"

"You don't have to make excuses with us, Creighton," Jameson said. "We won't tell Sharon."

Marjorie nodded in agreement. "Our lips are sealed. Although the next time you have the urge to 'sacrifice' yourself to a worthy cause, I suggest you do it in private. If Sharon or her parents had caught you, it would have been the Great War all over again."

Creighton sighed in exasperation; he didn't give a hang about the Schutts. The only reason he courted Sharon was to make Marjorie jealous: a plan that had, thus far, fallen short of its mark. "Thank you. I'll keep it in mind. So, why did you rescind your offer to run the kissing booth? I thought you did it every year."

"I do, but Robert and I discussed it and we concluded I should give this year a miss." She grabbed her escort's arm and beamed at him.

"Robert and I discussed it?" Why was she permitting that presumptuous little toady to influence her decisions? "Why in heaven's name not?" the Englishman demanded as he glared at the detective.

Jameson flashed a luminously white smile. Everything about the man's appearance was irritatingly perfect. He was the Hartford County Police's answer to Errol Flynn — minus the comedic wit.

"Because," Marjorie replied between

16

giggles, "we didn't think it was a suitable job for the future wife of a policeman."

"Future wife?" Creighton managed to utter.

"That's right," Jameson affirmed. "Marjorie and I are engaged to be married."

Marjorie held out her left hand to display a golden ring into which had been set a diamond slightly larger than a chip. "Isn't it beautiful? Robert gave it to me last night. It was all very romantic. He even got down on one knee when he proposed."

Creighton struggled to find the appropriate response to this bit of news, but he could find none. His thoughts were concentrated only on the injustice of the situation. Surely, this wasn't happening. Today he was to tell Marjorie he loved her. It was to be his day, not Jameson's. His day! There was a sudden pain in his abdomen, as though someone had just kicked him in the stomach, and it was becoming increasingly difficult to breathe.

Marjorie stared at him worriedly. "You look funny, Creighton. Are you feeling all right?"

Creighton wanted to answer, but he was unsure as to whether he possessed enough strength. Just in time, he felt a hand on his arm. It belonged to Mrs. Emily Patterson, owner of the boarding house where Creighton had stayed when he first arrived in Ridgebury. "He's fine," the elderly woman assured Marjorie. "He's just surprised. As I was."

"You know?" Creighton asked.

"They told me last night," she stated, her hand still on his arm.

"We would have told you last night, too, Creighton," Marjorie explained, "but by the time we left Mrs. Patterson's it was late."

"I understand."

Marjorie looked at him hopefully. "Well, aren't you going to congratulate us?"

"Of course, how stupid of me. Congratulations, Jameson." He shook the policeman's hand and then stepped forward to kiss the young woman softly on the cheek. "Congratulations, Marjorie."

"Thank you," the couple responded in unison.

"When's the happy day?" the Englishman asked, though he was sure he'd rather not know the answer.

"As soon as possible," Marjorie replied. "Perhaps even during the next few weeks."

"What's the rush? Afraid someone might snatch her away from you, Jameson?" Creighton gibed.

The detective flashed a knowing smile at

his competition. "Could you blame me?"

"No," Creighton answered in earnest, "but I don't think Marjorie should be forced into settling for a slapdash wedding just because her fiancé is intimidated by the possibility of competition."

"I'm not being forced into anything," Marjorie spoke up. "It was my idea to get married quickly."

"Your idea?" Mrs. Patterson repeated in disbelief. "Marjorie, dear, I'm amazed. You're usually so cautious."

"What is there to be cautious about?" Marjorie scoffed. "When something is right, you just know it. There's no need for hesitation." She smiled lovingly at Jameson, who absently returned the smile and then glanced at his watch.

"As much as I'd like to hang around here," he excused himself, "I'd better get going. I have to be at headquarters in fifteen minutes."

"Oh, do you have to go?" Marjorie asked disappointedly.

"You know I'm on duty this weekend," he admonished gently. "But I'll see you tonight."

"I'd rather see you today," she added peevishly. "We could spend the day together, here at the fair."

"Now, you know that can't happen. I'm a policeman; it's my duty to protect this town. I just can't call in and say I won't be reporting for duty because my girlfriend wants me to take her to the church fair."

"Fiancée," Creighton corrected. "And you might be able to get away with it. All of Ridgebury is bound to turn out for the fair today. If something were to occur, it would take place here, not on the other side of town."

"He's right," Marjorie agreed. "The police station is miles from here. If something did go wrong, it would be several minutes before you'd be able to arrive on the scene." She nodded in the direction of her abettor. "Thank you, Creighton."

Jameson shot him a withering glance. "Yes, thank you, Creighton."

He tipped his hat in response. "Glad to be of service."

Mrs. Patterson spoke up. "Well, I think I'd best be running along. I'm signed up to watch one of the bazaar tables." Like the mother of a wayward boy, she took Creighton by the arm. "Come along, Creighton. I think you've stirred up enough trouble for today. It's time we leave these lovebirds alone. Good day, Detective Jameson. Marjorie, I'll see you later."

Creighton bid his adieus and followed Mrs. Patterson across the fairgrounds to a table laden with doilies, lace-trimmed handkerchiefs, and other crocheted items. "So," she began as she reached into a bag beneath the table and brought up a large pocketed apron, "what are you going to do about this?"

"Do about what?"

"Marjorie and the detective's engagement."

"Do? There's nothing to do."

She tied the apron strings about her waist. "Yes there is! Stop the wedding. Break up the engagement."

"But Jameson . . . the fellow's already bought the ring."

Mrs. Patterson waved a reproving finger. "That's an engagement ring, not a wedding ring. There's a big difference between the two."

"Granted. But it still signifies Marjorie's acceptance of Jameson's marriage proposal."

"Are you telling me that you've never heard of a couple breaking off an engagement? Even after the ring has been bought?" She picked up a collapsible lawn chair from its place beside the table and dragged it behind the display area.

21

"Of course, I have," he replied, gallantly snatching the chair from the woman's tremorous hands and propping it open. "However, in every instance, the breakup occurred because one of the parties involved was dissatisfied with the other. As much as I hate to admit it, neither Marjorie nor Jameson appears to be dissatisfied."

"Thank you." Mrs. Patterson lowered herself into the seat. "Oh, I think Marjorie has her doubts."

"She didn't strike me as having cold feet. In fact she seemed rather keen on the whole idea."

"Hmmm," she sounded in agreement. "Too keen, if you ask me. Don't forget, I've known her since she was a little girl. I helped to raise her when her mother left. I know she wants a nice big wedding just like most girls her age. But this — well, it's as though she wants to get the whole thing over with before she changes her mind. That's where you come in, Creighton. It's up to you to change her mind."

"And when I'm through with that, what's my next trick? Changing water into wine?"

"Oh, how you exaggerate." Mrs. Patterson waved her hand dismissively. "I'm not asking you to perform a miracle. Simply tell Marjorie that you're in love with her."

Creighton tugged uncomfortably at his shirt collar. "In love with her? Where did you get the idea that I'm in love with her?"

"Creighton Ashcroft!" she scolded. "You may only have lived here for three months, but I know you almost as well as I know Marjorie. Are you going to stand there and tell me that you don't have feelings for Marjorie?"

"Naturally, I care about her," he allowed. "She's a dear friend."

"Ha! 'Dear friend', my foot. Why, the first day you saw her, you thought she was a fine piece of crackling."

He burst out laughing. "Mrs. Patterson! Where did you hear that expression?"

"I get around, you know," she replied smugly. "I may be old, but I'm not dead."

Creighton caught his breath and relented. "Fine, I love her. Alright? There, I've said it: I love her. I care for her more than I've ever cared for anyone. That's why I'm not going to undermine her happiness. And if marrying Robert Jameson is what makes her happy, then so be it."

"Very noble. But what about you?"

"What about me?"

"If Marjorie and Detective Jameson marry, what will you do with the rest of your life? Lock yourself in that mansion of yours

23

and wither away, a lonely, bitter old man?"

He chuckled at her vivid description. "Mrs. Patterson, have you been reading Dickens again?"

She glared at him. "Laugh all you want, but it's a question you need to ask yourself. What will you do if Marjorie goes through with the wedding?"

Creighton breathed heavily. He didn't want to think of life if Marjorie married Jameson; so much of his future rested upon the belief that she would someday learn to love him. This morning's news had shattered that belief. "I'll probably get married . . . someday."

"To whom? Sharon?"

The Englishman gazed halfway across the fairgrounds to the bake-off booth, where the rotund figure of Sharon Schutt stood sampling, with gusto, a wedge of blueberry pie. She looked up from her plate and, upon seeing Creighton, smiled broadly, revealing a row of blue-stained teeth. Creighton gave a tepid wave and quickly swiveled back in Mrs. Patterson's direction. "Good heavens, I hope not."

"I wouldn't write off the idea so quickly," Mrs. Patterson warned. "Stranger things have happened."

She was right; truth was, very often,

24

stranger than fiction. Despite his objections, it was possible that he might wind up marrying Sharon Schutt, if only as a means to assuage his loneliness. Creighton shuddered as he envisioned awakening every morning to the sight of Sharon's pig-like countenance. "All right," he agreed hastily. "I'll do it. I'll talk to Marjorie."

"Good," the elderly woman proclaimed as she gazed across the fairgrounds. "You're just in time too. She's heading this way."

"What! You want me to talk to her now? Here?" he nearly shrieked.

"There's no time to waste, Creighton. We don't know when you'll get another opportunity." She rose from her post and moved toward a neighboring table.

The Englishman blocked her advance. "Where do you think you're going?"

"To talk to some of the other ladies from the parish."

"Now?"

"My dear child, this is a delicate matter between you and Marjorie. It's not my place to interfere." She pushed her way past him.

"Yes, well, you do have a point. . . . What!" he shouted after her. " 'You shouldn't interfere?' It's a bit late for that!"

"What's wrong?" asked Marjorie as she approached the shouting Englishman.

25

"Oh, nothing," Creighton replied in disgust.

"Where's Mrs. Patterson off to?"

"Joining the other hens for a little gossip."

"Hmm, Mrs. Patterson's with her friends, Robert's on his way to headquarters, and Sharon is quite engrossed with her role as judge at the baking competition. I guess that leaves you and me. What would you like to do first? Take a ride on the Ferris wheel, try our hands at some of the games?" She arched a sly eyebrow. "Or maybe you'd like to visit the kissing booth again? I hear Susie's been asking for you."

"Actually, I'd like to talk to you first, if you don't mind," he proposed.

"Sure," she amiably agreed. "What about?"

"Your wedding."

"What about the wedding?"

Creighton bit his lip and stared blankly at the young woman all the while berating his own cowardice. *Don't pick at it, man. Rip the bandage off.* "Marjorie, I don't think you should marry Jameson."

Marjorie was eerily calm. "Oh? Why not?"

"Because it's too soon," he sputtered. "You've only been seeing Jameson for three months. How much could you possibly know about the man?"

"Plenty." Her eyes narrowed in defiance.

"Really? Let's test this." He folded his arms across his chest and fired his first question with all the grace of an army drill sergeant. "When's his birthday?"

Marjorie mimicked Creighton's arm fold and thrust her nose in the air. "July 31."

"What year?"

"1899."

"What's his middle name?" he volleyed.

"He doesn't have one. His parents couldn't think of anything they liked."

"Ah, creativity runs in the family I see. What's his favorite color?"

"Brown."

"Brown?" He shook his head. "Sounds like an exciting fellow."

Marjorie dropped her arms to her sides and heaved a loud sigh. "Will you please get on with this silly experiment of yours?"

"Absolutely. Just one question left," he smirked, confident that his last question would be the stumper. "What was Jameson's boyhood nickname?"

"Boyhood nickname!" she shouted in annoyance. "What does that have to do with anything?"

Aha! Point! "Just answer the question, please."

Marjorie rolled her eyes and then finally

capitulated. "I guess Rob or Bob or Robbie or Bobby, or something like that."

"No, no, no," he corrected. "I mean a descriptive nickname. My chums and I all had them. If someone was intelligent, we called him 'Professor' or 'Egghead' or maybe even 'Sponge'. If he was tough, it was 'Butch', 'Spike', 'Killer'. That sort of thing."

"I don't know! But what does it matter, anyway?"

"It matters quite a bit. You can tell a lot about a man from the nickname his friends choose for him."

She placed a hand on a well-curved hip. "Is that so? And what, pray tell, was your nickname?"

Creighton cleared his throat with a sideways glance. "That's of little relevance to our conversation."

"I see. It must not have been very flattering."

He shot her a sour look.

"That's okay, Creighton. You don't have to tell me. I'll try to guess. Let's see . . . you were younger then, so you weren't quite as tall as you are now, but you were probably just as irritating, with the same uncanny knack for showing up in the wrong place at the wrong time. Hmm." She snapped her fingers. "I've got it. They called you 'Wart.' "

"Very funny. You're just sore because I proved you don't know Jameson as well as you claim," he taunted.

"I'm not sore. And just because I don't know Robert's boyhood nickname, doesn't mean I don't know him well enough to marry him." Her face saddened. "If anything, I'm disappointed. I expected Mrs. Patterson to have some reservations as to my marriage, but I thought you, at least, would be happy for me. What's the matter? Don't you like Robert?"

Aside from the fact that he was nauseatingly good looking, lacked a viable sense of humor, and was set to marry Marjorie, Creighton harbored no feelings of ill will against the detective. "He's okay," he shrugged.

"Then what's the problem? Why don't you want us to get married?"

He drew a deep breath. This was it. It was now or never. Taking her by the shoulders, he declared, "Because I love you."

Marjorie stared at him, open-mouthed and flabbergasted. Encouraged by her reaction, he was about to repeat the sentiment, but soon realized that the look of excitement upon her face was not due to his shocking revelation, but to the piercing scream that had drowned out his every word.

Marjorie stabbed at the air with her index finger and motioned violently toward the opposite end of the fairgrounds. "Over there, by the Ferris wheel. It's Mrs. Schutt. Come on!" She grabbed her companion by the hand and yanked his arm in the direction of the disturbance.

Creighton dug his heels into the ground and stood firm. Louise Schutt was the last person he wanted to see. "I'm sure it's nothing. Sharon probably has a hangnail or something."

"Oh come on. Mrs. Schutt doesn't scream like that over nothing — especially in public. You know how she is — trying to be a 'lady' at all times." With a spirited gleam in her eye, she gave his arm another tug. "Let's find out what it is."

Creighton recognized that look. It was the one that had drawn him to her — that look of curiosity and sheer determination. With a slight grin, he unlocked his knees and allowed her to drag him across the fairgrounds and through the throng of onlookers. They arrived at the front of the crowd to find a distraught Mrs. Schutt, a man's lifeless body lying face-up at her feet.

Marjorie gasped. "What happened?"

"I — I don't know," Mrs. Schutt cried. "I opened the door and he fell out of the car. I — I think he's dead."

Creighton took the gold calling card case from his jacket pocket, knelt down, and held it before the man's open mouth. The case retained its bright yellow gleam. "He's dead."

The words sent a shockwave through the crowd.

"Someone call Detective Jameson," Marjorie ordered.

"I'll go," came a voice from the crowd. It was the fifteen-year-old soda jerk at the local drugstore. "I'll go, Miss McClelland!"

"Thank you, Freddie," Marjorie shouted as the boy was swallowed up by the huddled mass of bodies.

He was replaced by the spherical figure of Sharon Schutt. "Mother!" she wailed as she waddled to her mother's side. "Mother, how horrible!"

The Schutt women embraced in a fit of tears as the tiny, bird-like figure of Mrs. Patterson appeared from amid the sea of worried onlookers. Like the fairgoers surrounding her, she wore an expression of concern. Her concern, however, was of a different nature. Waving her hands in the air, she flagged Creighton's attention and silently mouthed the question: "Did you tell her?"

Meanwhile, Sharon, through muffled sobs, sought to learn of her mother's condition. "You're not hurt, are you, Mother?"

The Englishman shook his head in response to Mrs. Patterson as the elder Schutt replied in a tone of feigned weakness: "No, dear, I wasn't hurt."

"Darn it!" The frail voice of Emily Patterson, oblivious to all but Creighton's failure, rose above the mutterings of the crowd,

The onlookers stared. Marjorie bit her lip to stifle her giggles.

"Oh!" Mrs. Patterson swiftly drew her hand to her mouth. "Oh! I am sorry! I didn't mean . . ." Flustered, she cleared her throat and called to Creighton. "Mr. Ashcroft, may I have a word with you?"

"Certainly." Under the careful scrutiny of the fairgoers, he joined the elderly woman near the now-vacated kissing booth.

"What's Plan B?" she asked.

"Plan B? Simple, there isn't any."

"What do you mean 'There isn't any' Creighton? There's no time to lose. Detective Jameson will be here any minute."

"So?"

"So, you must tell her now."

"Mrs. Patterson," he laughed, "Marjorie's

not going to listen to me now, not while there's a dead body sprawled at her feet. You know how she gets when there's a potential mystery afoot." He gestured at Marjorie, who was examining the ground surrounding the fallen man. "Just look at her. She's gone completely googly-eyed."

"Well, you'd better come up with something. If not today, then soon."

"I will. I'm formulating a scheme as we speak." There was no plan, but it would keep Mrs. Patterson at bay for the moment.

"I knew you'd come up with something. After all, this should be easy for someone of your intelligence."

"Oh yes, very easy." He added, sotto voce: "Like saddling a wild horse."

THREE

Marjorie watched intently as two uniformed interns lifted the corpse from the ground in front of the Ferris wheel and onto a stretcher.

Why she found herself fascinated by such grisly matters, she could not explain. She only knew that her love of the macabre, like her ardor for the English language, was a passion she could never quell. Nothing else set her pulse racing like the thought of a new mystery or the lyricism of a well-turned phrase. Not even Detective Robert Jameson.

She cared for Robert, to be certain, but beyond his police badge and matinee idol looks, he was a dull, ordinary fellow. Not that ordinary was necessarily bad, she reminded her ever-practical self. Marriage, after all, was supposed to be reliable and stable, not passionate and exciting.

Even if she were sometimes left with the

feeling that there should be more to their relationship, that feeling was still a sight better than the complete exasperation she felt when with Creighton Ashcroft. Despite his wit and charm, Creighton could be quite maddening. Initiating verbal tug-of-wars, complimenting her appearance one moment and teasing her the next, proofreading her manuscripts and *actually* making corrections, it was as if he presumed to know more about her than she did herself. But what was worse was that he very often did.

Yes, Jameson was the right choice for her. No surprises, no staying awake at night wondering what he was thinking about, no being on guard that your next word may be used against you. Just security, stability, and quiet time in which to write.

Thwap! The interns snapped the sheet open before lowering it over the body.

"Heart attack, most likely," the coroner declared, "but I still have to do the full workup."

"If you could look into it as soon as possible, Dr. Heller, I'd appreciate it," Jameson appealed.

Heller nodded his reply and signaled to the interns to load the corpse into the rear of the ambulance.

Heart attack? Marjorie reached into her

purse and fingered the discovery she had made while waiting for the police to arrive. "Robert," she spoke up, "I want to show you something."

"Not now, dear." He strode off in the direction of his right-hand man, Officer Patrick Noonan.

"But, it's important," she cried, trailing after him.

"So is this." Coming upon Noonan he asked, "What did you find out?"

The officer held up a manila envelope containing the man's personal effects. "Driver's license lists him as Alfred Nussbaum, age forty-six, from Boston."

"Boston, huh? What was he doing here?"

"Dunno, but I found a key in his pocket for a room at the Hideaway Hotel in Hartford."

"Anything else of interest?"

Noonan shook his head. "I haven't gone through everything, but so far just the usual. What does the doctor say?"

"Heart attack. Do me a favor. Cordon off the area and tell Reverend Price that if Dr. Heller's report is clean, he should be able to have the Ferris wheel up and running again tomorrow."

Noonan departed and Jameson hurried away to attend to his next item of business.

36

Marjorie tried in vain to get her fiancé's attention. "Robert. Robert!"

He ignored her and continued on his path toward Mrs. Schutt, who was precariously perched upon a short wooden milking stool. Sharon, juggling a cup of water, an embroidered pink handkerchief, and a dimestore Chinese fan, stood in attendance.

"Mrs. Schutt," Jameson addressed her with a slight bow. "You've had a bad shock. How are you feeling?"

"Not well, Detective. Not well at all." She closed her eyes and placed the back of a large hand against her forehead in a mock swoon. With the other hand, she gestured to her daughter.

Sharon obediently set the black, accordion-pleated fan in motion.

"Sorry to hear it. I hope I haven't kept you waiting long."

She recovered from her torpor long enough to glare at him. "As a matter of fact, you have."

Jameson cleared his throat. "Then, I'll be brief. If it's not too much for you, Mrs. Schutt, I'd like you to tell me what happened."

"By all means, Detective. I had just submitted my famous strawberry pie in the baking contest when Reverend Price informed me that the man who was scheduled to operate the Ferris wheel called to say he couldn't make it and would I be willing to take his place. Well, I say that if people have no intention of helping out, they shouldn't volunteer. It put us in a terrible position. Simply terrible. I told Reverend Price that I didn't know much about machinery and that I thought running a Ferris wheel was more of a man's job, but if the church needed me, I would be more than happy to oblige. That's the kind of person I am, Detective. I'm always there when people need me."

"That's very good of you, Mrs. Schutt."

"Yes it is. Others wouldn't have done, so mind you, but I did. The Reverend showed me how to work all the switches and how to lock and unlock the compartment doors so the passengers could get on and off. It was all very straightforward — but then, I always have been very clever — so I agreed to run the wheel until he could find a gentleman replacement. Everything was going quite smoothly. I gave three rides in succession without so much as a hiccup, and then, it happened. Oh! I can't bear to think of it!" She covered her eyes with one hand; the other reached up to take the cup of water from Sharon.

"Please, Mrs. Schutt," Jameson urged, "do try."

"If you insist, but it is so very difficult." Louise swallowed a sip of water and followed it with a dramatically deep breath. "When the fourth ride was over, I began to unload the passengers. No one was waiting to board, so it wasn't necessary to load any new passengers."

"That man," she gestured toward where the body had lain minutes earlier, "was the last passenger to be let off. I lowered the car to ground level and unlatched the door lock. I told him it was safe for him to disembark, but there he sat, staring blankly into space. I thought perhaps he had a hearing problem, so I repeated my words, only louder. Again, he did nothing, so I opened the door myself, and he came tumbling out of the car, landing on the ground exactly as you found him. It was all quite distressing." She motioned to Sharon to accelerate her fanning.

"I understand," the detective sympathized. "Just one more question and I'll be through."

"Yes, yes," the woman snapped impatiently. Sharon passed her the pink handkerchief, which she used to daub her wide, creased forehead.

"Did Mr. Nussbaum appear to be ill when he boarded the Ferris wheel?"

Mrs. Schutt stopped daubing. "Ill? No. I might have described him as agitated, but I suppose if one were to fall ill in a strange place, one would become anxious, wouldn't one?"

Jameson smiled. "Yes, I suppose they would. Thanks, Mrs. Schutt. That'll be all." He tipped his hat at Sharon. "So long."

The younger Schutt woman blushed bright red and giggled idiotically.

The detective gave her a curious look before turning on one heel to leave. Marjorie stood in his path: "Robert, I must speak to you."

"Not now, Marjorie."

"Please." She opened her eyes wide and tried on the most bewitching expression she could muster.

"Sweetheart, I'm very busy right now. I have to get back to the station and start on that paperwork. We can talk when my shift ends."

"But it can't wait that long."

"Then talk to Mrs. Patterson or Creighton. Whatever the problem is, I'm sure one of them can help you." He gave her a chaste kiss on the forehead and took off across the fairgrounds.

Marjorie, frowning, stared after him. *Discuss it with Mrs. Patterson or Creighton. Creighton . . .*

She raised an eyebrow as an idea took shape in her head. *Yes, talk to Creighton. That's exactly what I'll do!*

FOUR

Creighton was still standing near the kissing booth with Mrs. Patterson when he spotted Marjorie, running hell-for-leather in their direction. "Uh oh!"

Mrs. Patterson followed his line of vision. "My goodness, you're right. She has gone all googly-eyed."

"Creighton!" Marjorie cried when she was within arm's distance. "Creighton, I need you."

For three months he had longed to hear those words. The setting wasn't quite as he had anticipated, but beggars couldn't be choosers. He opened his arms wide. "Yes, darling?"

She stopped just short of his embrace and endeavored to catch her breath. "Dr. Heller's lab . . ." she gasped.

His blue eyes narrowed. "Hmm, 'Dr. Heller's lab.' Is that like 'Alexander's Ragtime Band?' If it is, it might be helpful if you hum a few bars."

"Stop goofing around. This is important. I might have found some evidence in the Alfred Nussbaum case."

"Ohhh, the Alfred Nussbaum case," he sang in mock understanding. He shrugged at Mrs. Patterson before asking, blindly, "Who's Alfred Nussbaum?"

"The man on the Ferris wheel," Marjorie replied impatiently.

"And you've discovered something related to his death?"

"That's right."

"I see," he stated. "Very interesting. Just one thing confuses me though: who is Dr. Heller?"

Marjorie clicked her tongue in exasperation. "Really, Creighton, you must try and keep up. Dr. Heller is the coroner examining Alfred Nussbaum. I need you to drive me over to his lab, so I can talk to him."

"The coroner? You're asking me to take you to the morgue?"

"That's precisely what I'm asking."

"Marjorie," Mrs. Patterson chastised. "The morgue? What would your father say if he were alive?"

"He'd probably congratulate me," she averred. "You know how Dad enjoyed a good riddle."

"Might I ask you something?" Creighton ventured. "Why do you want to talk to Dr. Heller when you possess influence over a certain member of the Hartford County Police Department?"

"Robert's too busy to listen to a word I say."

"That's ridiculous. You just got engaged. He should be giving you his undivided attention."

"Yes," Mrs. Patterson chimed in. "If he's like this now, imagine what he'll be like after the wedding."

Marjorie pulled a face. "True, but he is awfully busy. He'll learn to listen to me eventually. Especially when he finds out I'm usually right."

Creighton cleared his throat.

"What? I'm not usually right?"

"When it comes to murder," he answered evasively.

She smiled radiantly. "Then you'll take me to the lab?"

"That depends. What are you so keen on discussing with Dr. Heller?"

"A bunch of things. First, Nussbaum was on the Ferris wheel by himself, which, in itself, is very strange. A man wouldn't normally go on a ride like that by himself. With a child or sweetheart, maybe. But alone? Not likely."

"So, he lived locally, had no one to ride with and still wanted to have fun. Not a big deal."

"But he wasn't a local, Creighton. He was from Boston. What was he doing here?"

"Just passing through?" the Englishman offered.

"I doubt it. Then there's the way Nussbaum died. Robert's convinced that he suffered a heart attack while the Ferris wheel was in motion. But Mrs. Schutt described Nussbaum, not as sickly, but agitated and anxious before he boarded the ride. Why? Was he already feeling ill, or was there some other reason? And, if Nussbaum fell ill in the compartment as Robert assumes he did, why didn't he try to summon help? He may have been too weak to yell, but the cars are completely open. All he needed to do was turn around and gesture to the people in the car behind him, but he didn't. In fact, Mrs. Schutt claims that when she stopped the ride to let him off, he was seated in the upright position, face forward and eyes staring straight ahead, as though he were paralyzed."

Creighton stared at her pensively. "You have some good questions there, but I'm sure there are logical explanations for all of

45

them. Did Dr. Heller say anything before he left?"

"Only that he thought it was a heart attack," Marjorie replied reluctantly.

"Then it sounds to me as though you're grasping at straws. People do die from things other than murder, Marjorie. You can't live your life looking for wrongdoing around every corner. Pretty soon, you won't be able to watch a ball game without wondering if the bat was ever used to bludgeon someone to death." He grasped her shoulders and stated slowly: "Take it from me — sometimes a baseball bat is just a baseball bat."

"But," she countered with a gleam in her eye, "as my great-uncle Clancy could tell you, sometimes it's a shillelagh."

"I'm not going to argue with your great-uncle. With a name like Clancy, I'm sure he knows much more about shillelaghs than I ever will. However, I do know a thing or two about evidence, and yours is entirely circumstantial. Dr. Heller is a scientist; he deals with cold, hard facts, not speculation and conjecture. The only thing that interests him is physical proof, and if you can't provide any, I'm afraid he won't pay any more attention to you than Jameson did."

"And what if I show him this?" Marjorie

smugly extracted a wadded handkerchief from her purse and opened it. There, in the middle of the starched white linen lay a tiny, pointed brass object.

"Looks like a miniature dart," Mrs. Patterson declared as she leaned over the Englishman's shoulder to get a better view.

"Take a closer look at the tip."

As Mrs. Patterson adjusted her glasses, Creighton's eyes focused on a reddish-brown spot at the point of the object. "Looks like dried blood," he asserted.

The elderly woman gasped and took a step backward.

"Where did you find it?" Creighton inquired.

"On the ground near Alfred Nussbaum's body. When I was waiting for Robert to arrive, I happened to catch a glimpse of something sparkling in the grass. I thought it might be an earring, so I picked it up."

"Hmm mmm . . . you just 'happened' to catch a glimpse of it?"

Marjorie's face broke into a broad grin. "Okay, so I was looking."

"Sweetie, if you had been any closer to the ground you'd have been under it."

"Maybe, but not for my own sake. When I realized what this might be, I wrapped it up so I could give it to Robert."

"Only he didn't give you the chance," he completed the story.

"Right. So, now will you take me to see Dr. Heller?"

"Yes, but under one condition. We drop off the dart, or whatever it is, and then we leave."

Mrs. Patterson nodded her head in silent approval.

"Leave?" Marjorie repeated incredulously. "But this is my piece of evidence. I want to stick around long enough to know whether or not it's valuable."

"You can find that out from your betrothed, Detective Jameson."

"He won't tell me."

"That's your problem," Creighton replied unsympathetically. "All I know is I'm not about to get mixed up in police business again. I should think you'd feel the same way. Need I remind you what happened last time?"

"No, you needn't remind me. I remember everything." She gazed wistfully into the distance. "The thrill of the hunt, the anticipation of unearthing a long-buried secret, the giddiness we felt upon finding a new clue."

Creighton had to admit the whole thing was pretty damn exciting, and he might have said he enjoyed it too, if it hadn't ended so badly. "Do you remember how the case closed?"

"Of course I do. We solved it. And we did a brilliant job, if I do say so myself."

"Uh-huh. Anything else?"

"Yes. I'm working on a book detailing the case. My agent says it should sell like hot-cakes."

"Hotcakes? Wonderful," he proclaimed. "With all that money you're going to have in the bank, there's no need to tag along on another police investigation in search of a story."

"Oh, but Creighton," she moaned.

"Don't 'Oh, but Creighton?' me. You've conveniently forgotten one minor detail about the last case: you were nearly killed."

"Well, if you're going to hold a little thing like that over my head," she grumbled.

"A little thing? You spent three weeks in the hospital," Creighton shrieked.

"I'm feeling much better now. In fact, I'm stronger than I've ever been."

"Good, let's see that you stay that way."

"Oh, come now. What harm could possibly come from hanging around a coroner's office?"

"For a normal person? None. But I know you. You start out innocently enough, hang-

49

ing around the coroner's office and spewing a few wild theories. Before we know it, you're interrogating suspects and insinuating yourself into their homes. Pretty soon, that evolves into getting blitzed on sherry, accosting dogs with lemon drops, and accepting checks for fake charities. Then, before you can say 'Sherlock Holmes' — bang! Someone decides that the world would be a happier place without you in it."

"I admit I got carried away last time," she conceded.

"Yes. Into an ambulance, by a bunch of medics."

"All the more reason for you to come with me," Marjorie continued. "If I recall correctly, when I was injured last time I was completely alone, with neither you nor Robert around to help me. But if you keep an eye on me this time —"

"Save the doe eyes and innocent look for your future hubby," Creighton interrupted. "They won't get you anywhere with me. You can take care of yourself just fine. If anyone around here needs protection, I do."

"Protection from what?"

"You," he stated firmly, "and your overactive imagination. My word, you're good at twisting things. If your literary talent ever evaporates, you could easily find work as a pretzel-maker."

"Well," she huffed. "If you're going to be rude about it, I'll just find someone else to drive me to Dr. Heller's lab. I'm sure there are lots of men who wouldn't mind giving me a ride."

"That's what I'm afraid of," Creighton quipped. "I say, how do you think Jameson is going to react to you interfering with his investigation?"

"He'll be upset at first, but he'll get over it."

"I don't think he'll 'get over it.' Why, if he finds out you went to see Dr. Heller behind his back, he'll be — ugh!" He grunted as an elbow jabbed him in the ribs.

"He'll be furious." Mrs. Patterson lowered her elbow and gave a surreptitious wink in Creighton's direction. "Positively furious. He may even call off the wedding."

The Englishman returned his accomplice's wink. "Oh, I think you're overstating it a bit, don't you Mrs. Patterson? Jameson is a levelheaded chap; I don't see him reacting that strongly. Besides, Marjorie should set things straight before the wedding. Let her future husband know that she's not the type of girl who plans on sitting quietly at home. Right, Marjorie?"

Marjorie's face registered complete bewilderment. "What? Why, yes. Yes, he needs to learn that I'm my own person."

"Thatta girl! Well, don't just stand there dawdling. Let's get a move on."

"A move on?"

"Yes, I'm driving you to Dr. Heller's lab."

"You are? But you said —"

"I know what I said. You think women are the only people who are entitled to change their minds?"

"No, I don't, but —"

"Then let's go." Before Marjorie could protest any further, Creighton took her by the arm and began to lead her away from the kissing booth. Sharon Schutt, however, had different plans.

"There you are! I've been looking for you everywhere," she snorted. "Mother's tired and wants to lie down. I told her you'd drive her home."

"I would, Sharon, but I can't right now. Marjorie and I have some business to attend to."

She eyed Marjorie contemptuously. "Marjorie? What business could you possibly have with her?"

"Very important business. Now if you'll excuse us, we must be off." He gently stepped around her, towing Marjorie behind him.

"Off? Off where?"

With a devilish grin he shouted over his shoulder: "To find ourselves a shillelagh!"

FIVE

Marjorie and Creighton stood in the corner of the laboratory, drinking coffee from heavy earthenware mugs. They had been at the coroner's office for nearly two hours — a far cry from Creighton's original promise to deposit the evidence and then leave. What had occurred to change his mind, she couldn't say, and she certainly wasn't about to ask, but she had a sneaking suspicion that Creighton enjoyed a good mystery as much as she did. How else to explain the grin that crept across his face when Dr. Heller announced that the dart was, indeed, a party to murder? And, moreover, how else to account for the Englishman's jubilation when it was announced that Robert should be summoned, immediately, to share the news?

As if on cue, the detective breezed through the doorway. "I didn't expect to hear from you this soon, Doc. Must be something good." Upon glimpsing Marjorie and

Creighton his demeanor suddenly darkened. "What are you doing here?"

"That's a nice hunk of welcome for the woman you're going to marry," Marjorie quipped.

"I thought I asked you not to interfere," he countered.

"I wouldn't treat Miss McClelland too harshly, Detective," Dr. Heller interjected. "Her 'interference', as you called it, has proven vital in unraveling Alfred Nussbaum's true cause of death. In fact, her discovery is the reason I sent for you." The doctor waved his hand toward a tray of white cotton gauze resting upon the stainless steel counter.

Jameson leaned down and gazed at the object that lay on the blanket of white cloth. "A dart?"

"Yes," Heller affirmed. "Looks innocent enough from the size of it. But it's much more sinister than it appears. It's been dipped in an extract of Chondodendron tomentosum."

"Could you repeat that in English, please?"

"Curare," Marjorie spoke up. "A deadly neuromuscular poison used by certain Amazonian tribes on their hunting arrows. Medically, it's prescribed as a muscle relaxant, but just a few too many grains in the bloodstream can cause paralysis of all the body's muscles, including the heart and the lungs. The victim eventually dies of asphyxiation."

The three men stared at her in awe. "I used it in my second novel, *Peril in Patagonia*," she explained.

"So what you're saying, Doctor," Jameson picked up the conversation again, "is that Nussbaum was poisoned."

"That's precisely what I'm saying, Detective. In addition to the curare, I found particles of dried blood on the tip, type O positive: same as the victim. Moreover, the shape of the tip matches the shape of the wound found on the victim's body."

"Let me see if I understand this correctly: Alfred Nussbaum died because he came in contact with a dart laced with a South American poison?"

"More or less. Although to say that he 'came in contact' with the dart would imply some sort of accident. The wound I found was on the left side of the neck. One would be hard-pressed to call that an accident."

"Then he was shot?"

"Shot, pierced, struck, however you want to put it, the simple fact is he didn't do this to himself."

"Mrs. Schutt said he was alone the entire time he was on the Ferris wheel." Marjorie reasoned. "So he must have been shot by someone standing on the ground."

"Which means it could have occurred before he boarded," Creighton offered.

"Highly improbable," Dr. Heller dismissed with a shake of the head. "The effects of curare are instantaneous. Within seconds of being wounded, the victim would have been completely paralyzed. He was most definitely shot while on the Ferris wheel."

Robert stared at the dart as if intimidation might force it to reveal its secret. "Marjorie, where'd you find this thing?"

"On the ground near the body."

"Where near the body?"

She squinted her eyes and tried to remember. "Um, near his head. On his left side, I think."

"You think? You mean you're not sure?"

She didn't particularly care for the tone Robert's voice was taking. "I'm nearly one hundred percent certain that's where I found it," she said defensively.

"Nearly one hundred percent? Why'd you pick it up in the first place? You know better than to tamper with evidence. There's no way this would be admissible in court."

Marjorie felt her blood begin to boil.

"What does it matter if it's admissible in court? There are no fingerprints on it. All it does is establish wrongful death — which is already indicated by the wound on Nussbaum's neck."

"You didn't know that at the time."

"No, but I didn't know it was evidence either. I thought it might be an earring or a cuff link."

"Okay, so you thought it was an earring. But, when you looked at it and realized it might be evidence, why didn't you show it to me? I was at the fair. Why did you wait until now to bring it to Dr. Heller?"

"I tried to tell you about it, but you wouldn't listen to me."

"You should have tried harder to get my attention," he replied matter-of-factly.

Marjorie felt a throbbing at her temples so powerful she thought her head might explode. "Tried harder to get your attention? I could have done the dance of the seven veils and you wouldn't have noticed."

"I would have," Creighton offered.

"Me too," Dr. Heller rejoined.

"Oh, be quiet!" the young woman snapped.

"All right. All right," Jameson relented. "I'm sorry I didn't listen to you. As much as I would like to discuss this further, right now I have more pressing matters to think about, such as how a man could have ended up with a dart in his neck."

"You heard the good doctor. Someone shot him."

"Naturally, someone shot him," Jameson started, "but how did they do it? And how did they do it without being seen?"

"I don't know," she answered honestly. "Probably the same way most darts are fired."

"Swell," Jameson replied facetiously. "I'll have Noonan put out an APB for a man carrying a blow gun. That ought to be a cinch."

"Why must you interpret everything so literally?" Marjorie chided. "Just because the killer fired the dart doesn't mean he used a blow gun. I'm sure there are dozens of ordinary objects which could do the job just as well."

"Such as?" he challenged.

"Umm . . ."

Creighton came to her aid. "Isn't it enough that we've furnished you with the weapon and the possible means? Must we provide you with every detail? Next thing we know, you'll be asking us to find the murderer for you."

"No, Creighton," Jameson enunciated, "all I ask is that you leave and take Marjorie with you. Thank you for your help, but I can manage from here."

"But, Robert," Marjorie began to protest.

"No arguments. Noonan found Mrs. Nussbaum at that hotel in Hartford; he's bringing her around to ID the body. They should be here any minute. In the meantime, I'm going into the other room to look at that wound on Nussbaum's neck. When I get back, I don't want to see you here."

He motioned for Dr. Heller, who swiftly unlocked the door to the autopsy room and ushered the detective inside.

Marjorie waited until the door closed behind them to speak. " 'I don't want to see you here,' " she mimicked. " 'Take Marjorie home, Creighton.' "

"You heard the man," Creighton warned as he gestured toward the exit. "Shall we?"

"What, and miss out on meeting Mrs. Nussbaum? Not on your life."

"Rather poor choice of words considering the circumstances."

"Sorry," she apologized, "but I'm not leaving. This is just starting to get good."

"Good? If a man being murdered is good, I'd hate to find out what you consider bad."

"Bad is leaving here without getting the whole story."

Creighton was cautious. "Jameson is

pretty cheesed off at both of us already. Perhaps you should leave well enough alone."

Marjorie remained defiant. "Why? What is he going to do? Throw us in jail?"

The Englishman leaned against the counter and ran a hand through his chestnut hair. "He could if he wanted to."

"What are you worried about? You have enough money to post bail for both of us. Besides," she added, "Robert isn't going to arrest his fiancée. He'd be the laughingstock of the whole station."

He flashed a cunning smile. "What if you were no longer his fiancée?"

"You mean what if Robert calls off the wedding? You and Mrs. Patterson would like that, wouldn't you? Although, for the life of me, I don't understand why. He's treated both of you with nothing but —" Her words fell off as she suddenly remembered something. "Wait one minute. We were discussing this at the fair when Mrs. Schutt's scream interrupted us. You were trying to tell me something. What was it?"

Creighton glanced at his surroundings and shook his head. "This isn't the place. But I could take you somewhere more . . . er . . . appropriate."

"No dice," she refused. "You're not luring

me away from here that easily. Not so you can tell me I shouldn't marry Robert because I don't know his shoe size."

"So you're determined to stay here and incur your beloved's wrath."

"That's right," she folded her arms across her chest. "Like you said earlier, I have to set the ground rules sometime."

"Well, you'd better break out your lesson book," he replied, nodding toward the door. "Dreamboat will be back any second."

Marjorie glanced at the door, her heart full of dread. "Yes, I know."

Creighton's face broke into a grin. "What's wrong? Scared of what Jameson's going to do when he finds us still here?"

She tried hard not to frown as she weighed the situation. Creighton knew of her stubbornness and accepted it, perhaps even reveled in it, but Robert was another matter entirely. She had never pushed him this far before and was uncertain how he would react. In spite of her fear, she affected an air of indifference. "I'm not scared. I'm just afraid that Robert may not speak as freely if we're here. Same goes for Mrs. Nussbaum. There may be some facts about her late husband she wouldn't want to discuss in front of complete strangers."

He moved to make his exit. "Then it's

settled. We'll go."

She grabbed his arm. "No, I want to stay."

The Englishman rolled his eyes. "Make up your mind. Either we leave now, or we stay and make a poor widow feel uncomfortable."

"We stay," she stated firmly as a thought flashed into her brain.

"Then you're willing to face Jameson."

"We won't have to," she explained breathlessly. "I have an idea."

Creighton drew his hand over his face. "Oh, no."

"Stop being so wishy-washy and come on," she ordered. Then with a twinkle in her eye she asked, "Have I ever steered you wrong?"

Six

Creighton essayed to squeeze his six-foot two-inch frame onto the lower tier of the gurney. He would have preferred to have left the laboratory — to escape to somewhere peaceful where he could tell Marjorie what he had tried to tell her at the fair — but being in such close quarters with the young woman was not without its merits. Still, he felt obligated to complain, lest he be considered a pushover.

"Why do I let you talk me into these things?" he grumbled. "I feel like a passenger in a clown car."

"Relax, it could be worse," Marjorie assured him as she pulled the sheet down to conceal their hiding place. "I could have picked a table with a body on it."

"Remind me to thank you when I get this crick out of my neck." He settled into the spot beside her, his legs bent at such an angle, he could rest his head on them. "Now

I know how the Dionne quintuplets felt inside their mother's womb."

"At least the Dionne girls didn't have to worry about sitting on each others' dresses," Marjorie grimaced as she tugged at her skirt. "Lift up, will you."

The Englishman obeyed and hoisted himself up on both arms, taking care to bend at the neck so as not to hit his head on the tier above him; in this position, their faces were only an inch apart. With a flick of her lithe wrist, Marjorie swept the hem of her garment out from harm's way. "Thank you," she croaked awkwardly.

"You're welcome," he whispered as his azure eyes locked onto hers. It was intoxicating, being this close to her: the loveliness of her face, the warmth of her body, and something else, something that could only be described as an electrical spark. Was this spark the byproduct of months of pining, a hobgoblin of his fertile imagination, or did she, too, sense it? There was only one way to find out. He would kiss her and then . . .

The door of the examination room slammed shut and he heard the clicking of men's shoes against the terrazzo floor. Marjorie turned away quickly, leaving her companion with a mouth of blonde, marcelled hair.

Creighton cursed his fate as yet another opportunity slipped through his fingers.

"It appears your friends took your advice and left," the coroner noted.

"Yeah," Jameson replied, "I'm surprised they gave in that easily."

"They realized you meant business," Dr. Heller explained.

"Humph," Robert snorted. "You don't know Marjorie."

"Tenacious, is she?"

"Let's just say that only passing acquaintances address her as Miss McClelland. In more intimate circles, she's better known as Miss Never-Say-Die."

Marjorie, satisfied with her new sobriquet, smiled beatifically.

"Soon to be 'Mrs.' Never-Say-Die," Heller prompted.

"Don't remind me," Jameson quipped.

Marjorie's smile dissipated, replaced by a visage of utter indignation. Like a jungle cat preparing to pounce, she raised a hand to claw the sheet in front of her and opened her jaw wide as though to emit a mighty roar. Creighton grabbed the young woman by the waist and clamped a hand over her mouth.

"Second thoughts?" the doctor asked.

"No," he answered decisively. "No second

thoughts. Marjorie's absolutely wonderful. The most beautiful woman in the world."

Marjorie's body relaxed, and Creighton loosened his grip on her.

"It's just that sometimes I wish she were more like other girls. You know, content to sit home with her knitting and sewing. A homebody."

"A homebody? Not that one," Heller laughed. "Not with her green eyes and her temper. No sirree, she's a sharpie if I ever met one."

"Yes," Jameson agreed with pride in his voice. "Yes, she is."

Creighton completely relinquished his hold on the young woman and let his arms drop to his sides. Up until now, he had viewed Jameson as an emotional nonentity. This sentimental scene had put a different spin on things. It was quite clear from the detective's statements that he cared for Marjorie deeply: a fact that made Creighton feel like a heel.

"Speaking of sharp people, you might want to put your best men on this." There was the crinkle of paper. "I found it in Nussbaum's shirt pocket."

"It's all numbers," Robert noted.

"That's right. A page, covered front and back with numbers, some of them are

circled but all of them are listed in seem-
ingly random order, and none of them are
higher than 99. The only letters used are in
the signature at the end."

"Matt," Jameson read aloud. "Very interesting. There's a date in the lower left
corner. '5/21.' "

"That was three weeks ago," Heller stated.
"You think this thing might lead us to the
killer?"

"Can't say for sure until we decode it."

Creighton heard the swish of the laboratory door as it opened. Peering through a
gap in the sheet, he recognized the ruddy
complexion of Officer Noonan. The policeman held the door ajar and allowed the
woman accompanying him to enter. She was
a lanky redhead in her late twenties, flashy
rather than truly attractive, with bobbed
hair and scarlet painted lips and fingernails.

"Mrs. Nussbaum, I'm detective Robert
Jameson with the Hartford County Police.
I'm sorry to have to put you through this,
but it's necessary that we get a positive
identification from a family member."

Jameson needn't have apologized; Mrs.
Nussbaum was quite blasé about the whole
affair. "It's okay. Where's he at?"

"This way," the detective replied. Noonan
ushered the young widow from Creighton's

range of sight.

When the door to the autopsy room was safely closed, Marjorie whispered to Creighton excitedly. "I only saw Mrs. Nussbaum from the rear. Did you get a good look at her? What was she like? She sounded young. Was she young?"

Creighton grinned at Marjorie's zeal. "Around your age."

"My age? Wow, there must have been a difference of about twenty years between her and her husband. Though I guess it's not uncommon for a middle-aged man to marry a younger woman, especially if she's pretty."

He shook his head. "She may be pretty when she's all dolled up, but I'd hate to see her when she takes off that make-up. My grandfather warned me about women like that. He said, 'Creighton, my lad, before you get married, make sure you see the girl with her face scrubbed clean. You want to be sure you know what you're getting. You don't want to wake up with more of your wife sitting on the nightstand than lying in bed next to you.' " Creighton chuckled, "I remember he even made up a little saying about it: 'Lipstick, powder and a little bit of paint can make a girl look what she jolly well ain't.' "

"How charming. A poet in the family," Marjorie remarked in mock admiration. "Did your grandfather write anything else?"

"A little rhyme concerning a man from the town of Wick, but, um," he cleared his throat, "I don't think it's appropriate for mixed company."

The autopsy room door reopened and Creighton heard the shuffling of feet against the hard, terrazo floor.

"That's Alfie all right," Mrs. Nussbaum confirmed, her steely voice giving no intimation of grief. "Poor fella. How'd it happen?"

"We believe he was murdered," Jameson broke the news.

"Murdered!" she exclaimed in the greatest outburst of emotion she had emitted since entering the room. "Who'd wanna do a thing like that?"

"That's what we're trying to find out. Tell me, Mrs. Nussbaum —"

"Josie," she swiftly corrected. " 'Mrs. Nussbaum' makes me sound so old."

"All right, Josie. Did your husband have any enemies?"

"No, Alfie was just your run-of-the-mill sort of guy."

"What did he do for a living?"

"Salesman. Worked for Alchemy Enterprises. They're a chemical company in Boston."

Creighton pricked up his ears; the owner of Alchemy Enterprises, Vanessa Randolph, and her recently deceased husband, Stewart, had been friends of the Ashcroft family for years.

"Your husband was in Hartford on business?"

"Oh no, we live here," she corrected. "Alfie and me lived in Boston before we were married. That's where we met, in Boston. Alfie used to come and see me dance."

"Ballet?" Heller asked.

"Burlesque. Alfie came to the show every night for a week before he got up enough moxie to come backstage and talk to me. A few weeks later, he told me he was gonna move to Hartford and asked me to come with him. Said I didn't have to work no more. That he was gonna marry me and take care of me the rest of my life." She paused, "A girl like me don't get offers like that every day, you know."

"Excuse me, Josie," Jameson interrupted. "But if your husband worked for a company in Boston, why did he want to move to Hartford?"

"Cause he did a lot of moving around with

his job. One day in Boston, the next day in New York, the day after that in Hartford, then back to Boston, and so on and so on. It's hard, you know, moving around that much, so he figured if he lived somewhere in the middle, it would make things easier on him."

"So you and, um, Alfie, lived in the Hideaway Hotel."

"That's right, but it was just for the time being, you see. Alfie had a house and other stuff in Boston. Once he got rid of them, he was gonna take the money and buy us a big house. Brand new furniture, too." She added bitterly, "But I guess that's not gonna happen now."

"I'm sorry, Josie," Jameson conveyed his sympathy. "Just one more question and then Officer Noonan will take you back home. Did your husband know anyone by the name of Matt or Matthew?"

"N — No," she stammered. "Why?"

"Because we found a document in your husband's shirt pocket bearing that signature."

"Well, I don't know who that is," she denounced vehemently. "Alfie knew a lot of people from his job, though. Maybe you should check there."

"I will. Thank you for your time, Mrs.

Nussbaum. And again, my condolences."

Creighton spied from his perch as Jameson followed the widow and Officer Noonan to the door.

"Set her up in another room until we can search theirs," the detective instructed the officer aside. "Then go back to the fair and find out if anyone noticed anything suspicious this morning."

Noonan nodded, and was dispatched with a pat on the arm. The detective closed the door and moved to rejoin Dr. Heller. As he did so, his eye slid to the stationary gurney.

Creighton shrunk back into the shadows, but it was too late — Jameson had spotted him. He watched helplessly as the detective's shoes stepped closer and came to a stop outside their hidden lair.

Marjorie squeezed her companion's arm with her right hand and started blessing herself with the other. Her prayers, however, were cut short, for within a matter of seconds, the gurney began to spin wildly. Creighton braced himself against a table leg, but Marjorie, caught unawares by the sudden movement, accidentally poked herself in the eye while invoking the sign of the cross. She uttered a tiny yelp before the force of the rotation flung her to Creighton's side of the cart, where her head hit him squarely in the nose. In reflex, the Englishman surrendered his grip on the table to grab at the injured body part, and the couple tumbled to the floor.

Marjorie immediately repositioned herself and pulled her skirt down over her knees. "Why did you do that?" she demanded while struggling to stand upright on wobbly legs. "We could have been hurt."

Creighton sat on the floor, awaiting the fireworks.

"Good. Maybe if you're bandaged up, you'll stay at home and leave me to my murder investigation."

"You're forgetting," she pointed out, still swaying, "if it weren't for me, you wouldn't have a murder investigation. You and your men would still be chasing your own tails."

"Yes, I know. You found the dart that proved Alfred Nussbaum was murdered. And I thank you many times over. But now your job is done. I no longer need your assistance. So get lost!"

"Maybe you don't need Marjorie," Creighton raised an index finger, "but you could use my assistance."

"You?" Marjorie and Jameson replied in unison.

"You're just as bad as she is," Jameson motioned toward his fiancée.

"I acknowledge that I displayed a serious lack in judgment, but in spite of my shortcomings, you may find it beneficial to keep me around."

The detective narrowed his eyes. "Why?"

Creighton rose to his feet. "Because I know Vanessa Randolph, the owner of Alchemy Enterprises — Nussbaum's employer. She and her late husband were close friends of my family."

"So?"

"So, between her illness and the loss of her husband, Vanessa is a virtual recluse nowadays. She won't open her door to strangers."

"Ten to one says a police badge changes that."

"No," Creighton shook his head. "Vanessa is a stubborn woman. She'll pass the matter on to her personal secretary, who will then pass it to the manager of the company, who will pass it to his secretary, who will pass it to the head of personnel, who will ask the file clerk to retrieve Alfred Nussbaum's records, leaving the file to travel all the way back up the chain of command. Meaning that you won't get those employment records for two, three days, tops. But —"

"I knew there had to be a 'but'," Jameson commented.

"But, if you speak to Vanessa directly, she'll ensure you get everything you need, and quickly. Moreover," Creighton flashed a boyish grin, "Vanessa might have access to information that might be found in any file."

There was a long pause wherein Heller and Marjorie took turns glancing between the two men.

"Okay," Jameson sighed, "you've convinced me. We'll drive out to Boston first thing tomorrow morning."

"Splendid. What time shall we meet?"

"How about seven? I'll pick you up at your house."

"Sounds good to me," Marjorie approved.

"Not you," Robert made clear.

"Aw, come on," she whined. "How can you break up our little trio? We work so well together. Why, we're like the Three Musketeers. The Rhythm Boys. The leaves on a shamrock."

"Consider your leaf plucked. Now, if you two don't mind leaving, I have some paperwork to do. Creighton, I'll see you in the morning."

Creighton nodded in agreement.

"I'll see you in the morning, too," Marjorie interjected.

"Marjorie," the detective warned.

"To see you off and wish the two of you luck," she amended. "Or is there something wrong with that, too?"

Creighton tried hard to suppress a laugh as he followed M̶̶̶ ̶ie out of the laboratory. He paused in the doorway and waved his goodbyes to the detective and Dr. Heller. Jameson, looking as though he had survived a cyclone, didn't return the wave, but sighed tiredly: "Here we go again."

SEVEN

Marjorie arrived on the doorstep of Kensington House at six thirty in the morning, clad in a belted navy blue dress with white pin dots and butterfly sleeves. Upon her golden head rested the same floppy white hat she had worn the day before, this time accented with a navy blue scarf tied about the crown.

"Good morning, Miss McClelland," greeted the butler as he swung open the heavy wooden door.

"Good morning, Arthur." Marjorie stepped over the threshold and into the paneled center hall. "How's that tooth of yours? Any better?"

"Yes, Miss," the middle-aged man smiled. "I saw that dentist you recommended and he fixed it right up for me. Thank you."

"Don't mention it. I'm glad he could help you. Last time I was here, it was obvious you were having a miserable time of it."

"Yes, I was in a bad way," he chuckled. "But now I'm right as rain."

"Good." She glanced toward the stairs. "Is Creighton around?"

"Mr. Ashcroft is still in his room, but he should be down shortly. In the meantime, Agnes is setting up breakfast by the pool, if you'd care to wait there."

"Sounds great," she agreed. "It's a beautiful day. You should try to get some sun later."

Arthur escorted her down the hall to the back door and onto the flagstone patio. "I'll try, Miss."

At a large teak table, Agnes, a plumpish woman in her early fifties, was arranging an assortment of homemade sweet rolls in a basket. "Good morning, Agnes."

"Miss McClelland," the cook greeted. "How pretty you look! Mr. Ashcroft told me you might pop in this morning so I set an extra plate."

"Thank you." Marjorie settled into the chair held for her by Arthur.

"I also took the liberty of preparing a little surprise for you." From behind her back, Agnes produced a silver bowl brimming with red fruit and placed it on Marjorie's plate.

"Strawberries," Marjorie sang with delight

as Arthur unfolded her napkin and placed it on her lap.

"Yes, Miss. I overheard you once, telling Mr. Ashcroft how much you love them, so I picked you some fresh this morning."

"Agnes, that's so sweet of you. But you shouldn't have gone to so much trouble."

"It wasn't anything," she dismissed. "Besides, I'd rather see you eat them than that Schutt girl. Demanding this thing and that without so much as a 'please' or a 'thank you.' "

Arthur concurred. "I don't know what Mr. Ashcroft sees in her."

Marjorie agreed, but deemed it unwise to comment. Despite the casual relationship she enjoyed with Arthur and Agnes, they were still Creighton's employees, and Sharon, whether they liked it or not, might someday be their mistress.

"Oh well," Agnes sighed as she headed back toward the house. "I'll leave you to your breakfast. And let me know how you like those cinnamon buns. I used a new recipe."

Marjorie gazed into the basket; the buns were a tempting shade of golden brown. "I'm sure I'll love them. I like everything you make. Which reminds me," she added as a thought leapt into her head, "I wanted to ask you something."

"Yes, Miss McClelland?"

"I know you're very busy here at Kensington House, and I don't want to add to your workload, but I love your cooking so much that I was wondering if you could bake my wedding cake."

The servants exchanged astonished glances.

"Your wedding cake, Miss?" Arthur asked, his eyes wide with surprise.

"Yes, didn't Mr. Ashcroft tell you?"

"No," Agnes replied giddily, "he must have been waiting for this morning to make a formal announcement."

Formal announcement? Marjorie knitted her brow. "I know the English are very much into pomp and circumstance, but why would Creighton make a formal announcement of my engagement to Detective Jameson?"

"Detective Jameson?" they cried in unison.

"Yes, Detective Jameson," she answered in bewilderment. "Who did you think I was marrying?"

At that moment, Creighton breezed onto the patio dressed in a summer-weight dark blue suit. "Good morning, all. Did I miss anything?" He plopped into the chair beside Marjorie and placed his napkin in his lap.

"No sir," disclaimed Arthur as he handed him a neatly folded newspaper.

Agnes began pouring coffee from a silver pot. "Miss McClelland was just informing us of her impending nuptials."

"Oh yes. What with yesterday's excitement, I forgot to tell you both about it. Marvelous, isn't it?" Creighton asked cheerfully.

"It is?" Marjorie asked in disbelief. *Was this the same man who had attempted to dissuade her from matrimony because she didn't know her fiancé's childhood nickname?*

"Of course it is," Creighton assured her, raising his juice glass, "and I'm sure I speak for both Arthur and Agnes when I wish you and the good detective a long, happy life together."

"Hear, hear," the servants replied mechanically.

"And I'd be happy to bake your wedding cake, Miss," Agnes added tepidly.

"You're baking the wedding cake, Agnes?" Creighton asked his cook.

"I hope you don't mind my asking her," Marjorie stated apologetically.

"Mind? I think it's a bang-up idea. Agnes makes the best cakes this side of the Atlantic. And don't worry about buying the ingredients, Marjorie. I'll take care of every-thing."

"Thank you," muttered Marjorie, dumb-founded by his change in attitude.

The Englishman turned around in his chair to face the cook. "And Agnes, I'll pay you double your wages for the time you spend."

"Thank you, sir," she answered softly. In spite of Creighton's generous offer, she seemed oddly despondent. "I'd better go tend to my dirty dishes," she excused herself and then went back into the house.

Arthur stood stiffly before his master. "Is there anything else you'll be needing, sir?"

"No, I think we're set. Thank you."

"Then I shall be inside." Arthur bowed and made his leave.

"Seems my engagement makes for un-popular news," Marjorie observed after the butler had left.

"What, that? They're just taken aback by the suddenness of the whole thing, but they'll settle down once they get used to the idea." He polished off his orange juice with one swig and smacked his lips together. "Why, just look at me. I'm a changed man."

Marjorie dipped a spoon into her straw-berries. "Remarkably so," she muttered sus-piciously.

He broke off a piece of a cinnamon bun and chewed it pensively before swallowing. "I daresay you've changed as well. It's unlike you to be thinking of anything so serious as a wedding when there's a murder mystery to be solved. Or have you decided to make your future husband happy by giving up sleuthing in favor of knitting?"

"What? And lose the title of Miss Never-Say-Die?" She picked up her coffee cup and took a sip. "Besides, I don't know how to knit."

"Really? I'm surprised. After all, you're an excellent weaver."

Marjorie replaced the cup on its saucer. "Weaver?"

With a boyish grin, Creighton picked up his own coffee cup. "Yes, of fantastic stories."

Marjorie smiled and watched as he drank his coffee and continued nibbling at his cinnamon roll. It was during moments like these when she realized how appealing her companion actually was. With his wit, charm, and urbane good looks, Creighton was very attractive indeed. Damnably attractive, she concluded, recalling the incident beneath the gurney. How far would things have gone had Robert and Dr. Heller not returned from the autopsy room?

She returned her attention to the dish of berries and chided herself for entertaining such ideas. After all, she was soon to be a married woman.

"So," he continued, "if you haven't given up the sleuthing game, then it's safe to assume that you're not here just to give Jameson and me a grand send-off. In fact you're not looking to send us off at all, you're looking to join us, aren't you?"

"Maybe," she replied evasively as she swallowed her last berry.

Creighton finished his roll and started on his grapefruit half. "And you think Jameson will go along with that?"

She finished her last drop of coffee and retrieved a roll from the basket. "Who says I'm asking his permission?" She tore the roll in half and placed part of it on Creighton's plate.

"What are you planning? To hitch a ride on a passing gurney?"

"Ha ha. There are other ways to get to Boston," she stated cryptically.

Arthur appeared in the doorway. "Detective Jameson is here to see you, sir."

The detective pushed past him and onto the slate patio.

"Morning, Jameson," Creighton called. "Come join us for some coffee."

Jameson silently eyed Marjorie and took the seat opposite her.

"Good morning, darling," she greeted sweetly. "What? No kiss hello?"

"No," he snapped. "No kiss hello."

Marjorie tried on a look of concern. "Dear, you look all out of sorts. Didn't you sleep well?"

He ignored her question and replaced it with one of his own. "Why are you here?"

"I told you yesterday; I wanted to see you off."

"The best send-off you could have given me this morning was for you to stay home in bed."

Marjorie smiled to herself. For her plan to work, she needed to leave Kensington House before Robert and Creighton did; now was her chance. She pushed her chair away from the table. "If that's the way you feel, I'll go home. I know where I'm not appreciated."

Jameson watched as she rose from her seat and headed toward the house. "So long. I'll call you when I get back tonight."

"Hmph," she grunted over her shoulder.

"Oh, and by the way," he added with a smirk, "I intend on performing a thorough check of the car before I leave to make sure you aren't stowed away anywhere."

Marjorie thrust her tongue in his direction and took her leave through the main house. Arthur and Agnes, busy with their chores, were nowhere to be seen. She let herself out the front door and scurried down the driveway and then up the road, where, as planned, she encountered Freddie, the drugstore clerk, waiting behind a cluster of trees.

Beside him was parked his trusty bicycle and, next to that, the 1911 Ford Model T once belonging to the late Mr. Patterson.

"Boy, you were gone a long time," the teenager exclaimed. "I was startin' to get nervous. Why'd ya need me to wait all that time, anyway?"

She removed her hat and threw it into the backseat. "Because, Freddie, you know I can't crank this car all by myself. I need the help of a strapping young man like yourself."

"Yeah, but I already cranked it once today," he whined. "Couldn't ya just have driven it here and left it running?"

"And run the risk of someone stealing it?" She pulled a pair of driving goggles from her handbag and strapped them on her head. "Convincing Mrs. Patterson to lend it to me was difficult enough. I don't need the added aggravation of telling her it was stolen."

Freddie inserted the crankshaft into the engine and began turning it. "One thing I don't get, though. Who's gonna help you start the car when you wanna come back from Boston?"

Marjorie grabbed an old cloche hat from under the driver's seat and pulled it onto her head. "Detective Jameson or Mr. Ashcroft, of course."

Freddie looked up from his cranking. "Huh? But I thought you were hiding from them."

Marjorie tucked her loose strands of hair under the hat. "That's only until I get to Boston. Once I'm there, I'll be joining them in the investigation. Now keep cranking. I don't want to miss them."

Marjorie jumped behind the driver's wheel and Freddie returned to the task of cranking, all the while shaking his head. "My mom's gonna be awful sore at me for sneaking out of the house this morning."

"Oh, stop complaining," Marjorie admonished. "You're making a dollar out of the deal, aren't you?"

"Yeah, but you ain't seen my mom when she's angry."

"Tell her you were helping a damsel in

distress," she shrugged. "That's at least partially true."

Freddie stopped cranking and went on whining. "But what do I tell her when she asks who the damsel was? I'm not even 'posed to talk to you, let alone help you start your car."

"You're not supposed to talk to me? Why not?"

The fifteen-year-old placed his hands on his hips and explained in a childishly blunt fashion. "Cuz my mom thinks you're nuts."

Marjorie raised an eyebrow in disdain. "Oh she does, does she? And I suppose your father agrees with her."

"Oh no, Miss McClelland. He doesn't think you're nuts."

"He doesn't?"

"No, ma'am. He says you're a good-looking dame. Tells all his friends that, too."

Marjorie blushed and sat back down. "A good-looking dame. That's what he says, eh?"

"Yeah, I heard him the other day at the drugstore, talking to my boss, Mr. Wallace. They saw you pass by the window and my pop said, 'Gee, that Marjorie McClelland is sure one good-looking dame. Screwy, but good-looking!' "

She glared at the boy from behind the

steering wheel. "Freddie."

He looked up at her ingenuously, "Yeah?"

"Shut up and crank the car."

Creighton sat in the passenger seat of the detective's squad car, savoring the warm air blowing in from the open window. In his rearview mirror, he could see an old jalopy following some distance behind. It had been doing so for the past hour since they left the house. *Was the driver doing so intentionally?* he wondered. *If so, why?* He glanced at Jameson, whose eyes were riveted on the road ahead of them.

"So," the Englishman asked, "what did Noonan find out yesterday?"

"For starters, Josie had been in the middle of packing when Noonan brought her down to identify Alfred's body."

"Noonan didn't spot that when he collected her?"

Jameson shook his head. "She didn't let him in. But when he went back with a warrant to search the place, he saw that all her things were packed away in suitcases."

"Odd time to take a trip. What was her explanation?"

"She said she was going to visit her mother. But a visit with the hotel clerk proved that Josie had already checked out earlier that day."

Creighton rubbed his chin. "So unless she's clairvoyant, it would appear that Josie knew Alfred wasn't going to be around much longer."

"It certainly casts suspicion in her direction. But all we have are a bunch of packed suitcases. No weapons, no bus or train ticket. No motive. No proof that Josie was at the fair. Nothing. Without sufficient evidence, Josie's packing could be written off as a marital dispute and nothing more. Regardless, Noonan put her in the fish tank overnight to prevent her from getting 'homesick' again. She's probably out by now, but if she tries to skip the state again we can lock her up a lot longer."

"And you said there was nothing else in the hotel room?"

The detective shook his head. "Nothing out of the ordinary."

"What about the fair? What did you turn up there? Did anyone actually witness Nussbaum's murder?"

"Not a soul. People saw Nussbaum get on the Ferris wheel, but after that, they draw a blank. No one seemed to notice anything suspicious. There was, however, a strange woman seen lurking around a nearby booth directly before the time of the murder."

Creighton narrowed his eyes. "A 'strange' woman? Strange how?"

"Well, Mrs. Hodgkin, the woman in charge of the booth, described her as tall, slender, and dressed in a long-sleeved white wool suit."

"Wool? It was probably eighty-five degrees yesterday."

"Exactly. Witnesses also claim she was wearing kidskin gloves."

Creighton rubbed his chin meditatively. "How old was this woman?"

Jameson shook his head. "No one knows. Mrs. Hodgkin was the only one to get a good look at her, and she said anywhere from her late twenties to her early fifties."

"Could she be more vague?" the Englishman cracked.

"The woman was wearing dark glasses and a hat with a veil, so no one really saw her face too clearly."

Tall and thin? An idea popped into Creighton's head. "What about her hair?"

"What about her hair?" Jameson returned the question.

"What color was it?"

"Black," Jameson replied, then cracked a knowing smile. "Hoping it was red?"

"Just a thought. You must admit Mrs. Nussbaum wasn't too broken up over the death of her husband. Add to that the fact that she was packing to leave town and . . ."

"Yeah, the thought occurred to me, too. But, just because the woman at the fair was seen with black hair doesn't mean it was her own. She could have been wearing a wig. And Josie just happens to own a trunk full of wigs and other costumes; Noonan found it during his search."

"Well, being a — how should I say? — an 'entertainer,' it wouldn't be unusual for Josie to have those sorts of things lying about."

"Mmm. That's precisely why I said we didn't find anything out of the ordinary in the Nussbaums' hotel room." Coming upon a slow speed zone, the detective shifted the car into a lower gear. "But we do have yet another clue to this woman's identity. She was a smoker."

"Oh good, that should make it a lot easier," he joked. "Hardly anyone smokes nowadays."

"I know, I know. It's nothing big, but hey, every little bit helps."

"Does it? For all we know, this mystery woman just has an abnormally low body temperature. She could have absolutely nothing to do with the murder." He glanced at the rearview mirror again; the jalopy was

93

gaining on them. "Are we sure she was the only stranger at the fair?"

"The 'only' stranger? Are you kidding? The fair is a big to-do. There were scads of people from towns as far as ten, twenty miles away. The Hartford Bus Company even added extra buses to Ridgebury just for this weekend. My men are wading through dozens of descriptions, right now, trying to see if the same person or people appear in more than one eyewitness account."

"Any luck so far?"

"As a matter of fact, yes. There were two men — business types — who rode the Ferris wheel right before Nussbaum did. Same exact car too."

"What did they look like?"

The detective shrugged. "All we can get out of anyone is that they stood out because they were wearing suits. Expensive suits, well-tailored. Not the type of thing a guy wears to a church fair with lots of sticky-fingered kids around. Apart from that, they were average looking, clean-cut."

"An average appearance is a criminal's best friend," Creighton commented.

"Humph," Jameson grunted in response. "Ain't that the truth."

"And what about Nussbaum?"

"What about Nussbaum?"

"You mentioned the bus company adding extra buses to their schedule. But how did Nussbaum get to the fair? He lives in Hartford — that's more than just a good stretch of the legs."

"I have Noonan checking on that right now. We found a driver's license in Nussbaum's wallet but, according to Josie, he didn't own a car."

"You think Josie can be trusted to tell the truth?"

"Maybe not, but we didn't find any abandoned cars this morning. So, for now, we have to assume that Nussbaum arrived by either bus, train, or cab. Noonan's showing Nussbaum's photo around. Maybe someone will recognize him." There was a long silence before he spoke again. "Creighton, I've been meaning to talk to you about something."

The Englishman knew what was coming, but he feigned nonchalance. "What is it?"

"It's about Marjorie," the detective started. "Listen, I know how you feel about her."

Creighton opened his mouth to object, but Jameson cut him short. "Don't bother trying to deny it, Ashcroft. We're way beyond that now."

95

He nodded solemnly. "All right. What's your point?"

"My point is that sometimes I think you doubt my feelings for Marjorie are real. Well, I'm telling you now that they are real. I love Marjorie and I'd do anything to make her happy. Even so, there are going to be times when she and I don't see eye to eye on things." His gaze slid to the man seated beside him. "I'd appreciate it if, during those times, you wouldn't interfere."

Creighton took a deep breath and focused on a spot on the windshield. He had been awake the whole night before deliberating his next move. Now it was time to follow through with his decision. "I understand," he stated placidly. "I haven't been very sporting toward you during the last three months, Jameson, and I'd like to apologize, particularly for yesterday. I brought Marjorie to Dr. Heller's lab with the sole intention of causing problems between the two of you. It was wrong of me, I know. However, I was under the illusion that I still had time to change her mind, to make her love me. But she doesn't love me, Jameson. She never will. You're the man she loves. You won her over, old boy, fair and square. It's you she's going to marry. It's you who makes her happy." He frowned as he realized the gravity of his next statement. "And I, like you, want her to be happy. That's why I'm bowing out gracefully."

Jameson slowed the car down to a crawl. Apparently, he hadn't anticipated his speech succeeding so easily. "Huh?"

"You heard me, Jameson. From here on out, I will no longer be a thorn in your side. No more hanging around Marjorie's house, no more invitations to Kensington for afternoon tea, no more horning in on your dates. I'll even surrender my role as Marjorie's editor. Of course, I don't plan on selling Kensington House, at least, not right now. That being the case, I shall still see Marjorie from time to time, and I shall always consider her a friend, but you can trust me not to do anything to compromise your marriage."

Jameson, stupefied, shook his head. "I don't know what to say, except thank you."

"Don't thank me," Creighton dismissed. "This is as much for my sake as it is for yours. I'm getting out while my pride is still reasonably intact. Call it cutting my losses."

"Just the same, thanks."

The Englishman stared into his mirror again; the dilapidated automobile was close behind them. He leaned closer to the reflection and tried to ascertain who was behind the wheel of the old clunker. All he could discern was a hat, a pair of driving goggles, and a thin, gauzy scarf, blowing in the wind. His jaw dropped. That was no scarf. That was hair. A wisp of wavy blonde hair.

Creighton closed his eyes to dispel the picture from his sight. When he opened them, Jameson had accelerated, leaving the Model T at a considerable distance abaft. *It was just my imagination,* he concluded. *A bad case of Marjorie-on-the-brain.*

The Englishman returned to the conversation at hand. "I just have one piece of advice for you, Jameson. I don't presume to understand everything Marjorie does, but I do know this: she does what she wants, when she wants. There are times when she needs affection, support, reassurance, but beneath that she's an independent woman, a free spirit, with a bit of the will-o'-the-wisp thrown in for good measure. If you try to break that spirit," he warned, "you'll lose her. You don't want that to happen. Take it from someone who knows."

"Thanks, I'll bear it in mind. You know, you're a good guy, Ashcroft," the detective admitted grudgingly.

"Not good enough, it seems." Creighton leaned his head back against the seat and sighed. "No . . . not good enough."

EIGHT

Marjorie pulled the Model T in behind the police car, stopping in front of a small, neat red-shingled house in the Brighton-Allston section of northwest Boston. She removed her hat and goggles and leapt from the car to meet Robert and Creighton.

"What are we doing here?" she asked of Jameson as he emerged from the driver's side door.

"A better question is what are you doing here?" he retorted.

"I drove," she gestured toward the Ford parked behind her.

Creighton stepped out of the squad car looking more drained than Marjorie had ever seen him. "So it *was* you," he murmured, then, doing a double take at Marjorie's means of transportation, asked, "Where on earth did you get that car?"

"Mrs. Patterson. Her husband bought it secondhand, but now that he's gone, she keeps it locked up in the garage."

"Wise decision," Jameson quipped.

"It's not that bad," she rebutted. "After all, I was able to keep up with you all the way from Ridgebury. I must say, Robert, you're not a very good detective; you didn't even see me following you."

"I saw you," he stated flatly. "I just didn't think anything of it."

"Why not? For all you knew, I could have been a dangerous assassin."

"In a rattletrap like that?"

"Oh I don't know, Jameson," Creighton submitted. "She could have suffocated you with the exhaust fumes."

The two men laughed loudly.

"Laugh all you want, but I might have been a sinister master criminal."

Jameson rolled his eyes. "Marjorie, I'm going to let you in on a secret. A master criminal wouldn't drive a car with a crank start. It would take way too long to make a getaway."

Unable to think of a witty response, she changed the subject. "You still haven't answered my question. What are we doing here? Surely, this isn't the home of Vanessa Randolph."

"It isn't," Creighton responded. "It's the home of Alfred Nussbaum."

Robert explained, "I figured as long as we were in town, we might as well check out Nussbaum's house. One of the neighbors might be able to tell us something."

"Good thinking. Well, let's get going. Unless," she added with a sly grin, "you're planning to send me back to Ridgebury."

The men exchanged commiserating glances.

"No," Robert finally answered, "I'm not going to send you back to Ridgebury. Not after you've driven all the way here. Besides, that car of yours should cool down before it makes another trip."

"Goodie," Marjorie exclaimed. "Our happy little trio is reunited."

She swung open the wooden front gate and led the procession up the front walk. Marching along the path that bisected the neatly manicured yard, she noticed that the windows of the house were open and were adorned with billowy, white curtains. "Considering Nussbaum spent the past few months in Hartford, this house looks awfully lived-in. I guess someone's acting as a caretaker."

"Or he's leasing the house out until it can be sold," Creighton suggested.

"Only one way to find out," Jameson concluded as he stepped onto the front stoop and rang the bell.

An adolescent boy appeared within the frame of the storm door. He was dark-haired, with a pronounced nose and thick, horn-rimmed eyeglasses. "Yes?"

"Hi, I'm Detective Jameson from the Hartford County Police. Is your mother or father around?"

Before the boy could answer, a spindly girl, no older than eighteen or nineteen, appeared on the scene. She shared her brother's dark hair and prominent proboscis, but her vision did not require spectacles. "Who is it, Herbert?"

Jameson held up the badge again. "Hartford County Police. We'd like to speak to your parents, if possible."

The girl's eyes grew wide. "Come in," she summoned.

They shuffled through the storm door and into a narrow sitting room. It was a pleasant space painted in a cheerful shade of yellow and, despite the shabbiness of its furnishings, immaculately clean. The girl leaned into the next room and shouted, "Mom, you'd better come here."

"What is it, Natalie?" a voice returned abruptly. A woman in her early forties entered the room; apart from the difference in age, she and her daughter were carbon copies. The sight of guests gathered in the sitting room gave her pause. "Oh. What can I do for you?"

"Detective Robert Jameson, Hartford County Police." He wearily flashed the badge for a third time. "Are you the house-keeper here?"

The woman smiled. "I do the housekeeping, yes, but not because I'm paid to do it. I live here."

"You rent the house from Mr. Nussbaum."

"Rent it?" her forehead creased. "No, I live here because I'm Mr. Nussbaum's wife."

Their jaws dropped open in unison. "You mean ex-wife," Jameson presumed.

"No, I mean it in the present tense," she corrected indignantly. "I *am* Mrs. Nussbaum."

"Mrs. *Alfred* Nussbaum?" the detective asked in astonishment.

"Yes." She raised a suspicious eyebrow. "What is this all about?"

"Mrs. Nussbaum, I don't know of an easy way to tell you this, but your, um, your husband is dead. We believe it was foul play."

"I'll be," the woman shook her head and clicked her tongue as if commenting on a bizarre newspaper headline. "When did it happen? How?"

"Yesterday. He was poisoned."

"Do you need someone to identify the body?" she asked coolly.

"Um, no, that's been taken care of."

"I see." She motioned them to be seated. They selected a printed sofa, long enough to accommodate all three of them. Mrs. Nussbaum sat on a chair opposite, and the children on an adjacent loveseat. "I suppose *she* identified him."

"She who?"

"That little red-headed tramp Alfred's been keeping on the side; the one who calls herself Mrs. Nussbaum. That's why you were confused, wasn't it? Because of her."

Marjorie nearly leapt out of her seat. "You mean you know?"

"About Josie?" She laughed and pulled a cigarette case from the coffee table and offered it to her guests, who refused. "Of course I know."

"When did you find out?" Jameson inquired.

"About a month ago, although I was suspicious long before that. When you've been married to a man for twenty-one years, you get to the point where you can see right through him. Alfred always traveled with his job, going back and forth between New York and here. About a year ago, the trips started getting longer. Then, it got to the point where he was away all week and came home only for a Saturday or a Sunday. I did some checking and found out he was shacking up with some floozy in Hartford. I don't know where in Hartford — if I had, I probably would have hopped a bus there and kicked the door in! According to the hall of records there, they had even gone through with a wedding ceremony. Not that's it's legal of course, since he was still married to me at the time."

Mrs. Nussbaum placed a cigarette between her lips and meticulously returned the case to its previous position on the coffee table. "I was jealous at first; the thought of him with that young chippy. But then the idea grew on me. It wasn't so bad," she declared unconvincingly. "In fact, it was the best of both worlds. Alfred paid the bills and yet he wasn't around all the time messing up the house."

Natalie clicked her tongue. "Typical. Father's dead and you're talking about him messing up the house."

Mrs. Nussbaum drew a long puff from her cigarette and ground it out in a spotless ashtray. "Must you always be difficult, Natalie? Why can't you be more like Herbert?

Even as a small boy, Herbert could occupy himself for hours. You, on the other hand, always needed to be the center of attention."

"If I looked for attention, it's because you never gave me any. Herbert has always been your favorite. The reason he stays home is to be close to you. If he were normal, he'd be outside playing ball like other boys his age, instead of reading those terrible books! Murders, autopsies, true crimes . . . it's enough to give you the willies!"

Herbert adjusted his glasses and gave his sister a coldly appraising stare. "Those books are case studies for my work. If you actually had an interest in something other than boys, you'd understand."

"Shut up, Herbert," his sister snapped. "You're always trying to show that you're smarter than we are."

"I am smarter. Mother always says I am. I know you're upset because you were Father's favorite," the boy went on, "but since he got a girlfriend, you and he hadn't exchanged more than a few words."

"I hate you, Herbert!" she shouted. "You're nothing but a horrible little monster!"

"You don't hate me, Natalie," Herbert calmly explained. "You're merely transferring your anger onto me. Father is the one you truly hate. I read about this sort of thing in the Lizzie Borden case. Lizzie hated her stepmother, but she really hated her father for —"

Natalie jumped from her seat. "You're right! I did hate Father. I hated him for leaving us. I hated him! I hated him! And you know what? I'm glad he's dead! Glad!" She burst into tears and ran toward the hallway.

"Natalie!" Mrs. Nussbaum shouted at her daughter. "Natalie, get back here. We have company! Can't you go one day without making a scene?"

"You'd like it if I kept my mouth shut, wouldn't you? The fact is you both hated Father as much as I did! You hated Father because he left you for that redheaded hussy. And Herbert, you hated him because he was always trying to force you to try out for sports."

Herbert was eerily calm. "Yes, I hated Father. I openly admit it. He never appreciated my superior intellect. Why, just last week —" Mrs. Nussbaum eyed her son as he clenched and unclenched his fists.

She glared at her daughter. "See what you've done now? You've gotten your brother all upset!"

"As if it would take much to rattle his tree!" Natalie shouted as she stormed from the room.

Mrs. Nussbaum slid an arm around her son's shoulders. "Herbert, dear. I think it's best that you go to your room. I'm afraid all of this has been quite upsetting for you."

The boy rose obediently from the loveseat. "Yes, I just got a new book from the library. It's about Jack the Ripper. I've been looking forward to reading it. Yes, that's just the thing to stimulate my brain for this case," he thought aloud before opening a door and disappearing down a hallway.

Mrs. Nussbaum rationalized her son's conduct with a nervous smile. "Herbert has always been an imaginative child."

"Yes, well, perhaps you wouldn't mind telling us just where that 'imaginative child' was yesterday morning, around eleven o'clock," Jameson replied.

"Same place he always is on the weekend: at home, reading."

"Were you with him?"

"No, I was out shopping. A new market opened up in the North End."

"Then he was here alone?"

"Yes." Her eyes widened as she realized the gravity of the question. "Oh, but you don't think — I mean Herbert can be a bit strange, but he wouldn't hurt a fly!"

"I'm sure he wouldn't," Jameson smiled.

"Do you know where Natalie was yesterday?"

"Natalie? Oh she was — she was with me, at the market."

"Can anyone place the two of you there?"

"I'm sure people saw us, after all, it was Saturday, so it was very crowded, but no one who knew us by name. As I said, it was a new market." Now that she was away from the judgmental eyes of her daughter, she lit another cigarette. "Why? Am I a suspect?"

"No, I just need this information for my records," he dismissed. "Mrs. Nussbaum, can you think of anyone who might want to kill your husband?"

"You mean other than myself?" she challenged. "You may want to try that Josie person. If she'll take another woman's husband, heaven knows what else she'll do."

Jameson nodded. "We found a piece of paper in your husband's shirt pocket signed by someone named Matt. Can you think of anyone your husband knew who goes by that name?"

She rubbed her temple as if in an effort to remember. "Name doesn't ring a bell, but between his job and his betting, Alfred associated with a lot of people."

"Betting?"

"Alfred played the ponies," she explained.

"He had a bookie down in Southie by the name of Murphy. Worked out of some gin mill down on Columbia Road."

Jameson stood up from his place on the sofa, prompting Marjorie and Creighton to follow suit. "Thank you for your time, Mrs. Nussbaum. By the way, what's your first name? For the records."

"Bernice."

"Bernice," he repeated as he pulled a small notepad and pencil from his suit pocket. "And your phone number?"

"We don't have a phone; we use the one down at the drugstore where Natalie works. I have the number, though." The first Mrs. Nussbaum recited three digits which Jameson hastily transcribed.

"Natalie works at the drugstore?" Marjorie spoke up. "I bet she makes a mean chocolate malted."

"Oh no, she doesn't work the soda fountain. She assists in the dispensary."

"Clever girl," Marjorie remarked.

Jameson raised an eyebrow in question. "Well, thanks again for your time, Mrs. Nussbaum. If we need anything we'll give you a call."

Bernice escorted them to the door and bid them adieu. As they stepped onto the front stoop, the woman made one last request of Jameson. "Oh, Detective, when will my husband's body be released? And who will it be released to?"

"I'll let you know when the coroner is finished with his work," the young man replied to the first part of the question as he pocketed the pencil and notebook. "As to who will get the body, I can't say. I never handled anything like this before, but if I had to make an educated guess, I'd say you, since you're his legal wife."

"Thank you," she replied in a tone of smarmy self-satisfaction before shutting the storm door.

The trio advanced down the front walk in silence, speaking only when they had reached the curb and were safely out of earshot of the occupants of the house.

"Nussbaum said he had a house and some 'stuff' in Boston to get rid of," Marjorie remarked. "Who knew the 'stuff' would be a wife and two kids?"

"Unbelievable," Robert responded.

"Two wives," Creighton sputtered in astonishment. "Two!"

"I know," Jameson commiserated. "Why would anyone want to do that? Marrying one woman is bad enough, but two? That's just asking for it."

Marjorie hauled off and hit him in the arm

111

with her purse. "One is bad enough?"

Jameson held up his hands defensively. "Okay, okay. I take it back. Just stop hitting me."

Satisfied with the apology, the young woman leaned back against the squad car and with her arms folded against her chest, stared at the tiny red-shingle house. "What do you fellas think? Is our murderer in that house?"

"It's possible," Creighton averred. "Natalie's job in the dispensary gave all of them access to the curare. Natalie could have swiped it while no one was looking. Or Mrs. Nussbaum could have taken it while under the pretense of bringing her daughter lunch."

"What about Herbert?" she suggested. "He sure is a creepy kid, with all that true-crime nonsense."

"Yeah, he's creepy, and he's smart enough to have come up with the dart idea, but I don't think he'd have the nerve to go through with it. He's all talk," the detective opined.

"I'm with Jameson," the Englishman agreed. "A boy like that wouldn't have been able to sneak in and out of those fairgrounds without someone noticing him. One slip of the lip and he'd leave an indelible impression on every person there."

"Are you kidding? Did you see how many kids were at the fair? Who would have noticed one boy more in that crowd?" Marjorie shook her head. "No, Herbert could easily have slipped in undetected, committed the murder, and quietly gone back the way he came."

"Perhaps, but Bernice seems the most likely," Jameson replied. "The fact that she knew about Josie gives her a pretty strong motive."

"She also had the means," Creighton added. "That story about the market is far from being a watertight alibi. I don't believe for a moment that Natalie was with her. She added that in to cover her own tracks."

"Or to cover Natalie's," Marjorie offered. "A mother will go to great lengths to protect her child."

Creighton pulled a face. "Bernice would go to great lengths to protect Herbert, but Natalie? I dunno."

"Mmm," the other man grunted in agreement. "Natalie's a little too nervy to have committed murder. Besides, Bernice Nussbaum fits the description perfectly: tall, thin, dark hair, smoker."

Perplexed, Marjorie straightened up and let her arms fall to her sides. "What description? Am I missing something here?"

Robert described the three mysterious persons witnessed at the crime scene as well as Josie's flight attempt. When he was through, Marjorie stared him down. "So you're looking for this lady in white, are you?"

"Yes, and the two men."

"But you think that the woman is most likely the killer, don't you?"

"Yes, I do."

"Why? It could just as easily be the two businessmen, couldn't it?"

"I guess so, but poisoning is traditionally a woman's crime, it being neater and all."

Marjorie screwed up her face. "That old saw applies to poison administered by food. And it has nothing to do with neatness. Anyone who has seen a victim of cyanide poisoning can tell you that it's anything but neat. But it does have everything to do with accessibility. Women, as the traditional keepers of the home, have always been responsible for cooking and cleaning, thus giving them control over the family's food supply as well as its stock of household chemicals. Therefore, if Dear John has been anything but dear, his wife could easily find herself sprinkling his pork chops with the rat poison instead of the salt." Her eyes twinkled.

Creighton leaned in toward the detective and whispered aside, "Make a mental note, old man: take your pork chops plain."

Jameson nodded. "Then you think the businessmen killed Nussbaum."

"I have no opinion one way or the other, but you shouldn't be so quick to write it off as a woman's crime just because it involved poison. Actually, to some extent, this case is better classified as a shooting."

"Okay, but so far our only suspect is a woman."

Marjorie could hardly believe her ears. "Only suspect?"

Robert jerked his head toward the house. "Mrs. Nussbaum."

"And what about the other Mrs. Nussbaum? You said yourself she was going to skip town."

"True, but she doesn't have a motive."

"What!" Marjorie exclaimed in disbelief. "Alfred's bigamy provides a motive for both his wives. If Bernice knew about Josie, there's a strong possibility that Josie knew about Bernice. I think we need to ask ourselves why the 'Lady in White' was wearing such an elaborate disguise. Black hair contrasted against a white suit? A long sleeved, wool jacket in summer? A large hat with a veil at a church fair? Whoever donned that costume did so for a reason — perhaps to incriminate Bernice. And, Noonan discovered, Josie has a variety of wigs, makeup, and costumes at her disposal."

"Yeah, you're right about the motive," Robert conceded. "Then, I guess we have two suspects."

"And what about Herbert?" Marjorie piped up. "You two may have written him off, but I certainly haven't. I think he could do anything he sets his mind to."

Jameson relented. "Okay, okay, we'll add Herbert. So, three suspects —"

"Better make that four," Creighton corrected, staring off into the distance.

Marjorie and Jameson followed his gaze to the side of the house where they spotted Natalie, standing in the vegetable garden. The girl was watching them intently, her face cold and expressionless. When she noticed them staring at her, she turned and walked away, dropping the object that had dangled between the first and middle fingers of her right hand.

It was a burning cigarette.

NINE

Vanessa Randolph wheeled herself into the drawing room of her elegant red brick Beacon Hill townhouse to greet her guests. "Creighton Ashcroft," she exclaimed. "When my maid handed me your calling card, I was completely bowled over. What a pleasant surprise!"

Creighton rose from his place on the Regency settee and met his hostess halfway across the room. "Vanessa, dear," he hailed as he bent down over her chair and kissed her on the cheek, "so good to see you again. You look wonderful."

"No I don't; I look old. I could pass for your mother."

Creighton didn't know what to say, for it was true. The ravages of illness had left Vanessa looking far older than her thirty-eight years — her body frail and tenuous, her brown hair flecked with gray, and her face pale and gaunt. Yet, in her voice, he could still hear the echoes of her indomitable spirit.

She grabbed his hand. "You, however, are more handsome than ever, if that's possible. Tell me, what brings you to Boston? The sights? The history?" She grinned. "The women?"

Creighton gazed into her smiling blue eyes and recalled the crush he had on her as a lad. "Now, Vanessa," he teased, "you know you'll always be my one true love."

"Still the charmer, I see," she pooh-poohed, and wheeled her chair closer to where her other guests were standing. "Darling, you must introduce me to your friends."

The Englishman obediently followed behind the wheelchair and gestured toward his female sleuthing companion. "Vanessa, I'd like you to meet Miss Marjorie McClelland."

Marjorie stepped forward and extended her hand. Vanessa clutched it firmly. "Marjorie McClelland. You're not the mystery writer, are you?"

The younger woman beamed. "Why, yes, I am. You've read my books?"

"Read them? I've devoured them. We must chat later, I have so many questions to ask of you." She relinquished her hand and wheeled closer to Jameson. "And who is this good-looking young man?"

"Detective Robert Jameson, Hartford County Police," he introduced himself.

"Police? This isn't a raid, is it?" Vanessa joked.

Jameson smiled. "No, Mrs. Randolph."

"Good, because I think I still have some bathtub gin in the liquor cabinet." Vanessa wheeled herself toward the mahogany cocktail table where the maid had placed a tray of sandwiches and a large pitcher of lemonade. "Please, sit down and join me for some refreshments." She began to serve.

Marjorie and Jameson sat side by side on the Sheraton sofa, while Creighton resumed his post on the settee. "Vanessa," the Englishman spoke up as their hostess presented Marjorie with a glass of lemonade and a sandwich. "Detective Jameson told the truth when he said this isn't a raid, but it's not strictly a social visit either."

Vanessa passed Creighton a linen napkin and a plate bearing a sandwich of roast beef and horseradish. "It isn't?"

"No," Jameson replied, "we're here on police business."

Vanessa handed the detective a sandwich and poured him a glass of lemonade. "You're from Connecticut. What possible

119

business could you have in Boston? Isn't it out of your jurisdiction?"

"The crime I'm investigating took place in Hartford County, but the victim came from Boston."

She looked up from the glass she was pouring for Creighton. "Victim?"

"Murder, Vanessa," Creighton answered as he leaned forward and took the drink from his hostess' hand.

She poured some lemonade for herself, then withdrew a small flask from a pocket in her dress, the contents of which she added to the glass. "Cuts the tartness," she explained, before replacing the cap and returning the flask to her pocket. "Murder, you say? I didn't think that sort of thing happened in the country."

"Only since Creighton arrived," Marjorie quipped and took a bite of her sandwich.

Jameson chimed in. "He's like a one-person crime wave."

Vanessa laughed. "Oh, I do like your friends, Creighton. It's nice to see someone give you a run for your money." She took a sip of her spiked lemonade. "I've never before spoken to anyone involved in a murder investigation. It's all too exciting. Would you think it excessively morbid of me if I asked for a few details?"

Creighton shook his head. "Not at all, considering that the victim was an employee of yours."

"An employee of mine? You mean this person worked at Alchemy?"

"Salesman," Jameson confirmed. "Name was Alfred Nussbaum."

Vanessa tilted her head back and stared at the ceiling repeating the name like a magical incantation. "Alfred Nussbaum . . . Alfred Nussbaum . . ." She snapped her head back. "Can't say I remember him, although Stewart used to do most of the hiring. And now, well," she waved a hand over her legs, "I can't get down to the labs like I used to, so most of what I know about the business is what I hear secondhand. Sorry I can't be of more help."

"That's all right, Mrs. Randolph," Robert excused. "However, I will need access to his records."

"Of course. I'll be sure you get all the paperwork you need, Detective. And do feel free to talk to anyone at the labs."

"Thanks, I appreciate your help." He raised his plate, "And the sandwiches."

"It's nothing, Detective. I enjoy the company. The house gets very lonely at times." She turned to Creighton. "Very lonely."

What was she thinking as she stared

121

through him, Creighton wondered. Was she reminiscing about the days they spent together as children? The countless tea parties she had forced him to endure at her family's house on Long Island's Gold Coast, the shooting competitions — Vanessa had been a crack shot — the horseback rides they had enjoyed at the Ashcroft estate outside of London? Perhaps she even remembered the kiss that he had given her one summer afternoon after a particularly exhilarating ride. How old was he then? Thirteen, maybe? Fourteen?

It was strange how, despite her physical changes, the sight of Vanessa could still inspire in him the same feelings of wonderment and veneration. How, after all these years, her very presence regressed him back to the clumsy, passionate schoolboy who had tried, rather awkwardly, to pin her and kiss her behind the stables of his father's home.

Marjorie, perchance sensing the uneasiness between Creighton and Vanessa, changed the subject. "You have a lovely home, Mrs. Randolph."

The woman emerged from her fugue-like state. "Thank you, and please, call me Vanessa."

"Only if you call me Marjorie," she stipulated. Having devoured her sandwich in record time, she stood up and walked toward the window. "That garden out there," she gestured to a vast landscaped area across the street, "does it belong to you?"

"Oh no, dear, that's Louisburg Square. It's a park."

"Really?" She paused a moment. "You must think me rude, but would you mind if I went over and checked it out? It's too beautiful a day to spend it indoors."

"Nonsense, you're not rude," Vanessa resolved. "You shouldn't feel obligated to stay here with me. I'd spend more time in the park myself, if I had more energy."

"Thank you." Marjorie picked her hat up from the sofa and glanced at Jameson. "Are you coming, Robert?"

"Now?" he replied in mid-chew as he held up half of a sandwich. "I'm still eating."

"Well, meet me in the park when you're done," she ordered as she sashayed out the room. "I'll be back in a bit."

No sooner had the front door slammed, than Jameson placed his sandwich on the table and rose from his seat.

"Going already?" Creighton asked. "I thought you wanted to finish your sandwich."

The detective shook his head. "I said that to get Marjorie out of my hair. With her gone, I can check out that bookie Bernice Nussbaum mentioned without her begging me to take her along."

"Are you adverse to tagalongs in general, or just Marjorie?" the Englishman asked.

"Just Marjorie. I don't think a bar that fronts for a bookmaker is any place to take a lady. But you can come along if you'd like."

"I would like," he asserted, "very much."

"But Creighton," Vanessa spoke up, "you only just got here. I was looking forward to a nice long visit."

"And we shall have one," he promised as he got up from the settee, "as soon as I get back. In the meantime, why don't you have a nap? Rest up for later."

"I suppose I am a bit tired," she admitted. "But what about your friend? Isn't she going to be angry when she finds out you left without her? I thought you were all partners."

Jameson smiled. "Yeah, that's what Marjorie thinks, too."

Creighton went on to describe how Marjorie had hidden beneath the gurney and tailed them in the Model T. Vanessa brought a hand to her cheek in disbelief. "You mean to tell me that sweet little thing is capable of causing that much trouble?"

Creighton put his hat on and grinned. "Does Will Rogers twirl a lasso?"

TEN

Marjorie hightailed it across the street and through Louisburg Square. When she reached the other side of the park, she ran to the sidewalk and hastily flagged down a cab. The taxi pulled to a stop in front of her. "Columbia Road," she directed as she climbed into the backseat and slammed the door behind her.

The driver pulled away from the curb and glanced in his rearview mirror. "Columbia's a big street. Any spot in particular?"

"Yes, I'm looking for a man named Murphy. He's in the wagering business. Works out of a bar. Have you heard of him?"

"Murphy? What does a nice girl like you want with a bum like that?"

"He and I have some private business to discuss," she answered evasively. "Can I assume by your answer that you know where to find him?"

"Yeah, I know where to find him, but —"

"Good," she interrupted, "then you can take me there."

"Lady, I don't think you should be hanging around that sort of place," he protested. "It's down by the shipyards. All kinds of rough characters down there."

"Sir," she stated firmly, "I'm not paying you for your opinion. I'm paying you to drive. As much as I appreciate your concern, if you're not willing to take me there, I'll find another driver who will."

The driver momentarily removed his hands from the wheel and shrugged. "Okay, Columbia Road it is, then."

He accelerated the taxi as he circled the park and drove past the Randolph home. Marjorie peered out the back window of the cab to see Jameson and Creighton emerging from the front door. She had a hunch that Robert might try to sneak away to see Murphy while she was out of the house, thus the reason for the subterfuge. The only thing she hadn't anticipated was that Creighton would accompany him. She was certain he would have remained with Vanessa to hash over the more personal details of their relationship. What the nature of that relationship was, she hadn't a clue, but it was apparent from the silence in the drawing room that their bond went beyond that of mere friendship.

Had they been lovers some time long ago? Marjorie had intended to ask that question the afternoon they had driven back from Dr. Heller's laboratory, but she found the notion of a romantic connection between Creighton and Vanessa so oddly unsettling, that she decided she'd rather not know the answer. Even now, the thought grated upon her.

However, she had no time to dwell on such matters. Right now, there were bigger fish to fry. "Could you hurry it up, please?" she urged the driver.

"Someone chasing you?"

"No," she watched as the figures of the two men faded into the distance, "at least, not yet."

After several minutes, the taxi dropped her off at Columbia Road, a few blocks away from her final destination. "Want I should stay here and wait for you?"

Marjorie handed him the money for the fare and exited the cab. "No thanks. I have some friends who will meet me here later."

"Have it your way," the cabbie shrugged again before driving off down the road.

She took a deep breath to strengthen her resolve, and proceeded along the sidewalk in the direction of The Rusty Anchor Bar.

Columbia Road was, as the driver described it, a less than savory neighborhood. Running parallel to the shore, the street afforded a view of Massachusetts Bay and the various maritime industries that had cropped up around it, shipyards, freight companies, and fisheries, along with the unpleasant mélange of the odors associated with them.

Marjorie, trying hard not to inhale, hurried along until she reached The Rusty Anchor. Waiting outside the door stood two men of enormous stature. She smiled sweetly as she breezed past them and into the building's interior.

After a few seconds, during which her eyes acclimated themselves to the dim lighting, she was able to discern certain details about her surroundings. The Rusty Anchor was a rough-and-tumble establishment with sawdust on the floors and nautical prints lining the walls. One could easily picture a tattooed seaman using the Anchor as a hangout. Right now there were no seamen present, just two landlubbing patrons dressed in suits and ties. One was seated at a round table near the back of the saloon, the other stood behind him protectively.

Marjorie made her way to the bar, behind which hung the tavern's namesake. "What'll it be?" the bartender asked as she hoisted herself onto a stool.

"A Singapore sling," she replied, recalling the name of an exotic beverage Bette Davis had ordered in the picture she had seen last week. The bartender nodded and then set about his work, leaving Marjorie to wait in nervous silence.

She could feel the men watching her, but watching from a distance wasn't enough. If the man seated at the table was Murphy, she needed to do something to catch his attention. Pulling her skirt up an inch or two, she crossed her legs and shot a come-hither glance over her shoulder.

No sooner did she turn around than she heard the sound of footsteps approaching. The bartender placed a glass filled with an unusual reddish concoction on the counter in front of her. "One Singapore sling for the lady."

"Put it on Murph's tab," came a voice from behind her. It was the man who had been standing guard at the back of the room.

"Thanks," she said appreciatively.

"Don't thank me, thank Murph," he gestured toward the table where, in the shadows, the second man sat.

Marjorie, drink in hand, slid down off her barstool and walked over to Murphy's table, while his friend stayed behind at the bar. Murph was a slightly overweight, middle-aged man, with dark hair and traditional Irish features. "Thanks for the drink," she acknowledged.

"Pleasure's mine." He pushed a chair away from the table with his foot. "Take a load off."

Resisting the urge to first wipe off the seat, she sat down and leaned an elbow on the shellacked wooden table.

"What's your name, doll face?" he leered.

"Marjorie."

"Marjorie what?"

She struggled to think of the name of someone she knew, but all she could remember was that of her pet cat. "Sam," she blurted, then quickly added, "son. Marjorie Samson. And yours?"

"Murphy. Just Murphy."

"Just Murphy. That's a strange first name — Just," she quipped in an effort to ease the tension.

Murphy cracked a smile. "I like my women sassy. Why haven't I seen you around here before?"

Marjorie took a long sip of her drink and found, quite happily, that it was fizzy, cherry-flavored, and extremely smooth. "I'm from out of town," she replied coolly.

"Yeah, that so? Need someone to show you around?"

"I'm not much into sightseeing." She raised a shapely eyebrow. "If you know what I mean."

"I hear ya."

"Besides," Marjorie continued, "this isn't a pleasure trip. I'm helping a friend of mine make funeral arrangements for her old man."

"Too bad," he remarked.

"Not really. The guy was bad news." She shook her head. "I warned her about getting mixed up with that low-life Nussbaum."

Murphy's eyes narrowed. "You say Nussbaum?"

"Yeah, Alfred Nussbaum. You know him?"

"Maybe," he answered evasively.

Marjorie winced ever so slightly at Murphy's response. If Murphy was going to tell her anything about Nussbaum's death, he had to trust her. She took another sip of her drink and plotted her next move. In her twenty-odd years, she had learned a great deal about the opposite sex. One of the more important discoveries she had made was that, no matter how resistible a man may be, when an attractive young woman tells him he's irresistible, he's bound to think her the most truthful creature he has ever encountered. Adhering to this theory, she reached over and placed her hand on his. "You're awfully cute, you know."

He leaned in closer. "You ain't too bad yourself, sister."

"It's surprising we haven't gotten together sooner, considering we both know the same people."

"We do?"

"Mmm-hmm. The Nussbaums."

"I don't remember saying I knew them," he contended.

"You did. Indirectly."

Murphy grinned. "Cute and sassy," he noted aloud. "Yeah, I knew Alfred Nussbaum. He and I did business together." He gnashed his teeth together. "The crumb owed me $5,000."

Marjorie struggled to hide her surprise; for most people she knew, $5,000 was the equivalent of five years' salary. "Puts you in a tight spot then, doesn't it? With Nussbaum dead, you'll never get your money."

"When a chump owes you that much money, you know you ain't gonna get paid. You're better off with him outta the way."

"Oh," she drew her hand back in fear.

Murphy put an arm around the back of her chair. "Settle down, sweetheart. I've got no beef with you. Ain't your fault your friend's husband was a deadbeat. Ain't no need to go spoiling the beginning of a beautiful friendship."

Marjorie relaxed and put her hand back on his. "How true."

"So, how long you known Nussbaum's old lady?" he asked in a conversational tone.

"Oh, Josie and I go way back," she lied. "I remember —"

"Hold on a minute," Murphy interrupted. "Who's Josie?"

"Josie Nussbaum."

"Tall, good-looking redhead? Helluva dancer?"

"Yes."

"Then you mean Josie Saporito," he corrected.

"Josie Nussbaum now. She and Alfred got married a couple months back."

"You say married? I thought she was still hitched to Mateo Saporito, the owner of the Svengali. You know, that club where she dances."

"Oh, she threw him over for Alfred," Marjorie explained as though she were an authority on Josie Nussbaum's love life.

"Really?" Murphy pulled a face. "That's strange. Mattie never said nothing about Josie dumping him. I saw her at the club last week, and she and Mattie still seemed pretty friendly. If you catch my drift."

"You know how fickle women can be," she shrugged, keeping her composure despite her excitement. *Wait until Robert and Creighton hear about this,* she thought. Then it dawned on her: Robert and Creighton. They would be here any minute. She couldn't let them blow her cover.

"You seem jumpy, doll face. Anything the matter?"

"Two cops have been on my tail since I came into town. They think I might know something about Nussbaum's murder. It could spell trouble for you if they find me here," she explained, trying to make her leave.

Murphy was unfazed. "I can handle trouble." He snapped his fingers and the man from the bar approached the table. "Two cops will be showing up here. Wait outside and keep a lookout. If they ask for me, tell 'em I'm not here," he instructed. "That should get rid of 'em for now."

The other man nodded. "How will I know 'em?"

"One is average height, dark hair, looks like a young Douglas Fairbanks," Marjorie described. "The other's tall, light brown hair, well-dressed and has an accent. Southern. New Orleans, I think."

"You heard the lady." Murphy dispatched his lackey and then turned his attention back to Marjorie. "Where were we?"

"I was just about to leave," she answered in an attempt to escape the bookie's clutches.

"Not without giving me your phone number," he stipulated.

"Of course," Marjorie smiled demurely. "Got a pen?"

Murphy reached into his jacket pocket and pulled out a gold-plated fountain pen.

The bookmaking racket must be very lucrative, Marjorie thought as she took the pen and etched three characters onto her beverage napkin: *2L8.* It was a trick she had learned to rid herself of unwanted suitors, and it usually worked, provided the would-be lover did not read the number aloud immediately upon receipt. To avoid this happening, she folded the napkin and slipped it into his pocket along with the pen. "I'd better go," she excused herself as she rose from her chair.

"How's about we get together tonight?" Murphy asked. "I'll call you later."

"I'll be waiting," Marjorie purred. Then, with a wink in the bookmaker's direction, she picked her way between the tables and through the door to the street.

Outside, she skipped past Murphy's entourage with a friendly wave goodbye and headed down the block, all the time her heart racing. *Hurry! Hurry!* she urged herself. She had to get out of there before he looked at that number. Keeping her eye out for a cab, she turned the corner.

Suddenly, she felt an arm grab her by the waist and a hand clamp over her mouth.

ELEVEN

Marjorie began flailing her arms and kicking wildly, but the man's grip only tightened.

"Shh," Creighton hushed. "It's me." He shoved her into the back of the waiting police car and climbed in after her. As soon as he slammed his door shut, Jameson, positioned behind the steering wheel of the automobile, accelerated down the street, away from The Rusty Anchor.

Marjorie, meanwhile, was incensed. "What do you think you're doing, scaring me like that? And how did you know I was here? I left my car at Vanessa's."

Jameson glanced at Marjorie in his rearview mirror. "I didn't know at first, but when those two thugs wouldn't let us in to see Murphy, it dawned on me that someone must have tipped them off."

"Why did you assume it was me? Anyone could have told Murphy you were coming. I wouldn't precisely call this a clandestine operation. After all, you're driving a marked car."

"I can't speak for Jameson," Creighton spoke up, "but for me, the alarm went up when those gentlemen advised me to give up police work, return to my native New Orleans and take up cotton picking." He glared at the young woman next to him. "There's only one person I know who's crazy enough to try passing an Englishman off as a Southerner."

"Sorry," she apologized, "but I had to do something."

"You should be sorry. New Orleans," he harrumphed. "They eat things like opossum and squirrel down there, don't they?"

"I'm not sure," Marjorie faltered. "All I know is I didn't want you two barging in on Murphy and me after I had worked so hard to win his trust."

Jameson glared into the rearview mirror. "How exactly did you win his trust?"

"Through the only means at my disposal: feminine wiles."

Creighton burst out laughing.

"What's so funny about that?" Marjorie demanded.

"Nothing," the Englishman replied. "I'm just picturing you as a gun moll." The detective joined in Creighton's laughter.

"Laugh all you want," Marjorie advised, "but I promise you won't be chuckling when I tell you what I found out."

Robert's laughter quickly faded. "What did you find out, darling?"

"Oh, it's 'darling' again, is it? From the beginning, you've been opposed to my involvement in this investigation, but now that I've uncovered a possible lead, I'm your fair-haired girl, and you expect to share in my success." She narrowed her eyes. "If I'm not mistaken, Robert, you seem to be operating by a double standard. However, I'm feeling generous, so I'll give you my findings in one luscious nutshell. Namely, we have two more people to add to our suspect list."

"Care to tell us the sordid details?" Jameson inquired.

"I'd be honored," she replied smugly. "Suspect number one is Mr. Murphy, or just plain 'Murph' as he prefers to be called. Motive: Alfred Nussbaum owed Murphy $5,000 in gambling debts."

The detective whistled. "That's a lot of money for a simple salesman."

"I agree, but how is that a motive?" Creighton argued. "With Nussbaum dead, Murphy will never get his money back."

"I thought the same thing, until Mr. Murphy kindly pointed out that in his business, the punishment for deadbeats is rather stringent."

" 'Stringent' as in . . . ?" the Englishman drew a finger across his throat.

"You've got it."

"I'm sure this Murphy guy has a record," Jameson mentioned. "I'll try to get a copy of his mug shot and have Noonan show it around. Someone at the fair might recognize him as one of the businessmen."

"Better get photographs of his associates too, while you're at it," Marjorie suggested.

"Only thing is," Creighton spoke up, "would Murphy or his associates have been so discreet as to use a poison dart? I don't doubt that he has access to all sorts of drugs, but death by poison doesn't seem violent enough for his type."

"True," Marjorie agreed, "but he'd also be reluctant to have the police breathing down his neck, especially if he's had trouble with the law in the past. He could have hired an outside party to make the killing look like someone else's handiwork."

Jameson nodded. "So, who's the second suspect?"

"Mateo Saporito, or 'Mattie', as he's known to friends and acquaintances."

141

"The 'Matt' from the paper in Nussbaum's pocket," Robert's voice exclaimed from the front seat. "Who is he?"

"He's the owner of the Svengali, the nightclub where Josie and Alfred met."

"Josie's boss," Creighton concluded.

"More than that," Marjorie added. "He's also her husband."

"You mean ex-husband," the detective corrected in the same tone he had used with Bernice Nussbaum only hours earlier.

"No, Murphy's positive that Josie and Saporito are still married. In fact, he's seen the two of them together as recently as last week."

"Josie's married to someone else, too?" Robert asked incredulously.

"That's right," she averred. "What we have here is a case of a bigamist marrying another bigamist. I wonder if there's a specific term for that."

"There is," Creighton declared. "It's called lunacy."

Marjorie nodded in agreement, then leaned forward, resting her arms atop the back of the front seat. "Are we off to the Svengali?" she asked of her fiancé.

"Yes, we're off to the Svengali."

"Me too?"

"Yes," Jameson sighed, "you too."

Marjorie, pleased as punch, clapped her hands together and leaned back in her seat, her arms folded contentedly across her chest. Creighton gazed across the seat at her. He had cashed in all hopes of ever marrying the young woman, but there was one question he still needed to ask. "Marjorie," he whispered so the detective wouldn't hear him, "if bigamy were legal, and you were able to have two husbands, whom would you choose?"

The question caught her unawares. "Huh?"

"We already know Jameson is your first choice for a husband, but who would be your second?"

Marjorie blushed. "Oh, you shouldn't ask me that. Not with Robert right in the front seat."

"You're not doing anything wrong," Creighton assured. "It's a purely hypothetical question."

"Purely hypothetical?"

"Purely hypothetical. Nothing you say will be held against you."

"All right, but I should think you'd already know the answer."

Creighton was overcome with a feeling of elation. Second place, at least, was better than nothing. "I think I know," he smiled back, "but I'd like to hear it from you."

"Okay." She drew a deep breath, "Clark Gable."

His smile evaporated, replaced by an expression of absolute abashment. "Clark Gable?"

"Of course," she replied matter-of-factly. "You know how I go for him."

"Clark Gable." Creighton repeated as he leaned back against the seat and croaked, "Of course."

Marjorie, Creighton, and Jameson entered the Svengali Nightclub, a large establishment that occupied three storefronts. An extensive stage replete with red velvet curtains stretched along the entire back wall. To the left was a bar lined with stools and on the two remaining walls, cushioned booths with round tables. The rest of the space was filled with the typical jumble of tables and chairs; at one of these sat an olive-complected man with a black pencil mustache.

He looked up from the ledger books he was reviewing. "We're closed. Come back in a couple of hours."

Jameson spoke up. "Mr. Saporito?"

"Yeah?" He took a gander at Marjorie. "If you're here for the dancer job, angel, you'd better get rid of these guys first. I don't deal with agents."

Marjorie pulled a face. "What?"

"I said I don't deal with agents. This ain't some audition for a Broadway musical."

"The lady isn't looking for a job," Jameson clarified, "and I'm not an agent." He reached into his suit pocket and pulled out his badge, but before he could display it, Josie appeared from behind the stage curtain. "Mrs. Nussbaum," the detective greeted. "Or should I say Mrs. Saporito?"

Josie stepped down from the stage and cautiously approached the table.

"You know this guy?" Mattie asked.

"Yeah, he's the cop I told you about. The one looking into Alfie's death. His goon is the one who put me in the clink last night."

"You mean Alfie's murder," Jameson corrected. Then flashing his badge, "Detective Robert Jameson. Hartford County Police."

Saporito smirked. "I'd ask you to sit down, Detective, but I'm a busy man."

Creighton couldn't resist. "Oh, that's all right. I'll do it." He pulled out a chair. "Marjorie, would you care to sit down?"

"Yes, thank you." She sat down and waved at the chair beside her. "Would you care to join me?"

"Don't mind if I do," he quipped as he

145

settled into it.

"Who are the clowns?" Josie inquired of the detective, who was still standing.

"Clowns?" Marjorie repeated indignantly. "We're not the ones wearing all the make-up."

"Now, now, Marjorie," Creighton minded. "Be nice to the suspects. They may bite."

"These are my associates," Jameson introduced his companions. "Miss McClelland and Mr. Ashcroft."

"Yeah, yeah, enough with the chitchat," Saporito impatiently dismissed. "What do you want?"

"Some honesty would be refreshing."

Josie rolled her eyes in exasperation. "Okay, so I didn't tell you about Mattie, but I didn't lie either."

"Yes you did," the detective averred. "You told me Alfred Nussbaum didn't know anyone by the name of Matt."

"He didn't," she insisted. "What d'ya think? The two of them got together every week to play poker? Are you nuts?"

"No, I'm not nuts, but I'm not stupid either. You told me you and Nussbaum met here, at this club. You said he was a regular customer who used to come and see you dance; that he came here every night before he finally got up the nerve to talk to you.

146

Do you expect me to believe that during that time, he and your husband never crossed paths? That as owner of the club, your husband wouldn't say 'hello' and introduce himself to a regular paying customer? Come on, now, Josie."

"Hey, back off, pal," Saporito warned.

"You're awfully protective of your wife aren't you? Considering she divorced you so she could run off with another man." Jameson raised an eyebrow. "Or did she actually divorce you?"

"What do you mean by that?"

"I have witnesses who've seen the two of you together as recently as last week. Witnesses who claim that the two of you never broke up."

"The two of us are friends, that's all," Josie shouted. "We had some good times together. It's only natural we still have a soft spot for each other. Since when is that a crime?"

"How sweet. I always do enjoy it when former loves are reunited in friendship. It's a shame that such strong affection so often seems to turn to hate. There's no need for it really. Divorce should be friendly," Creighton remarked as he examined his fingernails. "I mean, take Alfred and his first wife, for instance — oh wait, I'm wrong! That doesn't

147

count because they were still married."

Josie's face went completely white. "Still married?"

"Yes. Didn't you know? I thought for sure you did," the Englishman replied. "Nussbaum was already married when he eloped with you, Josie. Therefore, your marriage to Alfred wasn't legal."

"So?" she asked, her voice trembling.

"So, any documents you may have signed as Josephine Nussbaum, such as, say a life insurance policy, would be null and void."

Josie took a deep breath and clinched her fists. "Why that no-good, double-crossing, son of a —"

"Shut up, Josie!" Saporito urged. "They're bluffing. They haven't got a thing on us."

"Not yet," Jameson answered, "but once we decode that note you gave Nussbaum, I'm sure all will be explained."

"I don't know nothing about no note," Mattie denied.

"Oooh," Marjorie cooed, "nice alliteration. Unfortunately, you gave yourself away by using a double negative, thus implying a positive."

"No," Creighton contradicted, "he used a triple negative, which works out as a single negative since the first two negatives cancel each other out."

"Oh, that's right." She cheerfully waved a hand in Saporito's direction. "Never mind. Go back to what you were saying."

"I can't remember," the bewildered man responded.

"Don't worry, I think we got the gist of it," Jameson reassured. "I just need to know one more thing before I get out of here. Where were you yesterday morning around eleven?"

"Upstairs in my apartment," Saporito replied. "Asleep."

"You always sleep so late?"

"In my business, you get to be a night person."

Jameson nodded and turned toward Josie. "And you?"

"I was at the hotel, doing my nails."

"Alone?"

"Yeah," she answered facetiously, "my manicurist couldn't make it. She was giving Lady Astor a pedicure."

"Thanks. You'll be hearing from me soon, so don't go scheduling any out-of-town trips," he warned as he headed toward the door. "Like the one to see your . . . ehem . . . 'mother' who, by the way, looks remarkably like Mr. Saporito."

Marjorie rose from her chair and trailed behind him. Creighton followed suit, but

149

not before delivering one last parting blow. With a tip of his hat, he asked the Saporitos, "Who are the clowns now?"

TWELVE

"Thanks." Jameson hung up the telephone in the hallway of the Randolph home with a loud click.

"Who was that?" inquired Marjorie.

"A friend of mine with the Boston Police. I asked if he could have a guy keep tabs on Saporito and Josie. Make sure they don't go anywhere. I also have him checking into their backgrounds."

"You think they have criminal records?"

"I wouldn't doubt it. Especially that Mattie. He's a slippery character if I ever saw one. He and Josie are hiding something. You mark my words."

"I think we've already established that," she stated. "From the way Josie reacted when she found out she was ineligible to collect on Nussbaum's life insurance, it's obvious she and Mattie were running some sort of scam."

Robert shook his head. "I'm talking about

more than just hustling a guy out of a few bucks."

Marjorie raised an eyebrow. "You think they killed Nussbaum?"

"Would it surprise you if they did?" he countered.

"After finding out that both Alfred and Josie were bigamists, nothing would surprise me. So, what's your theory?" she tested. "Was Josie the Lady in White? Or was Saporito one of the two businessmen?"

He shrugged. "Either. Both. Neither. Saporito could have hired the two men in suits to do the job. Running a nightclub, I'm sure he knows a lot of shady characters — characters who could obtain a lethal amount of curare. Same goes for Josie."

"Or you could be wrong and the woman and two men have nothing to do with Nussbaum's murder."

"Could be. I don't know." He shook his head again. "However, one thing's for certain. Saporito has a car. There's no other way he could have picked up Josie from jail and brought her back to Boston so quickly."

"Good point," Marjorie conceded. "Which means that it would have been easy for him to get to Ridgebury and back, but it also means that it will be very difficult to check his alibi for yesterday morning."

Jameson nodded. "If only we could crack the code on that note we found in Nussbaum's pocket."

"Yes, the note," Marjorie replied pensively. "Very strange."

"I can't guess what you're thinking, honey," Robert prodded.

"I'm thinking that note doesn't quite add up. What possible reason could Saporito have had for sending a note to Alfred Nussbaum?"

"Maybe he was arranging to meet Nussbaum at the fair."

"Fine," Marjorie allowed, "but why encode it?"

"I'm sure the letter wasn't strictly an invitation. It probably contained some personal content that Saporito didn't want prying eyes to see."

"Then why put his name and date on it? Why not sign it anonymously?"

"The note could have been meant for Josie and Nussbaum intercepted it," he offered, approaching the problem from a different angle.

The young woman still was not satisfied. "Saporito didn't need to write to Josie to communicate with her; he could have called her at the hotel. Nussbaum was a salesman; he was seldom around. Saporito could have called or even visited at any time. Furthermore, even if that note were meant for Josie, and Nussbaum managed to get hold of it, would he have been able to decipher it? You've had your best men on it for the past twenty-four hours, and not one of them has been able to make heads nor tails out of it."

"True," he acknowledged, "but can you come up with a better explanation for the note being in his pocket?"

"As of right now, I'm afraid I can't. There are a dozen possibilities, but none of them seem to fit."

Jameson put his arm around her shoulders and guided her back to the drawing room, where Creighton and Vanessa waited. "Don't use up all your brain power," he teased. "You still have a wedding to plan."

She smiled distractedly. "A wedding, yes." Her mind was still speculating the origins of the cryptic note.

"Detective Jameson," Vanessa said as they entered the drawing room. "I have that file you requested." She passed him a green folder containing varying sized sheets of paper. "Can I help you with anything else?"

Jameson took the folder and gave its contents a cursory glance. "No, this should do it. Thanks for your help."

"It was no trouble at all, Detective," she

replied graciously. "Now, if you're through with business for the day, I'd like to invite you all to stay for dinner. I've instructed my chef to create an absolutely sumptuous feast."

Marjorie's eyes lit up. It wasn't every day that one had a chance to dine with such an illustrious hostess. Besides, her repertoire of inexpensive, one-pot meals had grown tiresome as of late. "We'd love to," she started to reply, but Jameson spoke up before she had a chance.

"As tempting as that sounds, I'm afraid we're going to have to turn you down. My folks live here in Boston and they'd be pretty cross with me if they found out I was in town and didn't stop by to see them. Especially since Marjorie and I are engaged and all."

His fiancée stared at him like a deer caught in someone's headlights. *Did he say parents? Oh no, and me wearing this old dress!*

"You're engaged," Vanessa exclaimed. "What a delightfully handsome couple you make. Congratulations."

Marjorie brought her hand up to her hair and began running her fingers through it self-consciously. *God, that was a mess too.* "Thank you. And thank you for your invita-

155

tion. I hope your chef hasn't already started cooking."

"Don't worry," Vanessa assured, "he's a marvel with leftovers. I'm just sorry I won't be able to spend more time with Creighton and his friends."

"Well there's no reason Creighton has to come with us," Jameson pointed out. "Not that he isn't welcome, but we do have two cars, so he can drive back to Ridgebury whenever he wants. Not to mention, by the time we finish with my folks, it'll be late, so it's probably best Marjorie and I stay in town for the night before heading back home."

"You may have something there, Jameson," Creighton agreed. "By the time we finish with dinner and enjoy our brandy, I'm not sure I'll feel like driving back to Ridgebury. You have several bedrooms in this house, don't you, Vanessa. Maybe I'll stay here overnight. Then Marjorie and Jameson can meet us for breakfast in the morning."

"That sounds like a perfectly lovely idea!" Vanessa declared. "I'd love to have a good long visit with you. To catch up on old times."

The Englishman smiled. "Then maybe I should extend my visit even more. Perhaps

I'll stay a few days. That is, if you don't mind me rattling around the house."

"Now, you know I don't mind," she replied.

Vanessa might not have objected to the idea, but Marjorie did. What was Creighton thinking, leaving during the middle of a murder case? Couldn't he see that she needed him? "But Creighton," she reminded him, "aren't you forgetting something? You didn't bring a change of clothes. Neither did I, or Robert."

"That's all right. I'll give Arthur a call and have him send over some of my things. As for you two . . ."

"Oh, I'm fine," Jameson spoke up. "I have some things at my parents' house. My mother may have something you can borrow, dear. Although she is a lot shorter than you are —"

"Why don't you stay here tonight, Marjorie?" Vanessa offered. "I'm a woman and I've been married. You don't want to face your future in-laws in the morning without the proper attire. I know I wouldn't have. How mortifying!" She winked in the young writer's direction. "Detective, bring Marjorie back here this evening. She can borrow one of my nightgowns and a robe to wear tonight and, as for tomorrow, I have a whole dressing table full of cosmetics and hairdressing items and my housemaid is a wonder with laundry. She can have your entire ensemble cleaned and pressed before noon. It'll be fun! As for Creighton, I have a pair of Stewart's pajamas he can use. The trousers may be a little short, but they'll be good enough for one night. And if either of you need anything else, I'll have my staff go out and get it for you."

"Thank you, Vanessa." Creighton smiled at Marjorie. "See? We're both in good hands. Go run along and meet your future in-laws."

Marjorie smiled at Vanessa. She still didn't feel comfortable leaving Creighton behind, but whatever may have occurred in their past, Vanessa's hospitality was beyond question.

Jameson glanced at his watch. "Yeah, we should get going, honey. My mom always puts supper on the table at six thirty. We want to get there with plenty of time to spare."

Marjorie stared blankly at Jameson, trying desperately to find the words that would make him change his mind and decide to spend the evening with Vanessa and Creighton. Something that would get her out of the meeting with his parents and back in familiar territory. She glanced at Vanessa. *True, she was generous, but what else was there about this woman that so enchanted Creighton? Could it be love?*

"Well, don't dawdle, Marjorie," Creighton goaded. "Go on. I'll talk to you tomorrow morning. Over breakfast."

"Breakfast," she repeated as though the word were foreign to her. "Yes, that's a good idea."

"Come on. Let's go," Jameson took Marjorie by the arm and led her through the hallway. After the two couples had exchanged farewells, he walked her to the police car and helped her into the front passenger seat. As she waited for Robert to walk around to the driver's side of the car, she gazed forlornly upon the Randolph house and the silhouette of Creighton Ashcroft framed in the front doorway.

Jameson sent the squad car barreling down the Boston roads at top speed, all the while relating happy tales about his family and his childhood. "You're going to love my parents, Marjorie," he said proudly.

Marjorie had been listening with only half an ear. "Hmm."

"And they're going to love you." He grabbed her hand and kissed it. "Almost as

159

much as I do."

"Hmm." Try as she might, she couldn't tear her thoughts away from the man they had left behind. "Sweetheart," she started, deciding to get Robert's take on the situation, "did you notice anything different about Creighton today?"

Jameson pulled a face. "Different how?"

"Quiet. Introspective."

"Yeah, he was a bit subdued."

"So you noticed it too," she sighed in relief. "I bet it has something to do with Vanessa. There seems to be a tension between them. It makes me wonder if they were old flames. Did Creighton tell you anything when you were alone with him?"

"Why are you so interested?" Robert scowled.

Indeed, why was she so interested? She sidestepped the question. "You know me, I'm interested in everything."

"No, Creighton didn't mention anything about Vanessa. We were too busy talking about you."

"Me?" she exclaimed in surprise.

"Maybe not you directly," Jameson amended. "Creighton just told me that he planned on resigning as your editor."

"What? Why?" she demanded angrily.

"Because he and I agreed that it would be

160

inappropriate for the two of you to work together after we're married."

"How very nice of you and Creighton to make decisions for me," she quipped.

"Now don't get angry," he beseeched. "We were just thinking of your reputation."

"Damn my reputation! What do I care what people think? The only opinions that matter to me are yours, Creighton's, and Mrs. Patterson's. Anyway, what's so inappropriate about Creighton and I working together?"

"It's not so much the work, it's the idea of the two of you alone, in the house, while I'm not home."

"I never thought you were the jealous type, Robert."

"I'm not jealous, but I'm not crazy about the idea of him hanging around all the time. After all," he blurted, "the guy is in love with you."

Marjorie was thunderstruck. "C— Creighton," she stammered. "In love with me? That's ridiculous."

"Oh, come on, Marjorie! Wake up. Haven't you noticed the way he fusses over you? The way he conveniently shows up whenever we're together? Heck, you can even tell by the way he looks at you . . ."

Marjorie, feeling as though the earth were

swirling about her, leaned her head back against the seat. *Creighton. In love with me. It can't be true!*

"But that's in the past," Robert continued. "We're together now and Creighton has given me his word not to interfere." He reached over and rubbed her arm. "Besides, what difference does it make if Creighton resigns as your editor? Once we're married, you'll have other things to occupy your time, such as children."

Marjorie picked her head up. "Children?"

"Yeah. You want children, don't you?"

"Well, yes . . ." In reality, she hadn't given the subject much thought.

"Good, because you know, I'm kinda used to having a lot of kids around."

"Yes, you told me you were one of six."

"Yeah, and I decided a long time ago that I wanted a big family of my own one day."

"What do you mean 'big'?" she asked, panic-stricken.

"Oh not six," he replied reassuringly. "Four would be fine."

"Four?"

"Yeah, well, unless you decide you want more and then we can negotiate."

Marjorie was too stunned to argue; she wasn't yet prepared to be a mother to one child, let alone four. However, even this crisis paled in comparison with Jameson's earlier revelation. She played the detective's words over and over again in her head: *'Can't you see the guy's in love with you?'*

She closed her eyes and hoped that when she reopened them, she would find herself back in her cozy little house, or Mrs. Patterson's kitchen. Anywhere, so long as it was away from the cramped interior of the speeding police car. Yet, she knew her wish would go ungranted. Opening her eyes and finding that her situation was unchanged, all she could do was watch mutely the blur of passing buildings outside the passenger side window and listen to the sound of the tires as they moved over the seams in the pavement, their rhythmic bumping seeming to chant, "Creighton loves you. Creighton loves you. Creighton loves you . . ."

She leaned back against the headrest and exhaled deeply. This was supposed to be one of the happiest times of her life. So why was it that she felt like crying?

Thirteen

After a delicious repast of caviar, chateaubriand with béarnaise sauce, and fresh
asparagus tips, Creighton followed his hostess to the study for cognac and coffee. It
was a masculine room, with dark wainscot-
ing and bulky furnishings. Vanessa hoisted
herself out of her wheelchair and into a
straight-backed Biedermeier armchair while
Creighton selected a plump, mahogany-
colored leather sofa. Coffee, cognac, and all
the accoutrements were laid out on the
cocktail table between them.

Creighton took to the task of serving while
Vanessa opened a hinged wooden box filled
with tobacco and rolling papers.

"Since when do you smoke?" he asked.

"I don't," she replied as she rolled a
cigarette between her gnarled fingers. "This
was Stewart's. Every night after dinner, he
and I would come in here and he'd have a
cigarette. It was his personal blend of

tobacco. I used to complain about the smell, but now that he's gone, I miss it." She placed the cigarette in a long, slender holder, lit it, and then balanced the whole instrument against a crystal ashtray on the table beside her chair. "It's ironic," she said with a wry smile. "I used to tell Stewart that these cigarettes would be the death of him, and it turns out I was right."

Creighton passed her a demitasse cup filled with coffee. "How? He died in a fire at the Alchemy lab."

"He did," she took the cup and added a lump of sugar to it, "but the fire marshal's report proved that the fire was caused by a lit cigarette." She sighed. "I don't know how many times I had warned Stewart against smoking in the lab area. And each time, he'd assure me that he was the soul of caution. He never smoked near any of the chemicals, nor when anyone else was in the lab."

"Then how did it happen?"

"An overturned ashtray as much as the fire chief could guess. Strange that Stewart should have gone that way. He was always in control; always did exactly as he pleased."

"Yes, good old Stewart. He was a strong man, but kind, too," Creighton settled back with a glass of cognac. "One of my deepest regrets in life, Vanessa, is that I wasn't here for his funeral."

"Don't be ridiculous," she dismissed. "You were in New York at the time, and you sent those lovely flowers."

"That doesn't justify my behavior. I should have delivered the flowers myself. But, instead, I acted with complete indifference. I only hope you can forgive me."

She gazed at him lovingly. "You, Creighton, I could forgive anything."

He took a swig of cognac. "Just because you can, doesn't mean you should. It was beastly of me, leaving you alone, especially in your condition."

Vanessa was quick to correct him. "My illness was somewhat under control at that point. Just before Stewart's death, I heard of this so-called 'wonder drug' that would alleviate my symptoms. Well, I walked straight into my doctor's office and demanded that he prescribe it for me, and let me tell you, it has helped immensely. I'm not cured, mind you, and I'll never be able to reverse the damage done, but at least the pain isn't as intense as it used to be. Why, if circumstances were different, I'd say I had been given a new life. So I don't want to hear you wallowing in your guilt over my condition."

He smiled. "I'm English, Vanessa. Obsessing over perceived impoliteness is my stock-in-trade."

"Then find something else to obsess about, because I won't have you beating yourself up any longer," she stipulated. "You were a different person then, Creighton. Working fourteen hours a day, seven days a week at your family's business. Traveling around the globe. You were beginning to turn into . . . well, you were beginning to turn into your father."

"Yes," he agreed, "what a narrow squeak that was."

"You seem more relaxed now; more like the Creighton Ashcroft I know and love." She drank some of her coffee. "What finally made you give up the business and move to Connecticut?"

"My thirty-fourth birthday. I spent it alone, in my apartment, looking out the window, watching the people on the sidewalk below scurrying about. Some had arms full of groceries, others carried small children, but they were all hurrying, as though there were someplace important they couldn't wait to get to, someone special they couldn't wait to see. And I realized that in my thirty-four years, I had never rushed anywhere. Sure, there were meetings and appointments, but I had never rushed for something that I had chosen to do, never with any true sense of purpose. I had spent my entire life trying to be someone I'm not, making other people happy, living up to expectations."

"So you resigned," she filled in the blank.

"The very next day. Then I called a real estate agent and went house hunting. I never liked the city. Noisy, dirty, full of those society phonies. So I searched for a house in the country. A house suitable for a wife and a family. Not that I had either of those things, but hope springs eternal." He fell silent as he became conscious of how hollow his words sounded. What hope? All his hopes had been dashed.

Vanessa, watching him, cited, " 'But when the feast is finished and the lamps expire, then falls thy shadow, Cynara, the night is thine, and I am desolate and sick of an old passion.' "

"Ernest Dowson," Creighton attributed.

She took a sip of coffee and then flashed him a look of pity. "The lady has quite a hold on you."

He was intentionally obtuse. "What lady?"

"Marjorie McClelland."

"No, Vanessa. If I'm sick and desolate of an 'old passion', it's you," Creighton chuckled.

"Watch how you use the word 'old,' " Vanessa laughed. "Seriously though, I was a crush, a schoolboy's fantasy. But Marjorie — you're in love with her aren't you?"

He polished off the rest of his drink, placed the empty glass back on the table, and rose from his seat. "What does it matter?" he replied impatiently as he leaned his arms against the back of the sofa he had just vacated. "She doesn't love me."

"I think she does," Vanessa countered. "She just doesn't know it yet."

"When will she know it?" he asked sarcastically. "When we're both too old to do anything about it? Eh, Vanessa? When will she know?"

"Maybe soon. Maybe never."

"Thanks for cheering me up." He retraced his steps to the other side of the sofa and plopped back into it. "Well, never mind. I've washed my hands of her. I decided last night that I wasn't going to sit around waiting for her to come to terms with her own emotions. If she wants to marry Jameson, then let him have her and I hope they're very happy together. I have a life of my own to live: a house, a car, an extensive library to read, and someday a wife." He set his jaw. "And when I do marry, it will be to a woman who knows what she wants, who

169

doesn't play games, who doesn't tease you half to death only to resuscitate you and tease you again. Someone reliable and sincere. Someone like you, Vanessa." His eyes grew large as an idea formed in his fevered brain. "Yes, someone like you." He lunged from the sofa and dropped to one knee before the Biedermeier chair. "And who's more like you, than you?"

She looked at him as though he were completely daft. "You're speaking in tongues, Creighton. I don't understand a word of what you're saying."

"I'm saying why don't you and I give it a go? We always said we'd get married some-day."

"We were children then!"

"Yes, but children sometimes see these things more clearly than adults do."

She shook her head. "You know that there was only one man for me, Creighton, just as there is only one woman for you."

"Yes, but you see, that's the beauty of it. Neither of us has any unrealistic expectations for our relationship. We care for each other, of course, but neither of us is under the delusion that we're in love with each other. Therefore, there are no hearts to break, no feelings to hurt, no dreams to go unfulfilled. Ours would be a marriage based on friendship and companionship." He grabbed her by the hand. "It could work, Vanessa. You could move to Connecticut with me. I have plenty of room and the fresh air would do wonders for your health." He added, to sweeten the pot: "And I would see that you wanted for nothing."

She stared at him for a good long while. "And what about Alchemy?"

"Sell it. We have enough money."

Her eyes misted over. "Oh, Creighton," she sighed. "I couldn't sell the company, nor could I move out of this house. Apart from that stupid box of tobacco, the house and the business are all I have left of Stewart. I would rather die than part with them."

Creighton went on, undeterred. "Then I'll sell my house and move in here. I could help you run the business."

She laughed. "And be back where you were a few months ago. Living in a big city and working around the clock at an office job you hate."

"But I wouldn't be back where I was," he explained. "I'd have you."

"And you'd be willing to sell your home and move here, even though you'd be miles away from Marjorie?" she challenged.

Creighton fell silent. The only thing sustaining him right now was the consolation that at least if he could not have Marjorie for himself, he could still be near to her.

"I thought not. It would appear that neither of us is willing to surrender our ghosts." Vanessa placed her hand on his cheek. "I thank you though, for asking. Maybe someday, when both of us have been nearly consumed by our loneliness, maybe then we'll be willing to cash in the ghosts of the past for a ghost of a chance." A tear slid silently down her face. "Until that day comes, I hope you'll keep me in mind."

He removed her hand from his face and kissed it. "You know I will."

"Good." She wiped her eyes and took a deep breath. "Then if we're finished with this foolishness, I think I'll go to bed." Using the arms of the chair, she raised herself to a standing position. Creighton rose and helped her into the wheelchair. "Try to get some rest, Creighton. I'm sure you'll have a better outlook in the morning." She turned her chair toward the door of the study. "I think you're all set. You already know where your room is; I had the maid lay your pajamas on the bed, and you'll find a spare toothbrush in the bathroom."

Creighton grinned. "You've thought of everything, haven't you?"

"Call it my maternal instinct," Vanessa replied as she wheeled herself out the door. "Good night, darling. Sleep well."

"I'll try." He followed behind her and watched until she had made it safely down the hallway, to her first-floor bedroom. When the door had closed behind her, Creighton returned to the study. During his conversation with Vanessa, he hadn't noticed the phonograph playing in the corner of the room. Now that he was alone he heard Bing Crosby crooning: *I thought at last I'd found you . . . but other arms surround you . . .*

Having refilled his cognac glass, he settled into the armchair that Vanessa had occupied and took a long drink.

Alone again, he said to himself wistfully. He had hoped that spending some time with Vanessa would help to fill the void he had felt since the announcement of Jameson and Marjorie's engagement, but witnessing his dear friend's debilitated state — a state exacerbated by grief — just made his heart ache even more.

Life, it seemed, was nothing more than a series of bitter ironies. Good men like Stewart Randolph always seemed to die young, while ruthless men like his father appeared to live forever. Vibrant, energetic women like Vanessa fell ill and became confined to wheelchairs, while the indolent shrews of the world remained healthy and complained incessantly over such maladies as indigestion and ingrown toenails. As if that weren't enough to rile his anger, Alfred Nussbaum, a middle-aged, balding man who had gambled away his last cent, had managed to find two wives, while Creighton didn't even have one.

He swallowed the rest of his brandy in one gulp and sighed. Life, to be certain, was not fair but, he mused, as he remembered the too-short existence of Stewart Randolph, it was still better than the alternative.

With this bit of wisdom firmly implanted in his mind, Creighton decided to go to bed. He placed his empty glass on the cocktail table and, reaching over to the crystal ashtray, rubbed out the still-smoldering cigarette.

As Creighton left the darkened room, Crosby's mellow voice continued to sing: *But what's the use of scheming . . . I know I must be dreaming . . . For I don't stand a ghost of a chance with you . . .*

Marjorie returned from the Jameson homestead to the relative quiet of the Randolph home just before eleven p.m. Robert's parents were pleasant enough, but it was apparent from his mother's questions and attitude that a daughter-in-law who was a mystery novelist wasn't what the petite, dark-haired woman had in mind for her son.

She could still hear Mrs. Jameson's words echoing in her brain, *"Of course, you won't have time for this mystery nonsense, once you have a family of your own"* alternating with the sound of Jameson's voice stating clearly, firmly, *"The man's in love with you!"*

But if she was in need of sanctuary, she was not to find it within these walls. For as she entered, she heard Creighton's fevered words floating from the study: *"I'm saying why don't you and I give it a go? We always said we'd get married someday."*

At once, Marjorie felt the earth spin beneath her feet. *This.* This was what she had dreaded. This was what she had sensed earlier. This was why she had wanted to stay behind. If Creighton had loved her once, she had pushed him away — pushed him into Vanessa's arms. But, perhaps, it was Vanessa he had loved all the time. Perhaps she was the passing fancy — a fantasy that Creighton had created in order to ease the pain he had experienced over Vanessa. And now that Vanessa was free . . .

Tears streaming down her cheeks, Marjorie decided not to wait for Vanessa's reply.

175

She quietly shut the front door behind her and, after removing her shoes, padded upstairs to her room, unobserved, unnoticed, and terribly alone.

FOURTEEN

Marjorie shuffled downstairs to the dining room at nine thirty the next morning. In truth, she had been awake most of the night, but she didn't want to see Creighton and Vanessa any longer than necessary and, therefore, delayed her "awakening" until she could be certain that Jameson would be present.

Clad in a robe whose sleeves she had rolled up and whose hem was too long by approximately four inches, Marjorie gingerly wended her way downstairs. Her entrance was well timed, for she stepped into the dining room to find the detective, seated to the left of Vanessa, happily drinking coffee and consuming a large plate of scrambled eggs, toast, and bacon.

She took a deep breath and breezed past Creighton and Vanessa to deliver a kiss that took her fiancé by surprise. "Good morning, darling!"

Jameson's eyes opened wide. "Why hello. You must have slept well."

Marjorie gave an elaborate demonstration of a stretch. "Yes I did. But, then again, why shouldn't I? It was a wonderful evening."

"Yes it was," Jameson agreed. "My father couldn't stop talking about you last night. I dropped you off and he stayed up just to tell me how nice he thought you were."

"How sweet! I liked him too."

Vanessa spoke up from her place at the head of the table. "I didn't even hear you come in. What time was it? It must have been rather late."

"About eleven," Jameson replied.

"Oh, it must have been later than that!" Marjorie argued.

Creighton slipped her a surreptitious glance.

"No," Jameson maintained, "it was eleven. I got back home at eleven thirty."

Vanessa pulled a face. "What were we doing, Creighton, that I didn't hear Marjorie come in?"

"Talking, most likely," the Englishman replied, staring at Marjorie the entire time. "Although we did have the phonograph on."

"Yes. Yes, we did. Although . . ."

Marjorie was relieved to see the maid so that she could take charge of the conversation. "May I have some coffee please? Thank you." The young woman filled her cup to the brim; so eager was Marjorie to change subjects, that she took a sip even before adding milk or sugar. "Did you hear from headquarters yet, Robert?"

"Yeah, I did. Noonan got a lead on the cab driver who took Nussbaum to the fair. I asked him to bring him into the station this afternoon so I can talk to him."

"May I join you?" Marjorie asked hopefully.

Jameson smiled. "I was counting on it."

Vanessa cleared her throat nervously. "Are you going to speak with this person too, Creighton?"

Creighton glared at Marjorie. "No, Jameson can handle it. This is my holiday, remember?" He returned his attention to his hostess. "There's nowhere I'd rather be than with you."

She cleared her throat. "Are you sure?"

Marjorie glanced at Vanessa. *What exactly was behind that question? Did she want Creighton to go? Or did she want him to stay? Was it a test? And what was her answer to Creighton's proposal?* Before Marjorie could say anything, the maid presented her with a plate of scrambled eggs and toast. "Thanks," she mumbled, and dug a fork into the fluffy yellow mass.

Vanessa passed a silver salver. "Bacon, Marjorie?"

"No, thank you." She added a teaspoon of sugar and a bit of milk to her coffee and took a sip before taking a bite of the buttered toast. She had always wished she were like other women who, in times of emotional distress, had no appetite for food, but, be it her Irish heritage or a sound constitution, Marjorie, in times of trouble, suffered absolutely no digestive ailments whatsoever. In fact, moments of extreme distress typically caused her appetite to be heightened to field-hand proportions.

She gazed at her full plate and wondered whether she would be able to finish the contents, but the thought was a fleeting one. All she had to do was glance at Creighton and Vanessa and her hunger grew by leaps and bounds.

"So, how was your evening?" Jameson asked innocently.

"Oh, it was wonderful," Creighton replied. "Dinner was marvelous . . ."

Marjorie salted her eggs and took a large bite.

". . . caviar and champagne . . ."

She doused the toast with a liberal teaspoonful of strawberry preserves.

". . . chateaubriand with béarnaise sauce . . ."

She spread the preserves evenly before devouring a corner.

". . . fresh, young, asparagus tips . . ."

She plunged her fork back into the scrambled eggs, all the while staring at Creighton, who returned her gaze with twice the intensity.

". . . and for dessert, chocolate mousse, followed by a fine cognac, coffee, and a wonderful conversation by candlelight — oh and Bing Crosby on the phonograph, of course." He punctuated the last statement with a broad grin.

Marjorie made a loud crunching sound as she took yet another bite of toast.

Her tablemates turned and stared.

Marjorie begged forgiveness. "Oh, I beg your pardon. The toast is well done. Not in a bad way. Just crunchy. Good and tasty and buttery and crunchy." She smiled demurely and stabbed another tidbit of egg.

Creighton smiled back. "And how was your evening? Did you 'kids' have a good time with the 'folks'?"

"We had a great time," Jameson was keen to answer. "Not quite as sophisticated as your night, but still just as good. My mother made liver and onions." He added aside to

Vanessa, "It's my favorite. Then we looked at family photos and had rhubarb pie with fresh whipped cream for dessert. Wasn't it fun, honey?" he asked of Marjorie, who had, by now, polished off most of her plate.

"Yes. Glorious," she replied. "I don't think I shall ever forget it. It's a story we can tell our children and our grandchildren. Now, if you'll all excuse me, I'm going to get ready for the trip back to Ridgebury."

Marjorie rose from her chair and curtsied for Vanessa. "Thank you for everything. It was very generous of you to have me stay the night and provide breakfast too. My compliments to your cook." She bestowed a hug upon her hostess and then proceeded to march around the table and toward the stairs. However, as she did so, her robe caught upon Creighton's chair leg. Oblivious to the potential danger and seeking to leave the room as quickly as possible, Marjorie soldiered on and wound up falling, face-first, onto the floor.

Creighton, albeit amused, leapt to her aid. "Are you all right?"

She pulled the flowing garment free from its snag and rose to her feet without assistance. "I'm fine. Thank you." With a deep breath and shoulders erect, she marched up the stairs and to the guest bedroom, the image of Creighton Ashcroft's complacent grin nettling her more and more with each step.

FIFTEEN

Raymond Maxwell was a tall, thin man with light brown hair that was graying at the temples. He rose from his seat by the front door as Marjorie and Jameson entered the station house at approximately one in the afternoon. Upon direction from Robert, he followed the couple to the detective's desk, where Noonan dutifully arranged an extra chair for Marjorie and then stood behind Jameson to observe the questioning.

"Mr. Maxwell," Jameson greeted. "Good of you to come. Before we begin, can we get you anything? Coffee? Water?"

The man nervously cleared his throat. "Um, no, thanks. I had a sandwich on the way over here."

Jameson nodded. "Then I'll get down to business." He extracted a photograph from a manila folder and placed it in front of the man. "You say this man was a fare of yours on Saturday?"

Maxwell took the photograph between a thumb and forefinger whose nails were lined with dirt. "Yes, sir. Yes I did."

"Do you remember anything about the fare? Where you picked him up, where you dropped him off — that sort of thing?"

"Yes, I do," he handed the photo back to Jameson. "I picked him up at the Hideaway Hotel. It's a dumpy place in Hartford. And I drove him to the fair here in Ridgebury."

"About what time was that?"

"Huh? Oh, I picked him up about ten thirty in the morning. He said he needed to be at the fair by eleven. I got him there at ten minutes to."

Jameson leaned back in his chair. "Did he mention why he needed to be at the fair?"

"No, I don't think — oh wait, I tell a lie. Yes, he did. He said he had some appointments to keep."

"Appointments?" Marjorie quizzed. "As in more than one?"

"Yeah, that's what he said. He was meeting someone at eleven and someone else at noon. He joked about it. Said that if the person at eleven didn't show he'd be in a huge fix with the person at noon."

Noonan pulled a face. "What the heck does that mean?"

The cabbie shrugged. "How should I

know? It's not like he told me what it was all about. Besides, with all the characters who get in and outta my cab all day, you're lucky I even remember this guy."

"That's a very good point," Jameson agreed. "Why do you remember him?"

"A few things. Off the bat, he was my first fare of the day. I usually remember the first fare. And the last one. I don't know why, but I always do."

Marjorie smiled politely and nodded.

"Then, the guy slipped me a twenty dollar bill if I'd wait for him. I mean, twenty bucks for an hour's work, that's a lotta cabbage for a slob like me."

"Hold on there a second," Jameson leaned across the desk. "You said you waited for him?"

"Yeah. A guy who gives ya twenty dollars to wait for him is probably gonna give you a good tip." He removed his cap and scratched his head. "Only the fella didn't come back. I waited and waited, but nothin'. Then I heard police sirens and I figured I'd better split. Twenty bucks is twenty bucks, but it ain't worth a run-in with the cops. Especially with my record. I'm straight now, you see — gotta nice little wife and two kids — but it wasn't always like that. I was a bit of a tough when I was younger. Used to mix it up a lot." He replaced his cap. "The police ain't got no beef with me now and I ain't got no beef with them. But I'm still a little gun shy, if you know what I mean."

"We know what you mean," Noonan confirmed. "Don't worry. You ain't a suspect. Just tell us what you know, we'll take your statement, and then you can get back to work."

Maxwell took his cap off again, this time out of tribute, and smiled. "Thanks, officer. That certainly does put my mind at ease."

Jameson flashed a brief smile. "Mr. Maxwell, before Officer Noonan takes your statement, you said there were a few things that made you remember this fare — the twenty dollars and the fact it was the first fare of the day. Was there anything else? Did you see something while you were waiting? Anyone suspicious?"

"Oh yeah," the cabbie nearly sang the phrase. "I hope I don't get in trouble for this, but there was a kid."

"A kid?"

"Yeah, I decided to beat it and this kid ran right in front of my cab. I almost hit him!"

"Probably Freddie, on his way to call you," Marjorie said to Jameson.

"No, Miss. He couldn't have been run-

187

ning to fetch the cops, 'cause I already heard the sirens. The sirens were what made me want to beat it outta there in the first place." He shook his head adamantly. "No, this kid was funny. He hightailed it outta the fair and ran in front of my cab. I had to slam on the brakes so I wouldn't hit him. I got out to see if he was okay, but he just kept running. Normally a kid would be shaken up, but not this one. This one just kept on goin' — didn't even look back."

"What did he look like?" Marjorie asked excitedly.

"Oh, about sixteen years old. Thin, dark hair, glasses and a pretty big . . ." He drew his hand outwards from his nose. "I'll never forget his face. He looked right at me as I slammed on the brakes. He seemed . . . I dunno, angry. But he didn't flinch. He didn't jump. He didn't even move a muscle. Nah, he's a cool customer that one."

Marjorie looked at Jameson with a combination of wide-eyed excitement and horror. "Yes, Mr. Maxwell," she agreed. "Herbert Nussbaum is precisely that — a cool customer."

Noonan escorted Mr. Maxwell to a back office, where they completed and filed the necessary paperwork. Marjorie had been feeling a bit drained from her sleepless night at the Randolph house, but the latest revelations in the Nussbaum case provided her with a jolt of energy that could have kept her awake for days.

She leaned an elbow on Robert's desk. "And you said Herbert Nussbaum wasn't a viable suspect!"

"Okay, so he was there," he admitted grudgingly. "But what's his motive?"

"Are you kidding? Herbert openly admitted that he hated his father. Nussbaum never appreciated the boy and his — what did he call it? — 'superior intellect.' Add to that the fact that Nussbaum betrayed Herbert's mother and hurt his sister, and the kid has a list of motives a mile long. Not to mention he also has the disposition needed to pull off the crime. You heard how Maxwell described him — that's exactly the type of person who would kill another human being. Cold, calculating . . . yet inside, almost simmering over with anger."

"I agree with you, honey. Herbert Nussbaum is definitely one strange kid. But just because he was running away from the scene, doesn't mean he committed murder."

"No, it doesn't," Marjorie conceded. "But it does make you wonder if Herbert was one of the people Nussbaum was on his way to see."

"If so, Alfred would have said he was meeting his son. He wouldn't have said he had two 'appointments' to keep."

"I'm not so sure about that. Nussbaum was living a double life. He wouldn't have told the cabbie anything that would incite a bunch of questions about his personal life. You know how those conversations go. Alfred mentions he's seeing his son, the cabbie asks him how many children he has and how long he's been married. I admit I don't know Nussbaum — I never will — but he doesn't strike me as the type who would have readily offered up that kind of information."

Jameson nodded. "You're probably right. But what reason would Nussbaum have had for meeting Herbert at the fair?"

Marjorie shook her head. "I don't know. But we can't ask Nussbaum."

He sighed. "No, we can't. We'll have to ask Herbert."

"You do that. I'll be at home listening to *Buck Rogers*." She rose from her chair and started to walk toward the door.

"Oh no you don't!" Jameson bellowed from his desk. "You wanted in on this investigation. Well, you're 'in' and that means talking to Herbert."

Marjorie pulled a face and moped back to her seat. "I know. I was joking . . . somewhat. That boy really gives me the creeps."

"Trust me, I'd rather be having a root canal than facing him again, but —" Before the detective could complete his thought, the phone positioned in the corner of the desk began to sound. He answered it on the second ring. "Jameson here . . . Oh hiya, Mike. What's new? . . . Oh yeah? . . . Really? . . . Hmmm . . . Yeah, we had a lead here too — Nussbaum's kid was at the fair. Cabbie saw him . . . Yeah . . . uh huh . . . Yeah, if you could bring them downtown that would be great . . . I'll be there in a couple of hours . . . See ya then. Thanks." He replaced the receiver in the cradle with a loud click.

"What was that about?" Marjorie inquired.

"Mike Logan, the friend of mine with the Boston Police Department, questioned the parking garage attendant where Mateo Saporito keeps his car. Seems 'Mattie' was out early Saturday morning and didn't return home until the wee hours of Sunday morning, when he had Josie in tow."

Marjorie arched a finely tweezed eyebrow. "He could have been in Ridgebury."

191

"Hmm mmm. Mike is picking up Mattie and Herbert, and bringing them to his station. I said we'd meet him there to do the questioning."

"Back to Boston!" Marjorie declared and then realized the significance of her words. "Oh, before we leave, could I stop at home for a minute? Just to freshen up. Vanessa has different coloring than I do and her lipstick just doesn't go well with fair skin."

"You look fine to me, sweetheart. But we can stop — so long as it's quick."

"Oh, it will be," Marjorie assured as she grabbed her pocketbook and left the station. "Or at least I hope so."

SIXTEEN

Creighton paced back and forth in the tiled lobby of the fourteenth district station of the Boston Police Department, pondering the telephone call he had received from Marjorie just hours before. What was the purpose of her call? Why did she ask him to come here? Now that she was engaged to Jameson she had all she wanted, hadn't she? Why rope him into her schemes? And yet, here he was, once again at her beck and call, awaiting her arrival.

Damnit, man, he thought to himself. *What in God's name are you doing here? She's set to marry another man!* He drew a deep breath and swung open the glass and metal police station door, only to find Detective Robert Jameson waiting on the other side.

"Creighton, what are you doing here?" Jameson asked in surprise.

The Englishman couldn't help but grin. True, he had relinquished all claims to

Marjorie McClelland, but the expression of surprise and shock on the detective's normally sanguine countenance was still cause for celebration. "Marjorie called me. She said I should meet you here."

Jameson turned his narrowed eyes toward his fiancée.

Marjorie, looking radiant, as well as defiant, in a green crepe dress that was a favorite of Creighton's, was prepared for the challenge. "I thought he should be here in case I forget anything. After all, I do intend on converting this into a true crime book, and Creighton, despite all arguments to the contrary, *is* still my editor." Her eyes sparkled with an electricity he had never before seen. "You are still my editor, aren't you, Creighton?"

He stared at her, unsure how to react. There was something different about her — that was for certain — but he had been led down this road before, only to meet with disappointment and frustration. "I'm your editor so long as you and the good detective wish me to be," he replied diplomatically.

Marjorie's lovely face was illuminated with a broad grin. "Of course I want you as my editor, Mr. Ashcroft. And so does Detective Jameson." She turned to her escort, "Don't you, Robert?"

Creighton grinned. When Marjorie was excited about something, when she had an objective to achieve, it was as if someone flipped a switch and every cell in her body was pulsing with life, her magnetism overshadowing every other being in the room. Detective Jameson didn't stand a chance.

"Ummm . . . yeah, yeah, I guess so," Robert answered. Creighton imagined he heard the sound of the detective's spine cracking under the steamroller force of Marjorie's vitality.

Marjorie smiled and smoothed the skirt of her dress — Creighton couldn't help but admire her curves. "Good. Now that that's settled," she proclaimed, "let's go see our suspects."

Detective Mike Logan was a giant of a man. Nearly six-feet-four-inches tall, barrel chested and broad shouldered, he met Detective Jameson at the front desk and offered a beefy hand in greeting. "Hey Bob. How are ya?"

Jameson shook his hand vigorously. "Good. Very good. Mike, I'd like you to meet my fiancée, Miss Marjorie McClelland."

Logan bowed slightly; that the younger detective had brought his bride-to-be with him on an interrogation gave him pause, but he offered a warm welcome. "Fiancée? You're finally getting hitched, huh? That's fantastic! When's the lucky day?"

"Oh, we haven't set a date yet," Marjorie responded.

"You haven't? Are you crazy, Bob? You don't want a pretty thing like this to get away." He gave Marjorie a playful wink before extending his hand to Creighton. "Is this your partner?"

The Englishman shook Logan's hand and immediately understood how and where the term "meat hooks" had originated.

"Yeah," Jameson replied half-heartedly. "Yeah, I guess you can say Creighton's my partner."

"Well, glad to meet ya!" Logan pumped Creighton's arm up and down enthusiastically.

"Likewise." So spirited was the detective's pumping, that Creighton wondered if he should shoot water out of his mouth.

As if sensing the Englishman's pain, Logan dropped his hand and his smile ran away from his face. "Say, Bob, I rounded up those two like you asked. Saporito didn't give us much trouble, but that Herb kid and his mother? What a scene that was! The kid's busy quoting the Massachusetts state penal code while the mother's clinging onto my leg, begging me to let go of her baby." He shook his head. "Some baby! When we went into his room, he was working on these." Logan held out a handkerchief containing two small brass objects.

"Darts!" Marjorie exclaimed.

"Yeah, he was making them from pen nibs he flattened out with a ball-peen hammer."

"Talk about incriminating," Marjorie observed.

"You'd better mind that leg of yours, Logan," Creighton quipped. "Because if we have to arrest this kid, his mother will do a lot more than cling to it."

"Yeah, don't I know it," Logan chuckled.

"Did you find out anything else on Saporito?" Jameson inquired.

"Oh yeah. He and Josie definitely have criminal records. I don't have the details, but New York's sending the files — I should have them tomorrow."

Jameson nodded. "Thanks, Bob. I appreciate your help." He motioned to the back of the station. "Where are our suspects?"

"The kid's in room 'A' and Saporito is in room 'B.' " He patted Jameson on the back. "If you need my help, let me know."

Herbert Nussbaum sat, perfectly erect and

completely composed, at a small, rectangular table. His mother, Bernice, sat beside him, her face pinched with worry and indignation. She stood up as Marjorie, Creighton, and Jameson entered the room. "What is this about? You can't keep my son here. He knows nothing about his father's death. I told you he was home that morning."

Jameson placed Raymond Maxwell's statement on the table before Bernice and then sat down at the head of the table; Marjorie and Creighton sat opposite Bernice and Herbert, respectively.

"We have a witness who says otherwise," the detective countered.

Bernice read the statement, and slowly sat back down. "What? What is this?" She turned her gaze toward her son. "I didn't know you were . . ." Her voice trailed off, but within seconds she stood up again. "Who is this cab driver person? And why are you taking his word over mine?"

"Mr. Maxwell was the cab driver who took your husband to the fair the day he was killed," Jameson replied. "He claims that, as he drove out of the fair parking area, he had to slam on the brakes to avoid hitting Herbert, who was running away from the fairgrounds just as the police were arriving."

"That's impossible!"

"Your son looked right at him as he hit the brakes. He has no reason to lie, Mrs. Nussbaum."

She threw her hands in the air. "No reason to lie? He was Alfred's driver. Alfred's driver! Do I have to spell it out for you? He picked Alfred up at that dumpy hotel he lived in and, while he waited for Alfred to get ready — Alfred was never on time — Josie got to him and paid him to say he saw Herbert at the fair. It's obvious!"

Marjorie was incredulous. "What? Why would she do that?"

"Because she murdered Alfred and wants to pin the blame on someone else! I told you my son was at home that day. Weren't you, Herbert?"

The spectacled young man squirmed in his seat.

"Mommy's defending you, Herbert. Now, tell these people you weren't at the fair," Bernice demanded.

"I wasn't at the fair," the boy replied mechanically.

Mrs. Nussbaum smiled beatifically.

"It doesn't much matter what either of you say when I have these." Jameson presented the handkerchief-wrapped darts.

Bernice's smile turned into a scowl.

"Where on earth did you get those?"

"Your son was working on them when Detective Logan went to collect him for this evening's interrogation."

"T — Those were for my work," Herbert stammered. "I was re-creating my father's murder. To prove that I'm the world's greatest criminologist!"

"World's greatest criminologist, huh?" Jameson jeered. "Your father had arranged to meet two people at the fair that day. I say one of them was you, Herbert. Being well educated in the art of murder, you hatched the poisoned dart scheme, making the darts just as you did these and securing the curare from the dispensary where your sister works. While your father was waiting for you — or the other person he was meeting — you shot him with the poisoned dart and then faded into the crowd to watch the drama unfold. You enjoyed it at first, too, didn't you? Until you heard the sirens. Then you got nervous and ran."

Herbert grinned. "That's an interesting theory, detective, but first, why would I have met my father at the fair? I barely spoke to the man. Second, how did I fire the darts? And, finally, why, after having successfully killed my father, did I feel compelled to make more?"

"That's right, Herbert," Bernice exulted. "Oh, my brilliant boy!"

Jameson took a deep breath. "I must admit, I don't know the answers to those questions. But, mark my words, I will. And when I do, you'll be hammering license plates instead of pen nibs. Unless . . ."

Herbert's eyes widened.

"Unless you tell me what you know now. 'Hot tempered young man kills philandering father out of loyalty to beloved mother.' A jury is sure to look kindly upon you — if you turn yourself in."

"And if I don't?"

"I'm afraid it makes you look like just another Nathan Leopold or Richard Loeb. Another coldhearted killer trying to prove he's a genius."

At the mention of the infamous Leopold and Loeb, Herbert cracked a bit of a smile. "I have nothing to confess, Detective."

"Of course you don't, Herbert." Bernice rose from her seat for the third time. "And without more evidence, they have no reason to keep us here any longer. So if you're finished with your questions, Detective —"

Creighton, who had heretofore been silent, spoke up. "I have a question, Mrs. Nussbaum. Yesterday, you said you knew your husband lived in Hartford with Josie, but you didn't have an exact address. If that's true, how did you know the cab driver picked your husband up at a — what was the phrase you used? — a 'dumpy hotel'?"

Herbert and Bernice stared blankly at the Englishman, yet said nothing.

"No answer for that either?" Jameson remarked. "You Nussbaums can be a tight-lipped bunch when you want to be. But, have no fear, we'll get to the bottom of that, too. Until then, there's no reason for you to stay here. Good night, Herbert. Good night, Mrs. Nussbaum."

"Yes, good night." Creighton added, "And do have a restful sleep. I think you'll both be needing your energy — particularly you, Mrs. Nussbaum. You're looking a bit peaked."

Interrogation room 'B' was the mirror image of room 'A': a small rectangular table, five chairs, and a small desk lamp. Mateo Saporito sat in the spot that corresponded to the one Herbert had assumed in the previous interview. But that's where the similarities between the two suspects ended. Whereas the young Nussbaum was a picture of poise and careful good manners, Saporito was abrasively crude.

Slumped in his seat, his arm draped over

the chair beside him, Saporito was clad in black pants and a sleeveless white undershirt stained with bits of orange and red.

"Hey, angel," he greeted as Marjorie entered the room. "You know, you really oughta start hanging around a different class of people. These two monkeys give you a bad name."

"Not as bad as yours," she replied.

"Oh, yeah? What have they been saying about me now?"

Marjorie sat across from Saporito, flanked on her left by Creighton and on her right, at the head of the table, Detective Jameson who nodded his consent for her to continue the questioning. "Only that you weren't where you claimed to be on Saturday," Marjorie replied.

He smirked. "Oh? Where was I?"

"We hoped you'd be able to tell us. But we know you weren't at home, since the garage attendant says your car was out all day."

Saporito chuckled and shook his head. "Son of a . . . yeah, I went out. I went out for some air. Is that a crime?"

"Depends on where you got that air. If it was in the vicinity of Ridgebury, Connecticut, it could be."

"I didn't go to Ridgebury. I went to

Hartford. I saw Josie while the old man was out."

"You were with Josie?" Jameson stepped in. "If so, perhaps you know why she packed her bags and checked out of her hotel room before she even knew of Alfred's death."

"Easy. We were running away together. Josie never loved that Alfred chump. It was me she really wanted. We decided then and there to go back to Boston together."

"How romantic," Creighton commented. "I always do enjoy a good love story. However, I somehow doubt you'd let Josie walk away from what you Americans would call her 'meal ticket.' You both had a nice racket going with Nussbaum. Why would you upset the apple cart? Unless, of course, Nussbaum found out about you."

Saporito scowled. "Find out about us? That guy? Ah, he was as dumb as a brick. All Josie had to do was bat her eyelashes in his direction and he'd give her anything she wanted."

"Handy," Marjorie remarked. "Hard to believe she'd let that slip through her fingers. Or, more precisely, that you'd let Josie let that slip through her fingers. I'm all for hearts and flowers, Mr. Saporito, but Josie's the type of girl who likes silk stockings, perfume, and nice clothes, and I don't

204

think you have either the means or the wherewithal to give them to her."

"Meaning?"

"Meaning that with Nussbaum around, you could have your cake and eat it too. He footed the bills and you could have Josie without having to pay for her maintenance. I'd go so far as to say that you probably profited from the arrangement too. After all, any extra money Josie may have acquired, she'd most certainly share with her 'Mattie.' "

"You're a good-looking woman. Smart too. But don't think you can ride too far on that ticket. I don't like mouthy dames."

"I don't think you like dames in general, Mr. Saporito," Creighton spat back vehemently. "Anyone who'd send his wife out to marry and fleece another man can't have much respect for the fairer sex. And for him to do it more than once —"

"What do you mean 'more than once'?"

Jameson took over. "We know you and Josie have a criminal record. The files from New York will be here tomorrow, but I'm feeling generous, so I'll give you the chance to tell your story, before we receive them."

Saporito mulled this over. "What do I get in return?"

"A chance to tell your side of the story

205

before I get the files and form my own opinion." Jameson leaned forward. "We know you and Josie were never divorced. We know that Josie was preparing to leave Hartford before Alfred was even dead. We know Alfred had arranged to meet two people at the fair on Saturday and that you have no alibi, except for what Josie can give you. You want me to draw my own conclusions? Because I will."

Saporito sat up and placed his hands on the table. "If you think I'm going to jail, you'd better guess again."

"If you killed Alfred Nussbaum, you're going to jail anyway."

"I didn't kill Nussbaum!"

"Then tell us where you were. If you killed Nussbaum, I'll find out one way or another. But, if all you were doing was running a scam, I'll put in a good word. You'll serve nine, ten months, tops."

"Ten months? Easy for you to say. You've never been in the pen." He shook his head. "No dice. I'll take my chances."

"Oh yeah? I wonder if Josie feels the same way. Creighton," Jameson addressed the Englishman, "call Noonan and tell him to pick up Josie. Explain to him what's been going on."

206

Creighton nodded and headed toward the door.

"Don't," Saporito nearly yelled. "Don't pick up Josie. She's innocent in all this."

The Englishman sat back down.

"It was my idea," Mattie continued. "I saw Nussbaum throwing money around at my club, so I figured he was loaded. I knew he had a thing for Josie; he never missed a show. So, I asked her to get friendly with him."

"Josie's your wife," Marjorie said, aghast.

"Yeah, but the club wasn't doing well. The bill collectors were at our heels. I thought the chump would give Josie a couple of furs and that would be the end of it. But this guy was serious. He said he wanted to marry her."

"And you couldn't refuse," Marjorie alleged.

"Look, angel, you may not like what I did, but it was our ticket out of Boston and out of that dive. Nussbaum gave Josie almost everything he earned."

"Yeah and left his wife and two children to fend for themselves."

Saporito looked down at the table. "I'm sorry about that. I really am. I don't like taking the food outta kids' mouths, but it's a dog-eat-dog world out there. And it's not like I took nothin'. Nussbaum gave it to Josie — so it's hers fair-and-square."

"How romantic," Creighton remarked again. "I'm sure Nussbaum would have been thrilled to know that Josie was sharing the money with her so-called 'ex-husband.'"

"Hey, it winds up Nussbaum wasn't on the level either. So now I don't feel so bad."

"You should," Jameson commented. "It means that any life insurance policies Josie took out are invalid."

Saporito laughed. "You really are a piece of work, Detective. You think I'd have chanced an investigation by an insurance company? Nah, I wanted my money up front. Josie told Nussbaum that she was still legally married to me — she was brilliant, really turned on the waterworks. I tell ya, she's a good dancer, but she's an even better actress. She told the old man that she wanted to marry him and that she lied about the divorce because she didn't want to lose him. He bought it, hook, line, and sinker!"

"I don't get it," Marjorie admitted. "What was in that for you?"

"I'm getting to it, angel. See, I was the heavy. Josie told Nussbaum that I wouldn't give her a divorce. I was heartless, cruel —

a real villain. Of course, Nussbaum took the bait and came to the club. I told him I'd give Josie a divorce if he gave me $5,000 in cash."

"How did you think he'd come up with $5,000?" Marjorie asked.

"Josie told me he had a big business deal he was counting on. She didn't know how much he was getting, but I named my price and he didn't even bat an eye. Made me think I should've asked for more. But, if there's one thing the extortion racket teaches ya, it's that ya can't be greedy."

"How very honorable of you," Creighton quipped. "I'm sure you'll be nominated for the Nobel Peace Prize for your humanitarian efforts. This exchange of money, however — where was it to take place?"

"The fair at noon. Nussbaum set the time and place. I was to meet him outside the Ferris wheel. It all sounded pretty Hollywood to me — money in a burlap sack and all that jazz — but I went along with it."

"And after you got your money, what then?" Jameson prodded.

"Well, that's the thing," Saporito minced, "I kinda lied to Nussbaum about the divorce. While I was getting the money, Josie packed her things. The plan was I'd pick her up at the hotel and we'd take off with the dough. I kinda felt bad for Nussbaum at the time, but now that I know he was still married, that changes everything. Honestly, some people are so crooked, they don't even take marriage seriously."

Creighton rolled his eyes. "Mmm. Like you said, it's a dog-eat-dog world."

"Ain't that the truth. But, live and learn," Saporito waxed philosophical. "Anyways, this should put me in the clear for killing that crumb Nussbaum."

"How?" Jameson challenged. "All your story proves is that you were at the fair on the day of the murder."

"What do ya mean? I had no gripe with Nussbaum. Why would I wanna kill him?"

"You may not have had a gripe with Nussbaum, but he may have had one with you. If he sensed that things weren't on the up-and-up with you and Josie, he could have caused problems for both of you. Problems that would have required him to be silenced."

"That's not how it happened," Saporito insisted. "I didn't get to the fair until eleven forty-five. Nussbaum was dead before I could even meet with him. Someone bumped him off before I could get the money. I swear to God! I may be a black-

210

mailer but I ain't a killer."

"We'll see about that," Jameson proclaimed. "I suppose no one can vouch that you arrived at the fair at eleven forty-five?"

"No, but —"

"I thought not. In which case, we're going totally by your word. Not exactly a watertight alibi. Besides, you still haven't explained that note." Jameson left the table and leaned into the hallway to summon someone.

"What note? I told you I don't know nothin' about a note!"

Jameson returned to the table and pulled the paper lined with numbers from a manilla folder. He placed it in front of Saporito.

"You think I wrote this? Like I'd write something in numbers. I hated math as a kid — numbers mean nothing to me!"

Detective Logan entered the room with a uniformed police officer.

"How do you explain your name as the signature?" Jameson probed.

"I dunno. But it's not me. I swear to God!" He invoked the sign of the cross. "You have to believe me. The plan was to get the money and run away. Nothing more. I wouldn't have put anything in code. I couldn't."

"What about Josie? Or is she still innocent?"

"Josie? I never . . . I never thought about her writing it."

Jameson nodded to Logan and the uniformed officer helped Saporito out of his seat.

"Angel," he implored of Marjorie. "Angel, have a heart. Tell him I didn't do it."

"I won't tell him anything of the sort. I don't even know you — except that you're a married man who let his wife live with another man to turn a profit." Marjorie pulled a face. "You should be locked up on that count alone." She waved Logan and the uniformed officer out of the room and then quickly summoned them back. "Oh, and if you want me on your side, don't call me 'angel'."

With that, she waved the suspect away without so much as a backward glance.

SEVENTEEN

The trio stepped out of the brick police department building and into the late afternoon sunshine.

Creighton glimpsed at his watch. "Five minutes after five. Perfect. Vanessa instructed me to invite you both back for dinner and drinks. That is, if you're off duty for this evening, Jameson. Which, according to my clock, you should be."

Jameson nodded. "Logan's out arresting Josie for her part in the extortion scheme, so there's nothing else for me to do today. Where did you park?"

"I didn't bring the car. Vanessa's house is just a few blocks from here — by the time I got that old jalopy of Mrs. Patterson's started I could have walked here and back three times."

"Ha ha," Marjorie scoffed. "You'll be surprised how smoothly that car drives when you take it back to Ridgebury."

"Yes, when it stalls and I have to coast downhill."

It was Jameson's turn to laugh. "We'll walk with you, Creighton. I parked the car in the station lot, so it'll be safe until we're done."

"Yes," Marjorie agreed. "We'll walk with you despite your shortsightedness. It's a beautiful day — and I could use some exercise and fresh air."

The trio started walking in the direction of the Randolph home. "I say, Jameson," the Englishman ventured, "I'm not one to question your methods, but why didn't you arrest Herbert Nussbaum? It seemed like we had enough evidence to hold him."

Marjorie concurred. "I'm surprised too. Logan found him working on the darts and the cab driver witnessed him at the crime scene. I know it's not enough to convict him, but aren't you afraid he and his mother may try to pull a 'Josie' and skip town?"

"That's why Logan has a bunch of his men trailing the Nussbaums. If any of them so much as look at a train schedule, they'll bring them in."

"Ok, but why not arrest them at the station?" Marjorie pursued.

"A couple of reasons. First, Herbert Nussbaum is a minor. If I arrest that kid before

I'm 100 percent certain he's the killer, the press, the mayor, my sergeant, and every child welfare organization in the country would have a field day — all at my expense. Not to mention I have proof that Mateo Saporito — a man with a criminal record — was at the fair about the same time Herbert was, and that he had an equally strong motive for murder. No, the first major arrest in this case is not going to be of a smart-aleck, sixteen-year-old kid. Not if I can help it." He paused. "Second, there are three people in that house, all of whom had a motive to kill Alfred Nussbaum. Even if Herbert committed the crime, we can't be certain he acted alone. Not after Bernice made that slip about the Hideaway Hotel. Herbert obeys his mother's every word. It's entirely feasible that she came up with the idea and asked Herbert to carry it out."

"It's a definite possibility," Creighton agreed. "We all saw how she bullied him into denying that he was at the fair." He did a dead-on impersonation of Mrs. Nussbaum: "Herbert, Mommy's defending you!"

Marjorie giggled. "Yes, but the fact that he was at the fair appeared to startle her. You saw how she reacted. That was genuine surprise. She even started to say something, and then thought better of it. 'I didn't know you were . . .' That's what she said."

"That doesn't prove anything," Jameson countered. "Bernice could have asked Herbert to make the darts and committed the crime herself. Herbert's a morbid kid. He could have sneaked off to the fair to watch his mother bump off his father, and Bernice would be none the wiser. Heck, even Natalie could be tied up in this somehow. It wouldn't have taken much coercion on her part to convince her brother to participate in an honest-to-goodness, real-life crime."

"Yes, but we have no evidence that either of them were in Ridgebury on Saturday," Creighton pointed out.

"Not yet, but I've had Noonan scouring train and bus stations to see if anyone remembers seeing Bernice or Natalie. They don't have a car and they don't have enough money to hire a cab all the way to Ridgebury. If either of them were there, it's a safe bet they took either the bus or the train."

"Hmmm. Had I known so many people were headed to Ridgebury, I'd have opened you a hot dog stand, Marjorie," Creighton quipped. "It's less work than these murder investigations and you'd have made a fortune."

Marjorie wrinkled her nose at the Englishman. "Well, at least we've figured out whom

Nussbaum was meeting at noon. Although, it pretty much exonerates Saporito from being the killer."

"What do you mean?" Jameson quizzed.

"No one can confirm Saporito arrived at the fair after the murder occurred. Likewise, we have no proof that Saporito was scheduled to meet Nussbaum at noon. He could have been the eleven o'clock appointment. Again, all we have is his word. Until we have evidence to substantiate his story, he's still a suspect."

"But why would he have killed Nussbaum before he got his money? It doesn't make sense."

"Again, there's no proof that Saporito didn't get his money. Nussbaum didn't have $5,000 in cash on him when he was killed. He had a pocket full of change and nothing more. It's easy to imagine Saporito taking his money and then killing Nussbaum to cover his tracks."

"Your reasoning makes sense," Creighton allowed. "But you're overlooking one thing. Do you really think Saporito is the type to use a poison dart? I would have fancied him the type to shoot someone with a gun or beat a fellow to death, but poison dart? Not only is it not 'tough' enough for him, but he's not smart enough to come up with it. I own suits with higher IQs than Saporito's."

Marjorie laughed out loud. "Creighton's right. Saporito hardly seems the type to devise something as exotic as a poison dart."

"Exotic," Creighton continued. "Yes, that's the word I was looking for. A poison dart has style, sophistication. But Saporito? When he wasn't calling Marjorie 'Angel,' he was referring to his wife as a 'dame.' It took every ounce of self-control I had not to punch him right in the nose, particularly when he called Marjorie a 'mouthy dame.' Of course, he has a weight advantage and could have given me a proper pummeling, but I'm wiry when I want to be." He executed a few boxing moves to punctuate his statement. "And, it goes without saying that I could have outsmarted him. Not that it's saying much — after all, a sheep could outsmart Saporito. Unless Saporito ate the sheep first."

Marjorie laughed again, and then stopped suddenly. She had, in truth, been quite annoyed at Saporito for the "mouthy dame" comment and had also been somewhat irritated that Jameson hadn't leapt to her defense. But Creighton had — a fact that hadn't gone unnoticed. She gazed surreptitiously at the tall man who walked beside her. *Would he have fought Saporito for her?*

Was Robert right — did Creighton care for her? Or had all of those feelings been replaced by his love for Vanessa? And what had been Vanessa's reply to his proposal? One thing was for certain, before the night was over, she would have to find out.

"It's lovely of Vanessa to invite us for dinner," Marjorie said. "I'm glad Robert doesn't have to work. I'd be awfully upset if we had to turn her down again."

"Oh, I don't think you could have gotten away with turning her down twice in a row. Vanessa was hell bent on having you two over for dinner tonight," Creighton answered. "Once that woman gets an idea in her head, she doesn't take 'no' for an answer. Like another certain someone I know . . ."

Jameson laughed. "You've got that right."

Marjorie, however, saw an opportunity to acquire the information she sought. "And what about you, Creighton? I don't figure you've heard the word 'no' very often in your lifetime."

"My dear Marjorie," he sighed. "If it weren't for the existence of the word 'no', the most important questions I've ever asked in my life would have gone unanswered."

■ ■ ■ ■

Vanessa wheeled herself to the front door and gave each of her guests a warm welcome. "Marjorie, dear." She kissed Marjorie on the cheek and then embraced Detective Jameson. "Robert. How are you? I do hope you don't mind me 'kidnapping' you, but when I heard you were both in town, I thought it would be a wonderful opportunity to make up for the dinner we missed."

She ushered them into the living room, where the housemaid offered martinis on a silver tray. Creighton passed the drinks around. "Martha makes the best martinis this side of the Mississippi," he teased the maid, who blushed a bright crimson. "Probably the other side too, but I've never been there, so I can't rightly say, can I?"

Martha left the room, pink faced and giggling.

"Creighton has always had a way with the ladies," Vanessa commented. "I swear, since he's been here, I can't get Martha to listen to a word I say. I have to pass all my instructions through him. It was always that way — even when we were young. You always charmed the socks off of my nurses and tutors, Creighton. And then when I told them about how you teased me so, they just wouldn't believe a word I said. I must say, I was shocked when you came here and told me you weren't married. I thought surely someone would have captured your heart by now — or at the very least, you would have captured theirs." Her blue eyes twinkled as she cast a brief glance in Marjorie's direction.

"Vanessa, dear, you know I've been waiting for the right woman," Creighton replied sweetly, although his face belied his true feelings.

Marjorie could look at neither of them as she felt her heart sink. She stared into her martini glass and wondered what she was doing here. She had hoped this evening would be fun. So far, however, it was turning out to be anything but.

"Enough small talk. Let's make a toast," Mrs. Randolph declared as she raised a glass triumphantly. "To love. The one thing in the world worth living for, worth fighting for, and worth dying for."

The foursome clinked glasses as Jameson replied with a resounding, "Hear, hear." They sealed the toast with a drink.

"Creighton, darling, why don't you show Detective Jameson the billiard room?" Vanessa suggested. "I'm sure he'd like to unwind and take off his tie after a hard day at work. And I'm dying for the opportunity to discuss Marjorie's books with her — if she's willing to indulge me."

The young blonde smiled. "I love discussing my books. I seldom get the opportunity."

"There you are, gentlemen," Vanessa stated. "I'll have Martha refresh your drinks. She'll call you when dinner is ready. I do hope you have no aversion to fish, Detective Jameson. We're having sole meuniere, followed by lobster thermidor, and for dessert, coffee, brandy, and an authentic Key lime pie." She turned to Marjorie. "It arrived from Florida this morning, along with some orchids I had flown in from our ranch in Argentina. I can't travel there any more, but I just love having fresh orchids on my table."

"That sounds fine, Mrs. Randolph," Jameson assured. "I'm Boston born and bred. Most of what I ate as a kid on came from the sea — nothing as fancy as what we're having tonight, but fish nonetheless. Except for brown bread and beans, although I'm sure you've never had to eat those." He smiled graciously. "It's awfully nice of you to do this for us, Mrs. Randolph. I know I speak for Marjorie when I say that we truly appreciate all you've done for us."

Vanessa waved a hand. "It's my pleasure.

I enjoy having people around me. It's been such a long time since I've entertained. Stewart — my husband — and I used to have parties all the time, but since he passed, well, nothing is quite the same. But you men pay no mind. You go to the billiard room and enjoy yourselves while Marjorie and I talk about 'girl things', including the wedding plans. I just adore weddings! But I'm sure you gentlemen would be bored to tears, so hurry along."

Jameson went on to the billiard room, chatting animatedly, while Creighton lingered just long enough to give Vanessa a stern look and silently mouth the word, "No."

Out of the corner of her eye, Marjorie witnessed this warning and assumed that Vanessa had been sworn to secrecy about the possibility of her own wedding plans. Once the men were out of earshot, she said, "You miss your husband very much, don't you?"

Vanessa drank the rest of her martini in one gulp and rang Martha to bring more. "Yes, I do. He was — well, he was everything to me. He understood me as no one else did. He could be cantankerous and short-tempered, but that's only because he didn't suffer fools gladly. To me, however, he was the sun, the moon, and everything in between. He could drive me crazy as no one else could, but he could also make me happier than anyone else could. But, you're engaged to be married," Vanessa added. "You know what I mean."

Marjorie paused a long while, during which she polished off her martini. "Yes, I do know what you mean. He finishes my statements, completes my thoughts, and knows me better than I do myself. He's in love with me." Realizing that her words described Creighton better than they did Robert, she added, "Whether or not I always realize it."

Martha arrived with a large cocktail shaker and proceeded to fill the women's glasses. Vanessa instructed her to leave the shaker. "We're discussing 'girl' things, Martha. And so very often, 'girl' things require the assistance of liquid courage. Women are the strong ones in life, don't you think, Miss McClelland? Men rule the world, but it's women who are left to pick up the pieces — lost sons, lost husbands, lost lives. As little girls, we dream of someone who will sweep us off our feet. We grow up and swear off love and marriage. Then we meet 'him.' We fall in love, we marry. Wars come, wars go. The men we love disappear, and yet we remain. It doesn't seem fair does it?" Vanessa's blue eyes focused on the figure of the young maid standing before her. "Martha?"

"Yes ma'am?" she replied obediently.

"Are you to see your friend, Tom, this evening?"

Martha blushed. "Yes, ma'am, we're going to the pictures."

Vanessa smiled radiantly. "Good. I made sure cook made a little extra of the sole and lobster. She can have some for supper, and you and Tom have the rest for a quiet dinner before you leave, or when you get back — I don't care. Cook can leave it in the oven for you and it will keep that way for quite a while before it's overdone." Mrs. Randolph took a sip of martini. "I could be wrong, Martha, but that Tom seems to be wild over you. I should start looking for another maid, because heaven knows the boy could pop the question at any moment!"

The maid tee-heed at the image of her 'Tom' proposing. "Oh, Mrs. Randolph. You are the limit! Truth be told, I'd be lost without you and Randolph House, but if Tom were to ask . . ."

"And that's the way it should be," Vanessa proclaimed. "Now run along and get the 'boys' their drinks and then get ready for your date."

"But, I — I thought I'd be serving."

"Not tonight. I'll instruct cook to bring everything out to the table and I shall serve my guests. You get ready for your young man, and put on your best dress," Vanessa giggled like a schoolgirl. "I'm willing to wager that tonight is the night!"

Martha ran out of the room like a chicken without a head. "Yes ma'am! Thank you, ma'am!"

When the maid had left the room, Vanessa sighed. "Ah, young love! But enough of Martha. I want to hear about your writing. What books do you have in the works?"

"I'm working on an account of the Van Allen case."

"Oh yes," Vanessa responded. "I read about that in the papers a couple of months ago. You were nearly killed, weren't you?"

"So I'm told," Marjorie replied humbly.

"Is it true that when someone dies, their life passes before them?"

Marjorie reenacted the scene in Kensington House in her mind. "I can't say for certain, but I know I saw my father, and the house where I spent most of my childhood," she said, and then recalled the feeling she experienced upon seeing the cerulean blue sky. *That blue,* she thought, *was it not unlike*

226

something she had seen before? That blue was what had given her the strength to survive. But what did it mean?

"I'd like to think that Stewart saw something similar before he died. I'd like to think he saw my face and knew how much I loved him."

Marjorie's eyes glazed over. "I'm certain he did, Vanessa. If not at the moment he died, then shortly afterward. In fact, I'm sure he's with you every day, watching you. Loving you."

Vanessa gazed upon her guest. "You're a good person, Marjorie. One can sense that the moment they meet you. It's no wonder Creighton loves you so."

"You mean Robert. 'It's no wonder *Robert* loves me so,' " she corrected.

Her hostess was unmoved. "I meant what I said."

Marjorie's eyes glazed over. "Oh Vanessa! You're mistaken. Why, he hasn't known me long enough to love me. I'm a passing fancy, but you — it's obvious he's cared about you all his life."

"Exactly. He's cared about me. It's you he's in love with. Haven't you wondered why he's been keeping his distance from you and Robert? Because it's tearing him apart to see you together. Creighton wouldn't do anything to compromise your marriage to Robert, if that marriage is what you really want. But if Creighton stands a chance, you owe it to him, and yourself, to tell him."

Marjorie was about to answer when Martha reappeared. "Dinner is ready, ma'am. I already called the gentlemen. I told them to meet you ladies in the dining room."

Vanessa wheeled herself out of the living room, leaving Marjorie to ponder her predicament alone.

Dinner was superb. Marjorie, her appetite whetted by both the alcohol and Vanessa's revelations, cleaned both her plates — first of the sole and then of the lobster. Vanessa rang for the cook to clear the dishes and then asked Jameson to escort her into the library. "Now, Robert, I want to hear about your juiciest cases and I do hope you don't edit out the good parts. Creighton," she summoned the Englishman. "Marjorie was very interested in the history of this neighborhood. Why don't you take her for a walk down Willow Street and then go to the Old Meeting House? Being from Boston, I'm sure Detective Jameson has already had the pleasure, but Marjorie, I'm sure, will find it quite lovely, especially at this time of the evening."

"Vanessa," Creighton argued, "Marjorie's had a long day. I'm sure she just wants to relax."

"Nonsense. She may say that now, but she won't later. Oh, be a good sport, Marjorie — you won't be sorry."

Marjorie grinned awkwardly. *What a terrible position Vanessa had put her in!* Not wanting to arouse Robert's suspicion she agreed. "Of course not. No one can accuse me of being a spoil sport."

"That's a girl!" Vanessa cheered. "Take your time and when you get back, we'll have coffee and dessert. How does that sound to you, Detective?"

Jameson was his usual cheerful self. "After that meal you gave us? How can I refuse?"

Vanessa smiled at Creighton and Marjorie. "See? The Detective doesn't mind. You kids take your time and have fun. And, remember," she added jokingly, "don't do anything I wouldn't do."

Creighton and Marjorie walked across Louisburg Square, the summer sun lying low in the sky, bathing the world in its golden glow. The breeze, which had been warm earlier in the day, now held a bit of a chill. Marjorie shivered as it blew across her bare arms and watched as lovers, oblivious to the weather, strolled hand in hand, stopping only to exchange a few fleeting kisses.

Creighton removed his suit jacket and gallantly draped it over Marjorie's shoulders.

"Thank you," she mumbled.

"You're welcome," he replied. "Wouldn't want you catching cold. Not with a wedding in the works. Speaking of which, how are the wedding plans coming along?"

"We haven't made any plans yet. What with the Nussbaum case, we've been too busy to discuss anything that's not related to the investigation."

"Well, if I were you, I wouldn't dilly dally," he warned. "Jameson's keen on the whole marriage thing — you'd better strike while the iron is hot. You wouldn't want him changing his mind. After all, this is what you've been dreaming of since you first met him, isn't it?"

"I don't know about that. I liked Robert from the moment I met him, but I didn't know him well enough to think of marriage."

"Women are always thinking of marriage, whether or not they care to admit it," Creighton asserted.

"If I were always thinking of marriage," Marjorie pointed out, "then Mr. Schutt would have no reason to call me a spinster."

"If you are a spinster, it's only because the right man didn't come along until now."

"He hasn't?" Marjorie prodded.

"No. You've only met Robert a short time ago."

"Yes," she replied. What she had expected Creighton to say, she hadn't the faintest idea. She only knew that she was inexplicably disappointed. "What about you and Vanessa? You make a very nice couple."

"Vanessa and I have always gotten along rather well," he chuckled. "I suppose that's why we've remained friends all this time. We seldom argue or bicker. There are times when we don't see eye to eye, but we've never lost our tempers with each other. Not like you and me."

Marjorie feigned a laugh. "True. We have had our moments, haven't we?"

"Moments? My dear Marjorie, if ever there were two people who were destined to eternally butt heads, it's you and I."

She felt her face grow warm. "I wouldn't go that far —"

"Far? Please, Marjorie," Creighton chuckled. "We are the essence of incompatibility."

"No we aren't. We don't argue that often, and when we do, it's not for very long. Nor do we fight when we're working. When we're working toward a common goal, we get along well. Extremely well, in fact. You can't deny that!"

"Working? Is that what you call what we do? I thought it was more like you and Jameson making eyes at each other while I tagged along," he shook his head. "If that's your idea of work —"

Marjorie stopped dead in her tracks. "What about the books? Surely you can't —"

"We haven't written a book together, Marjorie. You've given me some snippets to review. I've given my opinion and you've gone ahead and done whatever you wanted to do anyway. That's about the extent of 'our' book writing."

"What about the Van Allen case? And this case, so far? We think alike, don't we? And we have fun, or at least I thought we did."

"Yes, visiting you in the hospital for three weeks after the Van Allen case was a laugh a minute."

"Aside from that," she argued. "What about Mal, that silly little dog? And Gloria Van Allen's party? Our day at the fair? Those are good memories."

"Oh, yes. Wonderful. Of course, all those occasions ended with death or someone being pretty darned near close to it so they were, indeed, quite memorable, but not particularly enjoyable." He shook his head. "No, I'm afraid those things may be fun for you and Jameson. I, however, am the quiet type. I enjoy my wine collection and library. But, now you and Jameson are going to be married. He can chase after and worry about you, and listen to your tales of intrigue, while I seek out a bit of peace and relaxation."

Marjorie stared at him in disbelief. *This was the man Robert and Vanessa had claimed was in love with her?* "Well, I'm sure you'll find relaxation with Vanessa. Did she accept your proposal?"

Creighton's jaw dropped and the color drained from his face. Marjorie wanted to take back the question as soon as she said it, but it was too late now.

"So you heard that, did you? I thought you might have from the way you acted the next morning. As a matter of fact, she did, Marjorie. She did accept."

Marjorie felt the tears well up in her eyes. *She had accepted. She had!*

"Not that it matters to you," Creighton continued. "You're right. Gloria Van Allen's party was memorable. It was memorable because it was then that I realized that all you were concerned with was your own pride. You're crying now — not because I've proposed to Vanessa, not because she accepted. My engagement doesn't mean a damn to you except that it shows I'm not sitting around, pining away with unrequited love, like all the other stooges you bat your eyes at. That's why you're crying, Marjorie. You don't actually want me — you just want me to want you!"

Marjorie, her tears having subsided and now replaced with righteous indignation, hauled off and slapped the Englishman hard across the face. "You're right, I don't want you! How could I? You come across as so sweet and charming, but underneath it all, you're conceited and arrogant and just plain mean! How could I want you? How could I ever possibly want you?" Sobbing, she removed his jacket from her shoulders and threw it on the ground before running across Louisburg Square and into the gathering darkness.

EIGHTEEN

Marjorie and Jameson arrived back in Ridgebury some time around eleven o'clock. After being deposited at her front doorstep, Marjorie waited until the police car was out of view then ran diagonally, across the village green, to the other side of Ridgebury Road. She had noticed, as she and Robert drove into town, that the lights in Mrs. Patterson's house were on, signifying that the elderly woman was still awake.

Breathlessly, Marjorie sprinted up the steps to the gingerbreaded porch of the blue Victorian dwelling and knocked on the frame of the old storm door. She listened patiently to the sound of approaching footsteps drifting through the open windows of the house. Within seconds, the white-haired woman appeared in the doorway, wearing a pink seersucker dressing gown. "Marjorie, dear." Mrs. Patterson swung open the screen door to allow the younger woman admittance. "You didn't have to come over. Creighton has been keeping me posted. He told me he's driving the car back, oh, and about your dinner tonight."

Marjorie stepped over the threshold and into Mrs. Patterson's front parlor. Regardless of what might be happening in the world around her, she always felt safe within these walls. "I didn't come about that. I thought maybe we could talk. That is if you're not going to bed."

"No, I already tried to sleep but it's too warm upstairs. There's a nice breeze outside but this old house gets so stuffy. I considered lying out on the porch swing, but at my age, I'm not too sure I'd be able to get out of it in the morning." She chuckled and shuffled off toward the kitchen. "Come along, I was just boiling some water for tea."

Tea was Mrs. Patterson's panacea and she served it, highly sweetened and piping hot, no matter the season. Marjorie recalled the night, five years ago, when she discovered her father, dead of a stroke, crumpled on the living room floor of their cottage. She had stayed with Mrs. Patterson that night, and finding it impossible to sleep, had staggered downstairs to the kitchen where the rosy-cheeked old lady sat up with her until the wee hours of the morning, dispensing

236

cup after cup of the steaming beverage, wiping her tears and holding her hand.

Like she had done that night years ago, Marjorie extracted two jade green cups and saucers from one of the kitchen cabinets and then settled down at the green-and-white-striped cloth-covered table to watch Mrs. Patterson perform the familiar ritual of measuring loose tea leaves into the earthenware pot. "Creighton told me Detective Jameson took you to meet his parents last night."

"Yes," Marjorie sighed.

"You don't sound very happy about it. Did something go wrong?"

"No, not 'wrong' per se. It was a lovely evening. Robert's parents are very nice people."

"Why do I sense a 'but' coming?" Mrs. Patterson quipped.

"No. No 'but'," Marjorie denied. "They were both quite kind. Robert's father and I got along famously. However, his mother seems a bit worried. I sense she doesn't like the fact I'm a writer."

"After meeting Robert, I half-expected that. He's quite old fashioned in his ways, so I imagined his mother wouldn't be very forward thinking." She chuckled. "She's a mother, so she's concerned about her son's happiness. But once she gets to know you better, and sees how well you two get along, she shouldn't be a problem."

"I suppose not."

"Is there something else?" Mrs. Patterson quizzed as she measured the tea by the rounded teaspoon.

"I just — I just want to ask you something and I need an honest answer."

"Of course, dear. What is it?"

"You speak with Creighton on a regular basis," she prefaced. "Has he ever told you how he feels about me?"

Mrs. Patterson stopped what she was doing and looked up from the teapot. "What do you mean?"

"I mean that I know he and I are friends, but has he ever alluded to you that his feelings for me might be deeper than that?"

The woman was nonplussed by Marjorie's question. She gazed at Marjorie for a moment then turned her attention back to the teapot. "I don't know where I left off now." She emptied the tea leaves from the pot back into the tin and started the measuring process again.

Marjorie waited until the elderly woman was finished counting before pressing her for an answer. "So?"

Mrs. Patterson brought the kettle from

the stove and began filling the teapot with boiling water. "I think you're asking the wrong person. If you want to know how Creighton feels, ask Creighton." She returned the kettle to the stove and brought the teapot to the table to steep. "What makes you so interested in Creighton's feelings all of a sudden?"

"Oh, Mrs. Patterson," Marjorie started to cry. "I don't know where to begin."

The elderly woman handed her a crocheted handkerchief and sat beside her. Holding her with one arm and patting her back with the other, she soothed, "Shhhh. There, there, child."

Marjorie blew her nose in the handkerchief with a resounding honk.

"Now, tell me exactly what happened," Mrs. Patterson instructed.

"It started with Robert. We were on the way to see his parents and he told me that Creighton had resigned as my editor."

"Did he say why?"

"Yes. He said it wasn't proper because — because Creighton is in love with me."

"Oh," she exclaimed with a hint of surprise in her voice. "Go on."

"I tried to forget about the whole thing. We had dinner with Robert's parents and everything went . . . well, I told you about his mother."

Mrs. Patterson nodded.

"Robert dropped me back at Vanessa's house. It was quiet and dark and I thought everyone had gone to bed. And then I heard it. Creighton and Vanessa were in the library and he . . . and he proposed to Vanessa." She burst into sobs. "He asked her to marry him."

"How did she respond?"

"I didn't stay long enough to hear. I went up to bed, and I didn't come downstairs until morning, until I was sure Robert would be there. We left shortly afterward and came back to Ridgebury. But then, later in the day, Robert and I got a lead on the case. I called Creighton. I don't know why, but I called him and told him to meet us at the police station. I suppose I wanted things to be the way they had been last time — Creighton and I questioning suspects and gathering clues."

"But they weren't?" Mrs. Patterson assumed.

"They were at first. Then we went back to Vanessa's for dinner. That's when she told me . . ."

"Who told you what?"

"Vanessa," Marjorie answered quietly. "Vanessa told me that Creighton was in love with me. She said that he had been keeping his distance because the sight of Robert and me together tore him apart."

"What did you say? What did you do?"

"Nothing right away. Dinner was ready and I didn't want Jameson to find out what Vanessa and I had been discussing. Not that way; not yet. After dinner, however, Vanessa sent Creighton and I out for a walk and —" Marjorie's voice broke into sobs.

The older woman held her tightly. "It's all right, Marjorie. Go on."

"Creighton was downright mean. I tried to be nice to him. I really tried! I tried to give him a chance to tell me how he feels. I told him that I had a good time solving crimes with him and he — he acted as though it didn't matter, that it never mattered. He said that he needed a life of peace and quiet, and that he was going to marry Vanessa."

Mrs. Patterson appeared surprised. "He told you that she accepted his proposal?"

"Yes. And then it got worse. He — he said that I didn't care about him. He said that all I cared about was my pride and that I was more upset by the fact that he wasn't pining away for me, than whether or not he cared in the first place."

"What did you do?"

241

"I slapped him."

Mrs. Patterson's mouth formed a small 'o.' "You shouldn't have done that."

"I couldn't help it. He makes me so angry sometimes. I went back to the house and made a silly excuse for being upset. I said I fell and twisted my ankle and that Creighton had gone back to look for one of my earrings. He came back shortly afterward and I filled him in about the story. He played along and we spent the rest of the evening pretending nothing happened. However, I could think of nothing else. I'm sorry I slapped him, but he really knows how to drive me crazy!"

"Yes, I believe that. You're both stubborn, pigheaded people. I wouldn't want to face either of you in an argument, that's for certain."

"It's not just that. Here everyone keeps telling me that Creighton loves me. But first he gets engaged to Vanessa and then he goes and acts so rotten! I just don't know what to think anymore."

"I understand. What I don't understand is why Vanessa would tell you that Creighton loves you? Robert is easy — he trusts you and wants you to sympathize with his position. But Vanessa's behavior is puzzling. You're the mystery writer, Marjorie. What possible reason could she have had for telling you that her intended husband is in love with you?"

Marjorie shook her head. "I don't know, Mrs. Patterson. I don't know who or what to believe anymore. I just want . . ."

"You want to know if it's true," the other woman filled in the blank. "And what if it is? What if Creighton does love you? What will you do?"

Marjorie shrugged; she hadn't thought that far ahead yet. "I have no idea."

"Then that's the real question, isn't it? You ask me if Creighton loves you, but you can easily find the answer to that. Just open your eyes. Men don't say things the way women do. They don't act the way women do, but when they care, you can see it in their eyes. No, Marjorie, what you really want to know is whether or not you love Creighton."

The young woman leaned her elbows on the table and rested her head in her hands. Perhaps that was what she was asking, after all. "I'm just so confused. I'm not certain if what I'm feeling is cold feet because I'm getting married or if it's something more serious. Oh, Mrs. Patterson, what should I do?" she pleaded. "Should I forget about these feelings and hope they go away?

Should I marry Robert? Or should I break off the engagement, even though what I feel for Creighton might be nothing more than a crush? Should I let him break off his engagement with Vanessa?" She let her hands drop to the table. "What should I do?"

Mrs. Patterson patted her hand. "There, there, Marjorie. You're letting your thoughts run away with you. You don't need to make a decision tonight. You and Robert haven't set a wedding date yet. Take a few days to think about it and the answer will come to you."

"What if it doesn't? What do I do then?"

The elderly woman smiled. "Then you do what I did before I married Mr. Patterson. I had cold feet before our wedding. Very cold feet. So cold, in fact, that I nearly called the whole thing off. Well, my mother gave me some wonderful advice. She told me to picture my life without Frank in it, and that would help me make up my mind."

"Apparently it did. You and Mr. Patterson were married more than forty years."

"Yes, but you see, her advice worked because it failed."

Marjorie pulled a face. "What?"

Mrs. Patterson explained, "For days I tried to do what my mother had told me, but I just couldn't. Finally, out of frustration, I went to her and said 'Mother, I've tried to heed your advice, but I just can't imagine my life without Frank.' My mother looked at me and smiled, and I realized what I had said. She hugged me. 'Emily,' she said, 'that's exactly the way you should feel about the man you're about to marry.' "

Marjorie frowned; it was a pleasant little story but she wasn't sure how it would help her in her present situation. "So I should picture my life without Robert and if I can't, that means I should marry him," she rejoined skeptically.

"Not just Robert. You should try it with Creighton, too."

"What if I can't imagine life without either of them? How will I know what to do then?"

Mrs. Patterson began pouring out the tea. "You'll know, dear. You'll know."

NINETEEN

Marjorie awoke the next morning to the sound of someone knocking on her front cottage door. Still wooly eyed, she staggered out of bed, slipped into her dressing gown, and made her way into the living room. She swung open the door to find Robert standing on the front stoop.

He gave her a kiss upon entering. "Morning. What are you still doing in bed? You feeling okay?"

"Yeah, I'm fine," she rubbed her eyes and stretched.

"How's the ankle?"

"A lot better."

"I'm glad. I was worried about you last night. You looked like you were in a lot of pain."

"Yes, I was. Silly cobblestone streets," she replied. "What time is it?"

"Ten o'clock."

"I guess I was tired," she replied. Tired

was an understatement. In truth, she had been exhausted. "I'll put some coffee on," she offered.

"None for me, thanks," he declined. "I had some at headquarters."

Deciding not to make any for herself, Marjorie sat down on the chintz-covered sofa. Sam, her mottled-gray tomcat, rubbed against her leg. "How are things in police land?"

"Busy." He eased into a floral printed armchair. "Dr. Heller's report was on my desk this morning. It confirms that curare poisoning killed Nussbaum and that the wound on his neck matches the dart that you found."

"That was a foregone conclusion by now, wasn't it?" Marjorie picked up the cat and placed him on her lap. Sam, having nothing of this display of affection, wriggled free and jumped to the ground with a small meow.

"Yeah, but it's nice to know that the lab work backed up our theory — otherwise we would have had to start all over." He removed his hat. "By the way, Dr. Heller also released Nussbaum's body."

"Oh? And which Mrs. Nussbaum is the lucky winner?"

"Bernice. As we speak, Alfred's on his way back to Boston."

Boston, Marjorie remembered. *Boston and Creighton.* "Just as well," she commented, "since Josie's in the lock-up."

"Yeah, although her lawyer sent a request that she be released for two hours, under police supervision, for the funeral."

"Released?"

"Yeah, Logan has to play chaperone," he explained. "Speaking of Logan, he's sending over those mug shots of Murphy and his friends so we can show them around to everyone at the fair. I should have them by tomorrow."

"Tomorrow, yes," she replied distractedly.

"Noonan's checking out Nussbaum's financial records. I want to see exactly what kind of arrangement he had with Josie. I know Saporito admitted that they were trying to fleece the guy, but if we can prove there was a life insurance policy, it just strengthens our case. Noonan's also checking with bus companies to see if anyone answering to Natalie's or Bernice's description bought a ticket to Ridgebury or Hartford on Friday or Saturday. Like I said, it was the easiest and cheapest way for them to have made the trip."

"Sounds like you have all your bases covered," she casually remarked, disappointed that there wasn't some bit of police work that would help her get her mind off things.

"Not all of them. I'm going to check out Cullen Chemicals today. Nussbaum was employed there before he worked for Alchemy. I thought I'd see if he had any enemies: coworkers he didn't get along with, bosses who didn't like the way he looked, that sort of thing."

Marjorie raised an eyebrow; perhaps here was a distraction. "Cullen Chemicals in Hartford? They closed a few months ago didn't they?"

Robert nodded. "I called the Cullen brothers directly. Temporary shut down is how they described it, but it doesn't sound like they're bouncing back too quickly. They sold their estate and rented a couple of rooms at their men's club. I got the club's address and told them I'd stop by later."

"I'm surprised you're telling me about it. Aren't you afraid I'll try to tag along?"

"Not this time."

"Oh? Confident that the fact you're meeting in a men's club will keep me at bay?"

"Actually, we're meeting on a nearby golf course. Women are allowed there." Jameson smiled. "No, the reason I'm not afraid of you tagging along is I'm inviting you."

"Inviting me," she repeated. "Two days in

a row? Are you sure you're not the one who's sick?"

"I'm not sick. I'm just heeding the advice of a friend," he explained.

Marjorie narrowed her eyes. "Advice of a friend, eh? What precisely was this advice?"

"That I shouldn't try to break the spirit of an independent woman."

"Hmm, very wise man. I like him already. Is he married?" Marjorie asked.

"No, he isn't." Robert frowned.

"You'd better be careful then," she teased before heading off to the bedroom to change. "If I meet him, I might just be swept off my feet."

The Cullen brothers, Charles and Kenneth, were playing the sixth hole on the Grouse Hollow Golf Course when Marjorie and Jameson arrived, by cart, to speak with them. The men were fortyish and, apart from the bright knickers and tams they wore, were virtually nondescript in appearance, with plain, even features and mousy brown hair. In fact, the brothers blended with their surroundings and each other so harmoniously that the only way Marjorie could differentiate between the two was by the pince-nez clipped to the end of Charles' nose.

Kenneth requested the number one wood from the caddy and approached the tee. "So good of you to meet us here, Detective Jameson," he stated appreciatively. "I would've hated to have to cancel our golf game. Getting a tee time on this course is confoundedly difficult. Sometimes we have to make a reservation a week in advance."

"My pleasure, Mr. Cullen," Jameson replied. "I'm glad we have an opportunity to talk. You and your brother might be able to shed some light on this case."

There was silence as Kenneth addressed the ball and drove it about two hundred and fifty yards down the fairway. "Nice one," Charles commented enthusiastically. Then returning his attention to the matter at hand: "Yes, I couldn't believe the news when you told me, Detective. What exactly happened to Nussbaum? A botched robbery attempt?"

"No, a simple case of murder."

"Murder? But Nussbaum was such a placid man; I can't imagine him provoking anyone into taking such drastic measures. Are you sure it wasn't a robbery?"

"Positive. Nussbaum's wallet hadn't even been touched."

"Forget about it being touched," Kenneth

eagerly followed up. "Was there any money in it?"

Jameson hesitated. "No. Just some change. Why?"

"Because Nussbaum hardly ever carried cash in his wallet. It was a trick he learned from years of being on the road. A pickpocket, he said, will automatically go for a man's wallet. That's why he usually kept his cash in a separate pocket. Now, did you find cash anywhere else?"

Nussbaum had been wearing a white shirt and a pair of navy blue trousers, and the only items they had found in those pockets were his wallet, a few coins and the number-laden piece of paper.

"No, we didn't, but how much cash could a salesman have on him anyway? Not enough to kill for, certainly." He eyed the brothers suspiciously. "Now, if you don't mind, I'd like to ask the questions for a change."

"I'm sorry, Detective," Charles shot Kenneth a warning glance. "My brother sometimes fancies himself an amateur sleuth. Go ahead and ask whatever you like. Although I don't know how much we can help you. It's been months since we've seen Alfred Nussbaum."

"I realize that, but perhaps you can tell

me about the time he spent as your employee."

The caddy placed a second ball on the tee and handed Charles the driver.

"There's not much to tell, Detective," Kenneth interjected. "Like my brother said, Nussbaum was a quiet fellow. Kept to himself."

"He didn't socialize with any of his co-workers?"

"He didn't have an opportunity. He was a traveling salesman, you know." Kenneth held up a hand for silence, while his brother took his swing. The ball flew into the rough.

"Damn it!" Charles shouted and hurled the club to the ground in disgust.

"Quite a temper you have there, Mr. Cullen," Marjorie remarked. "You should try to keep it in check. It's not good for the blood pressure."

Charles glared at her over the top of his wire-framed spectacles.

"You were saying," Jameson continued, "that Alfred Nussbaum didn't have time to make friends at your company. Does that mean he also didn't have time to make enemies?"

The caddy packed up the clubs and the Cullen brothers proceeded to the green. "That's precisely what it means," Charles brusquely averred.

Marjorie and Jameson trailed behind them. "Why did Mr. Nussbaum leave Cullen Chemicals?" the young woman asked.

"Economics," Kenneth answered. "Nussbaum couldn't afford to wait for the company to reopen, so he looked for a position elsewhere. Luckily, Alchemy was in need of a new salesman."

"You mean lucky for Alfred Nussbaum," Robert corrected, "but not so lucky for you. From the way his records at Alchemy read, Nussbaum was very good at his job."

"He was."

"How did that sit with you," Marjorie pursued, "Nussbaum working for the competition?"

"We were disappointed," Charles admitted, "but my brother and I are not in the habit of keeping employees against their will. We understand our workers have mouths to feed."

"Some more than others," she remarked, recalling Nussbaum's colorful family life.

"You weren't at all resentful that Alchemy, aside from having beaten you at the chemical business, had taken one of your best employees?" Jameson prodded.

"If we did harbor resentment," Kenneth

allowed, "it was toward Alchemy Enterprises, not Alfred Nussbaum. Our relationship with him remained amicable. So amicable, in fact, that he visited our office several times after he had left."

From the corner of her eye, Marjorie saw Charles signal to his brother to stop speaking.

"I thought the two of you hadn't seen Nussbaum in months," she challenged.

"We hadn't," Charles maintained. "We were traveling in South America for some time, looking for inexpensive suppliers — you know, to cut down operating expenses so that we could reopen. Our secretary told us he had visited."

"Remarkable timing," Jameson commented. "Just for the record, where were the two of you the day before yesterday, around eleven in the morning?"

"Just for the record, in our room, reviewing our finances."

"Was anyone else with you?"

"No, our finances are our own concern and no one else's." They had reached the area of the green where Kenneth's ball had landed. "Now, before we get on with our game, is there anything else we can help you with, Detective?"

"Yes, Nussbaum's employment records.

Could I have them, please?"

The bespectacled man wrinkled his nose. "That's going to be a bit tricky. Our files are at the office."

"All right, we'll come back after you've finished your game and the four of us will go the office and pick up the file."

"It's not that easy. You see our facility, along with all its contents, was seized yesterday and Kenneth and I have been barred admittance. So, I'm afraid you're going to have to go through different channels if you wish to retrieve that file."

"I thought this was a temporary shut down," Jameson quipped.

"Yes," Marjorie concurred. "You led us to believe the company was going to reopen soon."

"It will," Charles assured. "It's simply been postponed."

"Until when?" she inquired.

Kenneth took the putter from the caddy and hit his ball across the green. It rolled straight for the hole and looked like it might sink, but then at the last minute, it uncannily bounced off the rim. Kenneth sighed angrily, and stomped off to the ball's new location.

Charles turned from the scene and peered

at Marjorie over the top of his spectacles. "Until our luck changes."

TWENTY

After an early supper and a leisurely stroll along the village green, Marjorie and Jameson returned to her cottage at dusk, just in time to hear the telephone ring. Marjorie ran to the large walnut secretary where she kept the sonorous black instrument and picked up the receiver. "Hello?"

"Hello," the operator replied. "Long distance for Miss Marjorie McClelland."

"This is Miss McClelland."

"Thank you, Miss McClelland. Please hold while I connect your call."

"Good afternoon," came a clipped British accent through the line. "Is this the Mc-Clelland Detective Agency? This is Cedric St. John Snell, the World Class Tiddlywinks Champion. I require your services in the recovery of a missing object: my tiddly. I awoke this morning and it had disappeared, which is rather puzzling since my winks are still intact."

Marjorie grinned and played along, glad to hear that Creighton was back to his old tricks. "What about your marbles? Do you still have them, or have you lost those, too?"

"My marbles? Oh, I lost those a long time ago. This loss occurred quite recently. Although I do seem to recollect a small tornado crossing my path yesterday evening, or perhaps it was more like a small hurricane — as I recall it did have a female name. Margaret? No. Maeve? No? What was it?"

"Marjorie?"

"That's it! And what a violent little tempest it was. Didn't stick around for long though. At least, not long enough for me to make amends. I was a right bounder last night. The heat I suppose. Makes everyone a bit stroppy."

"Well, the storm didn't give you much of chance to apologize, did it? But if it means anything, I'm sure she's sorry too. I, um, I expected you to call later this evening," she said, hoping that he would call her back when Robert wasn't present.

"Expected? You expected me to call — oh, Robert's there, isn't he? Sorry, but Vanessa and I have a late dinner date tonight. We made reservations for nine at a restaurant downtown that has quite a reputation; haute cuisine, candlelight, violins, that sort of rubbish. We wanted to do something to celebrate the engagement."

"Sounds lovely," Marjorie remarked, more than a little envious that it wasn't she who would be joining him.

"How's the case coming along? Any new developments since yesterday?"

"A few," she replied as she watched Robert plop onto the living room sofa. "We just saw Nussbaum's former employers, the Cullen brothers. Nussbaum worked for them before he worked for Alchemy."

"Did they tell you anything?"

"Yes, although not intentionally. They speculated that Nussbaum's death was probably a case of robbery gone wrong and asked us, numerous times, if we had found cash on the body."

"Very odd," Creighton commented. "It sounds almost as though they're looking for something."

"I got the same impression," she agreed. "It was as if they were hoping Nussbaum had cash on him so that they could claim it; which, I suppose, isn't out of the question, since their business has been seized."

"Seized?"

"Uh hum. Yesterday. We asked them for Nussbaum's employment records, but the

Cullens can't even access their own office. Robert had to contact the IRS and request that the file be sent to him. Heaven knows how long that will take."

"Unless it's a file for Eliot Ness, I'm sure they'll take their time," Creighton remarked. "The Cullen brothers are hardly Al Capone or Frank Nitti."

"No, they're not clever enough," Marjorie deemed. "Do you know they actually let it slip that Nussbaum had visited their office on numerous occasions since quitting? Yet earlier in the conversation they claimed not to have seen him in months."

"How'd they get around that?"

"They claimed they were in South America at the time, looking for new suppliers. Curious though — since curare comes from South America."

"Yes. Certainly sounds like they're hiding something, doesn't it?" he responded. "Did you find out anything else?"

"No. Noonan spent the day looking through Nussbaum's financial records in search of more ammo against Saporito and Josie," Marjorie mentioned. "Oh, and Dr. Heller released the body to Bernice."

"Yes, I know. I saw the obituary in the late edition of the paper. The wake is tomorrow. Vanessa and I are planning to attend."

"Both of you?"

"Vanessa was his employer and I, well, I thought it might be interesting to see who shows up, who doesn't, and how everyone interacts."

"Good idea. Although I'm sure your presence won't go over very well with Bernice or Herbert. Or Josie."

"Josie? I thought Jameson had her arrested."

"He did. Her lawyer requested that she be allowed to attend the funeral. Logan is taking her," she explained.

"Lovely," Creighton remarked. "I'll borrow an iron glove from the suit of armor upstairs."

"A glove?"

"Yes, so Logan doesn't crush my hand next time he shakes it. Honestly, the man pumped my arm so hard I thought oil would shoot out of my head."

Marjorie laughed. "You'll have to tell us all about it. Perhaps in person," she added hopefully.

"Perhaps, perhaps not. Whichever way the wind blows," Creighton remained ambiguous. "Why are you so eager to have me back? You certainly didn't seem very pleased with me last night."

"Because if you marry Vanessa, you may

not come back again and I miss you." She looked up to see Robert with Sam on his lap, and staring directly at her. "I mean *we* miss you. Mrs. Patterson, Sharon . . ."

"Sharon! Heavens, I forgot all about her."

"You mean you haven't called her? She usually keeps you on a very short leash."

"Yes, well I guess it slipped my mind, what with the case, our argument, and then my engagement to Vanessa . . ." his voice trailed off.

Marjorie winced. *That damned engagement! Was it true or not? Was he going to marry Vanessa? And if so, how long before he forgot Marjorie the same way he had forgotten Sharon?*

"I'd better hang up," he told her. "Looks like Vanessa's ready to go. Bye, Marjorie. I'll talk to you soon."

"Good-bye," she replied, then quickly added, "Oh, and Creighton?"

"Yes."

There was so much she wanted to say to him, so many things that needed to be discussed, but now was not the time. "Have a good time tonight," she faltered.

"Thank you. You and Jameson do the same. And I'm sorry again about last night. I want you and Jameson to be happy. As happy as Vanessa and I are. Good night,

263

now." There was a soft click from the other end of the line and Marjorie wondered if it wasn't the sound of her heart breaking. With her back to Robert, she returned the handset to its cradle and blinked back her tears.

"What did Creighton have to say?" Jameson asked.

She took a deep breath in an effort to regain her composure, and turned around. "He and Vanessa are going to Nussbaum's wake tomorrow."

"Good thinking. A lot can be learned about people just by watching them."

"That's what Creighton thought. He said it might —" Her words were interrupted by the ring of the telephone. "Not again," she sighed before picking up the handset. "Hello?"

"Noonan here," came the gruff voice. "Is Jameson around?"

"Yes, he's right here. Hold on a moment." She held the receiver out to Robert. "It's for you. Officer Noonan."

Robert rose from the sofa, forcing Sam to hop to the floor. He grabbed the telephone from Marjorie's hand. "What is it, Noonan? . . . uh-huh . . . uh-huh . . . You don't say . . . When? . . . Where are you now? . . . Okay, I'll be there in a few minutes." He hung up the phone and headed toward the

264

door. "C'mon. Let's go."

"Where? What's going on?" she demanded as she grabbed her purse from the top of the desk.

"To the churchyard," he replied with a frown. "It's Reverend Price. He's been attacked."

The minister was stretched out on the sofa in the rectory office, holding an icepack to the back of his head. Despite the fact that she was a Catholic and he a Presbyterian, Marjorie had always held the clergyman in very high regard. She knelt beside the couch. "Reverend Price, are you all right?"

"A bit battered, but none the worse for wear," the gray-haired man assured her.

"What happened?"

Officer Noonan hovered over him, taking notes in a small reporter's notebook. "Some nut whacked him on the head. Knocked him out cold."

"I guess someone disagreed with one of my sermons," Price joked.

Jameson stood at the minister's feet. "Tell me exactly how it happened."

"I was overseeing the dismantling of the fair at the church today." He said to Marjorie, aside, "It was very successful, you know. We took in two hundred dollars more than last year."

"Very good," she said approvingly.

"It is, isn't it?" He turned his attention back to the policemen. "As I was saying, I spent the day overseeing the dismantling of the fair. We rent the rides from a local company, so their employees disassemble and tow them away, but the booths and concessions are our own and are packed away by volunteers. It's a long, tedious process that requires two to three days, at least." He cleared his throat. "Well, after working all morning and afternoon, the volunteers called it a day around six o'clock and went home to their families. I stayed behind to compose a thank-you letter to the community for publication in the local newspaper."

"At the church? Why not here, at your office?" Jameson inquired.

"I often do my work at the church. It's quieter there, easier to concentrate. Plus, being in the Lord's house inspires me, and any writer will tell you that inspiration is essential to their craft."

"True," Marjorie nodded.

"So you were in the church, writing your letter," Jameson prodded. "Then what?"

"I worked on the letter for the next two, two and a half hours, until I noticed it was getting dark. That's when I decided to come back to the rectory, fix myself a light supper, and then turn in for the evening. I packed up my letter and left the church through the door behind the altar, it being closer to the rectory than the front door. As I was heading down the back steps, I observed a shadowy figure lurking around the churchyard, near the Ferris wheel. I walked over to investigate, but before I could get very far, I felt a terrible pain at the back of my head and everything went black." He frowned. "When I awoke, minutes later, and realized what had transpired, I staggered back here to the rectory and telephoned the police. Officer Noonan took the call."

At mention of his name, the constable smiled proudly.

"This person who was lurking, was it a man or a woman?" Jameson asked.

The Reverend shook his head slowly. "I couldn't say. It was too dark. All I saw was a silhouette. A vague outline."

"Man or woman, whoever did it should be strung up by their toes," Noonan judged. "It's a sad world we live in when a preacher isn't safe outside his own church."

"In defense of my attacker," Price spoke up, "they might not have known I was a minister." He pointed to the black shirt he wore, which was unbuttoned at the neck. "As you can see, I'm not wearing my collar."

"Gee," Noonan remarked. "I didn't know you guys were allowed to take off your clothes."

The Reverend grinned. "Yes, well, we find it makes laundry easier that way."

A voice came from the door of the office. "I got here as fast as I could." It was Dr. Heller, toting his medical bag. "Where's the victim?"

Reverend Price looked up in horror. "You called the coroner?"

Heller corrected him. "I happen to be a board-certified physician, thank you. Now then, what seems to be the problem?"

"The Reverend received a blow to the back of the head," Jameson explained. "Knocked him unconscious."

"Hmm, let's see," the doctor approached the sofa. Marjorie rose from her spot on the floor and stepped aside to allow him access to the patient.

Upon seeing the young woman, Heller removed his hat. "Good evening, Miss Mc-Clelland. Putting in another performance as Miss Never-Say-Die?"

Marjorie smiled. "My favorite role, Dr. Heller."

The Reverend swung his feet to the floor and sat up gingerly. Dr. Heller settled onto the cushion beside him. "Let's take a look."

Reverend Price drew the icepack away from the back of his head revealing a patch of hair matted with dried blood. The doctor parted the hair to examine the wound beneath, and with careful fingers, pressed on the area, causing Price to cringe in pain. "The skin is broken, but the skull appears to be intact. No fractures as far as I can ascertain. Turn around," he ordered.

Taking a lighted instrument from his bag, he peered into the cleric's eyes. "Concussion," he declared. "Not terribly serious, but you should take it easy the next few days. And I don't want you left alone tonight. Do you have anyone to stay with you?"

"Mrs. Reynolds, my secretary, volunteered to stay in the guest bedroom. She should be here any minute."

"Good, I'll leave instructions with her." He returned the instrument to his bag and brought out bandages, gauze pads, and a bottle of Mercurochrome. "In the meantime, I'll clean up this wound."

As the doctor set to work, Jameson asked, "What sort of object could have caused that wound?"

Heller took a piece of Mercurochrome-soaked gauze and swabbed the reverend's scalp. "From the shape of the bruise, something long, blunt, and narrow."

"And sometimes it's a shillelagh . . ." Marjorie remarked.

Jameson gave her a curious look. "Any idea what it was made of?"

The physician shook his head. "I don't see any splinters, so my guess is it wasn't — wait a minute." He did a double take at the wound then reached down to fetch a pair of tweezers from his bag.

"What is it?" Price asked.

"Just a minute," the doctor shushed. Within a few seconds, he held up the tweezers to display a reddish brown flake he had extracted from the reverend's scalp.

"What's that?" Noonan asked.

"Hydrated ferric oxide or, in layman's terms, rust."

"The object was metal," Marjorie surmised.

Noonan exclaimed. "Geez, what a world we live in. Nothin's sacred."

Jameson objected. "This isn't a sign of a world gone mad, Noonan. It's a sign of desperation. Whoever attacked Reverend Price did it because they were desperately trying to find something and didn't want to be caught snooping around the fair-grounds."

"Or, more precisely, the Ferris wheel," Marjorie interjected.

"Do you think this is related to that man who died at the fair?" Price asked.

"It's too much of a coincidence for it not to be," she replied.

"Well, if there's something funny going on, our guys will get to the bottom of it," Noonan stated with confidence. "They're out there now, searching the grounds and talking to the owners of the houses bordering the churchyard. They'll get to the bottom of this. You'll see."

Jameson rubbed his chin meditatively. "A long, blunt metal object," he pondered aloud.

"If the weapon is out there, our guys will find it, boss," Noonan boasted.

"What could it be?" Robert continued, ignoring Noonan's claims. "The barrel of a shot gun? A section of pipe?"

"Perhaps the handle of a shovel," Heller speculated.

"Maybe it's a tire iron," Noonan proposed. "I read about a case where some broad used one to kill her husband."

"Could be a metal stake from one of the tents," Reverend Price suggested.

"A blowgun," Marjorie spoke up. The men stared at her as if she must be quite insane. She explained defensively, "The killer could have run out of darts."

Twenty-One

Creighton sat in the third row of Gittle-man's Funeral Home with Vanessa, in her wheelchair, positioned in the aisle beside him. "Why did we have to get here so early?" she complained. "The only other person in this room is the corpse."

"At least he's quiet," the Englishman reasoned.

"It's rude," she insisted, "being here before the family arrives. They deserve some time alone with their grief."

"Grief? I don't think you'll see too much of that today. Not with this bunch."

As if on cue, Bernice Nussbaum appeared in the entrance arch, accompanied by her children, Natalie and Herbert. The women made their way up a side aisle to the coffin positioned in the front of the room, while Herbert made a beeline for Creighton.

The boy slid into the chair next to Creighton with a broad grin stretched across his bloated countenance. "Have the police found out anything about my father's murder? Or does Detective Jameson still think I did it?"

Creighton watched as Bernice and Natalie, attired in simple black crepe dresses, bowed their heads over Alfred Nussbaum's body then coolly retired to the first row of seats. "Why don't you spread the joy, Herbert, and torture someone else? Quite frankly, I've had enough of you to last a lifetime."

"You're the one who insulted Mother," he replied. "You implied that she was lying."

"She *was* lying." Creighton narrowed his eyes and stared at the boy. "Isn't there something else you could be doing beside talking to me? I know Halloween is your busy time of year, but surely you can find more constructive uses for your time. Such as brushing up on your knowledge of the Donner party, for instance."

Herbert would not be put off. "Does the detective have any other leads on the murderer?"

"Detective Jameson has plenty of leads, some of which could land you and your 'Mommy' behind bars."

"You're bluffing," the boy said matter-of-factly. "Detective Jameson hasn't found anything or he'd be here right now."

"Not physically, but I'll have you know the detective has plain clothes policemen all over this place. Tell me, on your way in here, did you happen to see a man across the street, walking a dog?"

"Yes, I did."

"The man walking the dog is Officer Rennert. The man in the dog suit is Officer Johanssen. Short young man, Officer Johanssen," Creighton arched an eyebrow, "but highly effective."

As Creighton presumed, Herbert was completely unaccustomed to humor. The boy wasn't sure how to react. "I don't believe you."

"You should, Herbert. Rest assured, they'll find the killer. Especially Johanssen, that nose doesn't lie."

"How can you be so certain they can?" Herbert challenged. "Perhaps it's unsolvable. A perfect crime."

"Herbert, my lad, you read too much and have lived too little. Perfect crimes, though popular in fiction, are, in reality, quite rare."

"Oh, but they do occur, and they're easier to commit than one might expect. All that's required is a little planning and a steady nerve. Most criminals are caught because they're sloppy, and the reason they're sloppy is that they lose their resolve. But, if a fellow keeps his wits about him, there's no telling how long he might elude the authorities. Months, years, maybe the rest of his life." Herbert gazed at his father's body with a glint in his eye that gave Creighton goose bumps.

Could this boy — this strange, gruesome boy — have murdered his father? He didn't want to even entertain the idea, but he did want to get rid of the kid at any cost. "You know, Herbert, all I have to do is whistle, and this place will be swarming with police," he boasted.

The boy rolled his eyes. "Again, a complete exaggeration, if not an outright lie."

The Englishman brought the forefinger of each hand to his lips. Before he had a chance to blow, Josie entered, dressed to the nines in a red silk dress and a feathered hat, on the arm of Detective Logan. They were followed by the three plainclothes officers who had been following Herbert, Natalie, and Bernice.

Creighton smiled; for once fate conspired with him, rather than against him. "See?" he asked of his young companion.

Herbert turned beet red and clambered to the first row in search of his mother's protection. Speaking in hushed tones to her son, Bernice Nussbaum glanced behind her seat nervously. Spotting Vanessa seated in the aisle, she rose from her chair and greeted the wheelchair-bound woman. "Mrs. Randolph," she said, and then, her demeanor become colder, "Mr. um . . ."

"Ashcroft," Creighton volunteered with a broad grin. "We've met before.

"Yes, Mr. Ashcroft. I remember you. How could I forget?" she added frostily.

"I do make an impression," he gloated.

"Our condolences to you and your family," Vanessa extended a gloved hand. "If I can help you in any way, please let me know."

Bernice took the hand and briefly clutched it in her own. "That's very kind of you, Mrs. Randolph, but we'll be all right. We're going to live with my mother to cut expenses, and Alfred's life insurance policy should cover the cost of the funeral."

Vanessa looked around. "It's a lovely funeral home. If your husband is watching over us right now, I'm sure he's very pleased."

"Should be," Bernice sneered. "It's better than he deserved."

Vanessa stared awkwardly at the woman, trying to think of something to say. However, she needn't have bothered; Bernice's focus was fixed on Josie who had, until now, been seated at the back of the room, handcuffed to a less-than-enthusiastic Detective Logan. Presently, the younger "Mrs. Nussbaum" was making her way toward the coffin.

"Who's Satan's secretary?" Vanessa whispered in Creighton's ear.

"The other Mrs. Nussbaum," he replied.

"What do you mean 'other'? You didn't tell me Alfred had two wives."

The Englishman grinned. "I didn't want to spoil the surprise."

"Who's the man she's with?"

"Detective Logan. She's in jail for conspiring with her husband to take Alfred Nussbaum for $5,000."

"What?" She gestured toward the coffin. "But her husband —"

He patted her hand. "I'll explain later."

Josie, with Logan in tow, strutted up to the coffin. Much to Bernice's chagrin, the woman in red planted a kiss on the dead man's cheek. "Excuse me," Bernice pardoned herself from Vanessa and Creighton's company and marched over to confront the redheaded woman.

"Why you shameless little hussy!" Bernice exclaimed. "You have some nerve coming here, and dressed in red, no less!"

278

"Alfie liked me in red. And I have every right to be here," the younger woman maintained. "He was my husband, too."

"Your marriage was never legal, and you know it!"

Josie thrust her nose in the air. "I know nothin' of the sort. If you ask me, I was more of a wife to him than you were."

"How dare you! At least I married Alfred out of love; you only saw him as a meal ticket. I bet you're the one who killed him. Why else would you have a cop handcuffed to you? Why'd you do it? For the money?"

"You should talk! If anyone had a motive for killing Alfie, it was you. You couldn't stand the thought of the two of us together! You couldn't stand the thought of him being with a real woman."

This remark was the last straw for Bernice. She let out a piercing scream and lunged for Josie's throat, sending the woman careening onto Detective Logan, who, upon losing his balance, fell backward onto the floral arrangements. Bernice dove on top of both Josie and Logan and began to choke the younger woman amid a flurry of gladiola and chrysanthemum petals.

"Get her, Mother!" Natalie cheered, while her brother shook his head and adjusted his glasses.

"I never knew she had such pugilistic tendencies," Herbert remarked.

Creighton leapt from his chair and, grabbing Bernice by the shoulders, attempted to pull her off the younger, lighter woman. Logan, meanwhile, tried to restrain Josie by pinning her arms between her back and his chest. After several minutes, they finally succeeded in tearing the two apart.

The detective rose to his feet and thanked Creighton before yanking Josie off the ground. "Hey!" she shouted. "This is my best dress!"

Hearing the fracas, a short, middle-aged man wearing a blue yarmulke rushed into the room, shouting. "Mrs. Nussbaum! Mrs. Nussbaum!"

"Yes," Josie and Bernice answered in unison.

"Mr. Gittleman was talking to me," Bernice corrected.

"Mrs. Nussbaum, please!" Gittleman implored, on the brink of tears. "This establishment was founded to serve as a haven for grieving families. A haven! What will happen to my business if people find out that I have women wrestling on the floor?"

"If they're anything like the joints I raid, the joint will be mobbed," Logan quipped and then patted Creighton on the back, causing the Englishman to swallow his breath.

"No, sir, the joint will not be mobbed. My business will be ruined! Ruined!"

"We're sorry, Mr. Gittleman," Creighton rasped. He still clutched Bernice Nussbaum's arm. "We promise it won't happen again."

The funeral director threw his hands in the air. "He promises! Promises! I'm warning you, if it does happen again, I'm throwing all of you out!" He pointed toward the door. "Out!" The angry man stomped off through the archway into the anteroom.

"You heard him, ladies," Creighton announced. "Take your seats. Fighting's over for today." He guided Bernice back to the seat she had previously occupied, while Logan directed Josie to a place two chairs away.

"This row is reserved for family members," Bernice objected.

Josie spat back, "I am family."

"Enough!" the Englishman bellowed before another dispute erupted. "No one is asking you to be friends, but for today you can at least agree to disagree. And, in case you can't, you shall have to be separated." He nodded to Logan, who wedged himself into the chair between the two women. "Still too close," Creighton deemed. Spotting the Nussbaum boy seated to Bernice's left he instructed: "Herbert, switch places with your mother."

They obediently changed positions, thus creating a two-person buffer between the feuding Mrs. Nussbaums. Creighton surveyed the motley lineup. "What a lovely group. When this is all over, we really must get you all together for a family portrait."

He returned to his seat under the blistering gazes of the bereaved family. "Bravo," Vanessa welcomed him back.

Creighton shook his head and whispered, in an impersonation of Mr. Gittleman, "These people are crazy! Crazy!"

"You handled them quite well."

"Thanks, if my financial situation takes a turn for the worse, it's comforting to know I can find work in a sanatorium."

As he sat down, he spied, in the doorway, the two goons from The Rusty Anchor flanking a heavyset man with dark hair and a day's worth of stubble. *Murphy,* he thought to himself.

The entourage removed their hats and approached the casket. With bowed heads, they paid their respects to the late Alfred Nussbaum, reciting what appeared to be small prayers and invoking the sign of the cross. When they had finished, they donned their hats, and upon a nod from Murphy, the two goons pounded the corpse in the chest with their fists.

The women in the room gasped. Murphy apologized politely. "Sorry, ladies, but in my business you gotta make sure."

The men tipped their hats in unison and exited via the aisle nearest Creighton.

Spotting the Englishman on the way out, one of the men smiled. "Hey, it's that copper from The Rusty Anchor. Whatcha doing here, Copper? I thought I told you to go back home to New Orleans."

"You did," Creighton agreed, and then pointed toward the back of his mouth. "But I had a piece of possum stuck between my teeth and my dentist lives here, in Boston."

Murphy gave Creighton an appraising glance. "You're one of the flatfoots who stopped by the bar. Do me a favor, will ya? If you see that Marjorie dame again give her a message. Tell her Murph liked the fake phone number gag."

"Fake phone number gag?"

"Yeah. She'll know what I mean. She's sharp, that one. Doesn't miss a thing and recognizes a good-lookin' guy when she sees one. Cute, curvy, and a 'connisewer.' Just the way I like 'em." He and his goons chuckled lecherously and made their way out of the room.

No sooner had they left, than a pair of drab-looking men dressed in identical dark charcoal-gray suits arrived. If it weren't for the fact that one wore spectacles and appeared slightly older than the other, they might have passed for twins.

"That's Charles and Kenneth Cullen," Vanessa informed her escort.

"As in Cullen Chemicals?" he asked, remembering his conversation with Marjorie.

"One and the same."

"Ah, the competition."

"Barely," Vanessa scoffed. "They were never quite in the same league as Alchemy. Though, Lord knows, they did just about everything they could to compete."

"Some people just don't have a head for business," he remarked.

They watched as the men bowed before the casket then turned around to pay their respects to the family. The Cullens glanced at the two women in confusion before splitting up, the man with the glasses extending his hand to Bernice, while his brother offered his condolences to Josie, who discreetly concealed the handcuffs that bound her to Detective Logan.

Creighton strained to eavesdrop, but the softness of their voices, combined with the difficulty of listening to two conversations at once, made it impossible for him to pick out more than a couple words at a time. However, even without the benefit of hearing, it was apparent that the Cullen brothers were doing most of the talking, their busy mouths pausing just long enough for their perplexed listeners to shake or nod their heads in response. With little imagination, one could easily envision the siblings as detectives performing an interrogation rather than businessmen paying a sympathy call.

Creighton's brow furrowed. Were the Cullen brothers asking Nussbaum's widows the same questions they had asked of Marjorie and Jameson? If so, what were they looking for?

From her place in the first row, Natalie abruptly stood up and, in an obvious state of agitation, hurried down the aisle and toward the door. As she passed Vanessa and Creighton, she shot them an icy glance.

The Englishman rose from his seat. "I think I'll see what that's about."

"Let me go," Vanessa suggested. "You're already on Herbert and Bernice's list of least favorite people. And you just don't know girls that age. If they don't want to tell you something, they won't. They can be very stubborn and difficult."

"So can I. And I'm quite well-acquainted with stubborn and difficult women. Keep an eye on things for me, will you?" He stepped around the wheelchair and headed down the aisle, following Natalie through the reception area and outdoors, where she pulled a cigarette from her purse and tried, with trembling fingers, to strike a match.

Creighton gently plucked the matchbox from her hand, and with one deft motion, ignited one of the matchsticks. Cupping one hand over the flame, he leaned forward and brought it to the end of the young woman's cigarette.

She took a good long drag, then exhaled a stream of smoke. "Thanks."

Creighton extinguished the matchstick and let it fall to the ground. "You're welcome." He handed back the matchbox. "Are you all right?"

She took the matchbox and dropped it into her purse. "Fine. Why?"

"You seemed a bit rattled in there."

Natalie leaned her back against the brick wall of the funeral home and took another puff on the cigarette. "So?" she breathed.

"Are you going to arrest me for suspicious behavior?"

Creighton smiled and folded his arms across his chest. "No, I'm not a policeman."

Her eyes narrowed. "Then what were you doing at my house the other day? And what were you doing interrogating my mother and brother?"

"Helping Detective Jameson. He's a friend of mine."

"Yeah? Are you gonna have your friend arrest me?"

"No. You haven't done anything wrong."

"Haven't I?" she challenged. "I guess they can't arrest people for what's in their hearts, can they?"

Creighton shook his head. "If they could, we'd all be in jail."

"I guess so." The girl gave a flicker of a smile, and then stared at him appraisingly. "You married?"

"No."

"Planning on it?"

His thoughts slipped, for a moment, to Marjorie. "No."

"You're very smart then."

"Not inordinately."

"Yes you are," Natalie contradicted. "Marriage brings nothing but pain and unhappiness. And men are nothing but liars and cheats."

Creighton propped his shoulder against the wall beside her. "Do you think I'm a liar and a cheat?" he asked in earnest.

The young woman gazed into his blue eyes and immediately started to blush. "No," she replied, swiftly looking away, "but, then again, you can't tell by looking."

"No, I suppose you can't."

There was a long pause before the girl spoke again.

"Do you think there's a hell?" she asked.

The Englishman shrugged. "I don't know. I was taught, as a boy, that there is, but whether I believe it or not, I can't say."

"But you do believe that people are punished for their sins?" she prodded.

"Yes, I'd like to think that, in the end, the good are rewarded and the bad are punished."

"But sometimes the bad aren't really bad. Sometimes they're good people who have done something stupid."

Her comment was a thinly veiled confession. "If the person is truly good," he hypothesized, "then they should admit to their wrongdoing and ask for forgiveness."

Her eyes filled with tears. "What if the

person's scared of what might happen to them?"

He placed a hand on her shoulder. "Then they should confide in someone they trust. Someone who can protect them." He flashed a kind smile. "Someone who isn't a liar and a cheat."

"Oh, Mr. Ashcroft," she cried. "I've done something terrible. I — I —" A small spherical object flew past Creighton's face and hit Natalie square in the forehead.

They whirled around to see Herbert, standing near the door, a peashooter in his hand. "Natalie's in lo-ove," he sang.

The girl threw her cigarette to the ground and crushed it with the heel of her shoe. "I am not!" she screamed.

"You are too," he insisted. "You're using that man to replace father. It's quite natural, really. Look at Mata Hari and Rudolph MacLeod."

Natalie shrieked and hit her brother in the head with her purse. "I hate you, Herbert! I hate you!" she declared before storming back into the funeral home. The boy flashed a self-satisfied grin, tucked the peashooter into his pocket, and then ran off in pursuit of his sister.

Creighton stayed behind in bewildered silence. Natalie's near-confession had surprised him, but the sight of Herbert clutching the peashooter had left him shaken beyond words. How long had Herbert been standing there? How much of their conversation had he overheard? Had he orchestrated the attack with the peashooter to prevent Natalie from confessing what she knew?

Breathing deeply, he ran a hand through his hair and tried to think. Like flashes of lightning, images appeared before his eyes — images of the peashooter and Natalie's cigarette. Suddenly a strange idea occurred to him. *Was it possible?*

He looked down at the ground where Natalie's cigarette lay broken. *When I get home,* Creighton resolved, *I shall have to call Jameson.*

TWENTY-TWO

Marjorie carefully removed the bones from the fricasseed chicken, discarding them as she went along. Half of the meat she placed in a covered casserole dish to take to Reverend Price. The remainder went into a separate pot to serve as supper for herself and Robert. When all the meat had been removed, she added a helping of peas, carrots, and pearl onions to each container, gave the contents a liberal dousing of white sauce, put the lids on both of them, and hurried off to the rectory.

She arrived to find Reverend Price seated on the sofa in his office, reading a book. He looked up with a smile, "Marjorie, what a pleasant surprise."

"Hi, Reverend. How are you feeling?"

"Not bad." He placed his book on the seat beside him. "Splitting headache, but, otherwise, not bad. I sent Mrs. Reynolds home. No sense in her hanging around here."

"Yes, I thought you might have, that's why I brought you supper." She handed him the casserole.

"Thank you." The cleric accepted the dish and eagerly removed the lid to view its contents. "Mmm, chicken fricassee. And it's still warm. Would you mind if I started in now? I know it's only four thirty, but I'm famished. Mrs. Reynolds is a very nice woman, but not much of a cook."

"I'll get you a fork." She rushed into the adjacent kitchen, retrieved the utensil and a napkin and sat in the chair opposite Price.

The minister took the fork from Marjorie and dug it into the steaming vessel. "Delicious," he proclaimed after swallowing a mouthful. "Best I've had in a long time."

Marjorie grinned wearily.

Price frowned. "You look tired, my dear. I hope you didn't go through too much work just for me." The reverend took another forkful of food.

"Oh no, I wanted to do it." She mirrored his frown. "I've just had a lot on my mind lately."

"This murder business, no doubt."

"Mmm," she answered evasively.

He swallowed. "Something troubling you?"

"I guess you could say that."

"What sort of troubles could you possibly have? Certainly not man trouble — not with Detective Jameson around."

Marjorie silently bowed her head.

"Oh, so it is man trouble," he presumed from her reaction. "You know, Marjorie, the period of time before a couple gets married can be very difficult. Marriage is a huge commitment; it's not unusual for a bride or groom to have second thoughts." He took another bite of chicken.

"It's more than just second thoughts, Reverend Price," she explained. "I'm not sure, but I might be in love with someone else."

"Mr. Ashcroft," he ventured a guess.

"How did you know?" she asked in surprise.

The minister dabbed at the corners of his mouth with the napkin. "There aren't too many eligible bachelors in this town, Marjorie. Besides, reading your novels has honed my powers of observation. From what I can see, the two of you are very close."

"Yes, but that was just friendship, or at least I thought it was friendship. Now I'm not so sure." She pulled at her hair with both hands.

"Has Mr. Ashcroft said anything to you?"

293

"No, he wouldn't. He's a gentleman. He knows I'm engaged to Robert. He wouldn't want to put me in that position."

"Have you said anything to him?"

"No, I only just realized two days ago, when I heard him proposing to someone else."

"He proposed to Sharon Schutt?"

"No, Vanessa Randolph."

The reverend was mystified. "Vanessa Randolph? Who is that?"

"A childhood friend of his. She lives in Boston."

"Boston?"

Marjorie nodded her head. "She was Alfred Nussbaum's employer. The case reunited her with Creighton. He's staying at her house."

The Reverend pursed his lips. "Really?"

"It's all above board," she said, anticipating the gossip that would circulate.

"Oh I'm sure. I'm sure." He took a bite of chicken, a puzzled look upon his face. "This might sound like a dumb question, but how did you figure out that you might be in love with Mr. Ashcroft? Were you jealous when you overheard his proposal to Miss Randolph?"

"Mrs. Randolph," Marjorie corrected. "She's a widow. And no, that wasn't it. It was when Robert told me that Creighton is in love with me."

The reverend was completely nonplussed. "Detective Jameson told you that Mr. Ashcroft is in love with you? But he's your fiancé. Why would he do that?"

"To explain why Creighton resigned as my editor."

He shook his head. "And this Miss — sorry — Mrs. Randolph? Does she know that Mr. Ashcroft may be in love with you?"

"Oh yes. She told me about it too."

The elderly man did a double take at Marjorie. "What! But why?"

"I don't know. She is quite ill, whether or not that has anything to do with it, I don't know. But she's a good soul — very good. Only —"

"Only, you're not sure he should be marrying her." He took a forkful of chicken and chewed it with gusto, glad that he was finally able to anticipate Marjorie's next words.

"No, I'm not sure. I'm not sure about him and her. I'm not sure about Robert and me. I'm not sure about anything. Do I break off my engagement, only to find that I was wrong? Do I ask Creighton to break off his engagement? What should I do?"

"My dear, I can't tell you that. You have to figure that out for yourself. If you can . . .

heaven knows my head is spinning just listening to you." He reached to the book that had been lying beside him, and handed it to the young woman. "But here's something that you might find useful."

Marjorie took it in her hands and leafed through a few pages. "The Bible?"

The minister nodded and smiled. "Life is sometimes like fixing a broken toaster or radio. When things go wrong, it's often helpful to consult the instruction manual." He pointed to the book in Marjorie's hand. "That's your instruction manual."

With this piece of advice, Reverend Price gave her a playful wink and went back to devouring the chicken fricassee.

Marjorie left the rectory a few minutes later and trudged along Ridgebury Road back to her cottage, more than a bit disappointed in the guidance she had received from her elders. *Consult the owner's manual. Imagine your life without Robert.* What advice! Yet, so anxious was she to resolve her doubts about her impending nuptials, that despite her reservations, she opened the Bible the reverend had given her and perused it as she walked.

She had managed to read but one passage when she felt a heavy tap on her shoulder.

Marjorie turned around to see the corpulent figure of Sharon Schutt. She leaned her large, spherical head close to Marjorie's and whispered, so no one else would hear, "Marjorie, I need your help."

The blonde-haired woman reared back in a combination of fear and astonishment. Even on the best of days, Sharon never said more than two words to her, those two words being either "Hello, Marjorie" or "Get lost." Nevertheless, here she was, standing before her, requesting assistance. "What can I do for you, Sharon?"

"It's Creighton. I'm worried about him. He's been gone for days and I don't know where he is. He hasn't called or written, or . . . or . . . anything." She broke into a sob.

Marjorie reached into her purse and pulled out a lavender handkerchief. The heavyset girl snatched it and proceeded to blow her nose with a resounding honk. Marjorie would never have thought it possible, but she felt a great deal of pity for Sharon — this poor lonely creature who was so terrified of being an old maid that she clung voraciously to a man who didn't love her.

Still, who was to say that Creighton didn't love Sharon? In his own way, the Englishman might care for the Schutt girl. But if he did, then why hadn't he contacted her and let her know his whereabouts?

Vanessa, she thought in answer to her own question. Perhaps that's whom Creighton truly loved — not Sharon, not herself, but Vanessa Randolph. Lord knew she had a strange hold over the man. After thirty-four years as a bachelor, Creighton had finally proposed, not to either of Ridgebury's maidens but to Vanessa Randolph.

Marjorie glanced at Sharon's sad round face; she hadn't the nerve to tell her the complete truth. "Creighton's in Boston, helping Detective Jameson to investigate the murder of the man on the Ferris wheel. It's all very hush-hush."

"So that's why he hasn't called!" she exclaimed in elation. "He's on a top secret mission! Oh, the poor thing, alone in an unfamiliar town, cooped up in some hotel room without a decent home-cooked meal. And without a friendly face."

Marjorie bit her lip. Should she tell the girl about Vanessa even though it might break the girl's heart? Or should she let Creighton do the talking when, and if, he finally returned home? She sighed. As unpleasant as the task might be, she couldn't, in good conscience, string Sharon along, only for her to be blindsided later. "Um . . . Creighton isn't in a hotel. He's staying with a friend."

"Oh good," Miss Schutt sighed in relief.

"A female friend," Marjorie amended.

"Oh," she replied, crestfallen. "Have you met her? What is she like?"

Under different circumstances, Marjorie might have built up Vanessa's image and enjoyed Sharon's devastated reaction, but Creighton's fascination with the widow Randolph was a subject too close to Marjorie's heart. "Her name is Vanessa Randolph. She's a widow and an old friend of the Ashcroft family."

"Old?" Sharon asked hopefully.

"Old, in that she's been Creighton's friend for a long time. There's only a few years difference in their ages, but they've known each other since they were children."

"Is she pretty?" she catechized.

Marjorie remembered the delicate features of Vanessa's face, the softness of her wavy brown hair. "She was once, I'm sure."

"Not anymore?"

"Mrs. Randolph isn't a well woman. Illness has taken its toll." Marjorie stared into space. "Not that anyone would notice, since she possesses a lot of vitality. Moreover, what she lacks in physical beauty she makes up for with her engaging personality. She's generous, witty, and altogether quite charming — the type of woman any man would find attractive."

Sharon sighed, and Marjorie awakened from her fugue state to see that tears had returned to the girl's eyes. "Not that Creighton necessarily would," Marjorie quickly amended for Sharon's benefit. "In fact, I'm sure Vanessa isn't his type. He likes the kind of girl who's a homebody."

"Like me!" Sharon dried her tears and fairly beamed. "Do you think you could give me the address of where he's staying?"

"I don't know how long he'll be there, but I'll see what I can do."

"Here," the Schutt girl thrust the hankie into Marjorie's hand excitedly and then took off down the street.

Marjorie clutched the lavender cloth between her thumb and index finger and held it as far away from her body as possible. "Where are you going?"

"Home to write a letter," she shouted over her shoulder. "And since Creighton's on a secret mission, maybe I'll even put it in code!"

Marjorie turned her sights from the retreating figure of Sharon Schutt to the damp handkerchief she had left behind. "Not even so much as a 'thank you'," she noted aloud, while pulling a face. "Typical."

Not fancying the notion of toting the Schutt girl's nasal emissions all the way home, Marjorie crossed the road to the green and deposited the handkerchief in a public trashcan. She then resumed the process of reading, all the while, Sharon's words echoing in her brain: *Maybe I'll even put it in code . . .*

A thought leapt into her head. *Code.* Could it be? Feverishly, she leafed through the pages of the oft-handled book until she found the item for which she had been searching.

"That's it!" she exclaimed aloud, much to the amusement and curiosity of passersby. She glanced at her watch. Five o'clock. Robert wouldn't be off duty until six thirty. "I have to get there somehow!"

No sooner had the words departed her tongue than she saw Freddie, the drug store clerk, riding his bicycle in her direction. She ran into the street and began waving her arms furiously to gain his attention. The boy looked right at her, his mouth in the shape of a tiny 'O'. Suddenly, he braked and turned his bike in the opposite direction.

"Freddie!" she screamed. "I know you saw me. Come back here!"

The soda jerk, realizing the futility of an escape attempt, braked again and pedaled back toward Marjorie, coming to a halt a few inches away from her. "What do ya want now?"

"I need to borrow your bicycle," she stated breathlessly.

The boy scratched his head. "Huh?"

"I need to borrow your bicycle," she repeated. "I have to see Detective Jameson. It's important police business."

"I don't care if you need to see J. Edgar Hoover himself! My pop spent a lot of money on this here bike, and if he finds out I let someone else ride it, he'll be fit to be tied."

"Fine," she stated as she climbed onto the handlebars. "Then you do the steering and the pedaling and I'll just sit up here."

"Aw, but Miss McClelland," he whined, "I promised my mom I'd go straight home from the drugstore. She's gonna blow her top if I'm not home soon."

"I'll have Detective Jameson write you a note."

"Fat lot of good that'll do. She's still sore at me for sneaking outta the house the other morning."

"What if I make it worth your while?" Marjorie offered.

Freddie's curiosity was piqued. "Yeah? How much?"

"Fifty cents" she proposed.

The boy shook his head. "Nope. Fifty cents ain't worth getting into trouble twice in one week. Not with my Mom's temper." He narrowed his eyes. "But four dollars . . ."

"Four dollars!" Marjorie shrieked. "I'm asking you to take me to the police station, not Medicine Hat!"

"Three dollars," Freddie suggested.

She pondered it for a moment. "Two," she haggled.

"Okay, two. But in cash."

"Yes, yes, in cash."

"In advance," he stipulated.

"In advance!"

The boy nodded, and she reluctantly pulled two dollars out of her purse. "You know this is extortion, Freddie," she said as she handed him the money.

"Oh, yeah?" he grinned. "Call the cops."

TWENTY-THREE

Jameson and Noonan were exiting the police station as Marjorie approached, riding on the handlebars of Freddie's bicycle. "Looks like your girlfriend's paying a visit," Noonan observed.

Freddie stopped the bike in front of them and Marjorie leapt from her perch. "I've done it! I've cracked the code!"

"You did, huh?" Jameson was skeptical. "And, uh, just how did you do that?"

"With this." Marjorie held up the book.

"The Bible?" Noonan asked incredulously. "What'd you do? Pray for the solution?"

"No, smarty pants. I was reading this Bible Reverend Price gave me, when suddenly it occurred to me: Matt isn't a person!" She grabbed Jameson by the shoulders. "He's an apostle!"

"An apostle?" Jameson asked.

"Look," Freddie spoke up, "apostles or no apostles, all I know about the Bible is that my mother uses it across my backside when I'm late. Can I go home now?"

"Yes, yes," Marjorie answered distractedly. "Go on home."

"She's all yours," the boy gave a nod of the head to Jameson before pedaling back up the road.

"Where was I?" Marjorie strived to regain her train of thought. "Oh, yes. Matt! Reverend Price gave me this Bible to . . . er, well, to look over . . . and it dawned on me that Matt — the Matt we were looking for — wasn't a person, but a book in the Bible, named after the apostle, Matthew! I flipped through to the book of Matthew — you know the first Gospel in the New Testament — and there it was, plain as the nose on your face — 5:21! It's not a date, but a chapter and verse." She opened to a marked page and began to read. " 'You have heard it said to those of old, 'You shall not murder, and whoever murders will be in danger of the judgment.' "

Jameson took the book from her hands. "Let me see that."

Marjorie leaned over his shoulder as he read. "What's more, on the way over here, I counted the number of letters in that verse — at least the best I could count while riding on the handlebars of Freddie's bike."

She paused and said, aside, "By the way, I hope that boy never gets his driver's license. Do you know, I think he was actually trying to hit the holes in the road?"

"Imagine that," Noonan teased.

Marjorie stuck her tongue out at the officer.

Jameson intervened. "Yes, yes, as you were saying, you counted the letters and . . . ?"

"Oh, yes, I counted the letters in that passage and there are exactly 99 of them, which would explain why none of the digits on the coded note exceed that number."

"Coincidence," Noonan jeered.

"No, it isn't" she countered. "Think about it. The person who wrote that note would want it to be decoded easily by the recipient."

"Obviously," the officer replied impatiently.

"So," she continued, "the key to cracking the code would have to be something accessible to both the writer and the reader. Let's assume that the reader in this case is Alfred Nussbaum — a man who lives in a hotel. If you're the writer of the note, what's the one thing you can be certain he'd have access to?"

"The Bible," Jameson responded.

"Exactly. The Bible — a fixture in every

American hotel room from here to the Pacific Coast. Not that I've personally been in very many of them," she cleared her throat.

The detective handed the book to Noonan. "Give this to the fellas working on the code and see what they can do with it."

"It's a crackpot idea," Noonan argued.

"Yeah, but sometimes crackpot ideas work," Jameson pointed out. "It's been four days since we found that note, and we still haven't been able to decipher it. At this point, I'm willing to try anything. Besides that line about murder is a little creepy."

"A little creepy?" Marjorie challenged.

"Okay, okay, just get her to stop," Noonan crankily complied, as he took the book into the station house, grumbling. "We'll give it a try, but I doubt it will work. Screwy dame — giving everyone a bunch of harebrained ideas."

Marjorie waited until the officer was gone before she spoke. "Did you get any leads from Nussbaum's financial records?"

Jameson leaned back against the hood of the squad car. "Leads? No, but we did find some pretty strong motives for both Mrs. Nussbaums. Josie took out a hefty life insurance policy on her husband just a few days after their wedding. Get this — a policy with a double indemnity clause."

"But Josie wouldn't have been able to collect on that clause," Marjorie stated. "She's still married to Saporito and Alfred was still married to Bernice."

"I wouldn't be surprised if Josie and Saporito had fake divorce papers made up. As for Alfred's bigamy — no one knew about that at the time."

"Mmm, but even if this hadn't turned into a murder investigation, the cause of Alfred's death would have been ruled a heart attack — nothing accidental about that."

"True," Jameson capitulated, "but it's possible that Josie and Saporito had intended for Nussbaum's death to look like an accident and something went wrong with their plan. Or, maybe they chickened out and decided not to be greedy and stick with the original settlement of $5,000, just to avoid an investigation that could have revealed that the Nussbaums' marriage was never legal in the first place." He arched his eyebrows. "Either way, the insurance policy proves that Josie entered into her marriage with more than just love in her heart."

"So? She married a man she didn't love — you certainly can't arrest her for that. She's not the first girl to do it, and she definitely won't be the last." Marjorie paused to think of her present situation, and then resumed. "What did you find out about Bernice? Did she too, have a large insurance policy on Alfred?"

"No, but she shared a bank account with him — an account Alfred had been bleeding dry for several months. Whether he made the withdrawals in order to pay gambling debts, or to keep Josie in lipstick, who knows. Either way, Bernice was left in pretty dire financial straits — something that didn't sit well with her, I'm sure."

Marjorie shook her head and leaned beside the detective. "Shame on Alfred for doing that to the mother of his children, but shame on her for not opening an account in her own name. One that he couldn't touch."

"Not every woman has your presence of mind, honey," Jameson said admiringly.

She smiled sweetly, pleased that he should notice one of her finer attributes. "What about the bus companies? Anything there?"

"Hmph. Turns out witnesses recognized both Bernice *and* Natalie."

"Both of them? Together?"

Jameson shook his head. "No, they were traveling separately, on different buses. Natalie left Boston Friday night and stayed in Hartford. Bernice left early the next morning. But they were both headed to Ridgebury."

"And Bernice and Natalie, as well as Herbert, had access to the curare. It's seems like too much of a coincidence that they were all there at the same time. Do you think they all could have been in on it together?"

"I don't know anymore," he threw his hands in the air. "That family makes my head spin."

"What about our other suspects? Does anyone remember seeing them?"

"Nope. But that doesn't put any of them in the clear. Murphy has loads of guys on his payroll — we could be looking for anyone. Josie has costumes and wigs, so she could easily have altered her appearance. Ditto for Saporito — Josie slips a wig onto that fat head of his, sticks a different nose on his face, and voila! No one recognizes Saporito's photo and, therefore, no one can tell us if he was there at eleven forty-five in the morning or at ten forty-five."

"How frustrating," Marjorie commented. "And what about the 'Lady in White'?"

"That was a wash too. It's as if she materialized out of thin air and then disappeared back into it. But," he continued, "there again, Josie dons a wig, white suit, gloves, and hat and brings along a change of clothes. She kills 'Alfie,' sneaks into the rectory or some tent to change clothes, and bang! So begins the legend of the 'Lady in White.' "

"Mmm," she grunted in agreement. "Although that story could apply equally to any of the women in this case. Josie, having easy access to wigs and costumes, is naturally the first to fall under suspicion, but, in reality, both Bernice and Natalie could have had an old wool suit and a matching hat hiding somewhere in their closets. They're both tall and thin and neither of them would have needed a wig."

"But this woman was described as being anywhere from her late twenties to her early fifties. Natalie is only nineteen."

Marjorie sighed noisily at man's utter ignorance of anything female. "This woman was also wearing a heavy veil and, most likely heavy makeup. It's not very difficult to make nineteen look like thirty."

"No, I suppose not," Jameson capitulated. "Though you know more about these things than I do."

Marjorie again grunted in agreement. "So, it sounds as though your day was a washout."

"Not exactly. I did happen to unearth

some very interesting information regarding the Cullen brothers."

"Oh? I thought you said you hadn't gotten any leads."

"Yeah," he replied, "that wasn't completely true. While reviewing the bank statements, we found that four months ago, two checks had been deposited to Alfred's account within days of each other. One of those checks is from Alchemy, the other is from Cullen Chemicals."

"So, Alfred cashed a check from one company while he was working for the other. That doesn't mean anything. His last paycheck from Cullen Chemicals probably overlapped with his first paycheck from Alchemy."

Jameson shook his head. "The check from Cullen Chemicals was too big to be a paycheck. Not unless he was earning the equivalent of six salesmen's salaries."

"Maybe that check was to cover a few weeks' pay. The Cullens hadn't been doing too well financially, it's plausible that they might have been arrears in paying their employees' salaries."

"The check was for $7,000," Robert revealed. "If that was for back pay, then Alfred hadn't received a weekly wage in a number of years."

"$7,000! Did you mention this to the Cullen brothers?"

"No, Noonan and I were headed there when you showed up."

Marjorie stepped aside from the vehicle. "Oh. Well, if you want to go see them, don't let me stand in your way."

"I'm not. I'm waiting to see if your code idea works out. If that note points to the Cullens as the murderers, then I'll cut out the guessing games and get a warrant for their arrest. If it fingers someone else, then I'll have saved myself a trip."

She nodded and leaned back against the squad car again. "Did you hear from Creighton?" she asked nonchalantly.

"Yeah, as a matter of fact I did. He called me right after the funeral."

"What happened?"

"What didn't happen?" Robert rejoined. "I'll give you the abridged version: Bernice and Josie got into a wrestling match, pinning Logan against the floor and upsetting the funeral director. Kenneth and Charles Cullen interrogated Nussbaum's widows. Murphy and his gang did a test to make sure that the corpse was indeed a corpse. Natalie was feeling guilty about something terrible she had done. And Herbert proved himself to be a crack shot with a

313

peashooter."

Marjorie stared at him wild-eyed. "What does it all mean?"

"The long and the short of it — everyone is still a suspect."

She rolled her eyes. "Swell. Although if Herbert is, indeed, a crack shot with a peashooter, that could be the murder weapon you're looking for. We already found him making darts. What else do you need to put him away?"

Jameson shook his head slowly. "Trust me, the same thing popped into my head. But then Creighton stopped me. He said he didn't believe it was the peashooter, but something else. Said that people would remember a kid with a peashooter and that the real murder weapon was more likely something less apt to stir suspicion."

Marjorie knitted her eyebrows together. "How odd. Did he say anything else?"

"No. He was in a hurry. He asked me for Mrs. Hodgkin's phone number and then hung up."

"Mrs. Hodgkin? She's the one who witnessed that mysterious woman at the fair." Marjorie's brow furrowed. "Why did he want her number?"

"He said he wanted to buy something for Mrs. Patterson, but wasn't sure of her size.

Figured Mrs. Hodgkin might know since the two of them get together for tea."

"Why didn't he call me?" she asked, still doubtful. "I would have been able to help him."

Jameson shrugged. "I don't know. Probably thought you'd be too busy."

There came a shout from inside the station house. "Detective! Come here, we've got it!"

Robert and Marjorie hurried inside, where they found Noonan and three other men gathered around a desk. Noonan was scratching his head in bewilderment. "It worked. That damned Bible worked. I'll be damned!"

"Keep calling it a 'damned Bible' and I'm sure you will be," the young woman noted.

"You cracked it?" the detective asked his men.

"Yes, sir," one of the men replied. "We started substituting the numbers with the letters from that passage and everything fell into place. The numbers that were circled, however, didn't translate into words, so we left them in their numerical form."

"And?" Jameson prodded.

"And it looks like some sort of chemical formula." He handed the piece of paper to his superior.

"Formula? That's what they give babies!" Noonan exclaimed.

Marjorie peered over her fiancé's shoulder. "I wonder what it's a formula for."

"I wonder why they call that baby stuff formula in the first place," Noonan marveled.

"I wonder why someone would have sent it to Alfred Nussbaum," Robert chimed in.

A light clicked on within Marjorie's brain. "Maybe they didn't. Maybe we've been approaching this from the wrong angle."

"What do you mean?"

"I mean that we're assuming Nussbaum was the recipient of that document, when he might have been the author."

"Don't be ridiculous!" Noonan scoffed. "Why would Nussbaum put a chemical formula in code? And who would he have given it to?"

"Someone who might have paid him a sizable cash advance," she intimated. "We all agree that whomever coded that piece of paper used the Bible because it was readily available. That holds true whether Nussbaum was the recipient or the writer." She smiled. "You'd put a formula in code too if you had stolen it from your current employer and were about to sell it to your former employer for . . . oh, say somewhere in the ballpark of $7,000?"

Jameson exchanged glances with Marjorie and then jolted to life. "Noonan, you and the other fellas go round up the Cullen brothers and bring them back here. They have a lot of explaining to do."

Twenty-Four

"Goodbye, Mrs. Hodgkin and thanks." Supplied with the information he sought, Creighton returned the telephone receiver to the cradle and left the study in search of Vanessa. Knowing that the funeral had left his friend in a weakened state, he went to her bedroom door and, finding it shut, knocked gently upon it.

"Vanessa," he called softly. There was no reply.

He turned the knob and pushed the door open about an inch. "Vanessa." Again, there was no answer.

Creighton pushed the door all the way open, expecting to see Vanessa, sound asleep on the bed. When he stepped inside, however, he found that the bed was vacant. There was an indentation on one of the pillows and the plisse bedspread was wrinkled from where a body had rested, but the person who had created the impressions had gone.

The Englishman looked around the room and saw that the bathroom door was closed. He walked over and gave the door a rap.

Again, silence.

Concluding that his friend must be elsewhere in the house, Creighton headed back toward the door that led to the hall. On the way, he accidentally bumped the corner of Vanessa's nightstand, upsetting the table and its contents. Reacting quickly, he caught the porcelain bedside lamp before it crashed to the floor; however, the nightstand, its drawer, and everything that had been inside it, were strewn about the Persian rug.

After righting the table and reinserting the drawer, Creighton replaced the lamp and knelt to gather up the other items — a handkerchief, a photograph of Stewart, a paperback novel, and a tube of lipstick. He replaced the objects in the drawer and then scouted about the floor for anything he might have missed. Recalling that he had glimpsed something roll under the bed, he lifted the dust ruffle and peered beneath it.

In the shadows, he could discern a small cylinder that he presumed to be an atomizer of perfume. Reaching as far as he could beneath the bed, he retrieved the cylinder and brought it into daylight.

What he saw when he gazed down at the object he had reclaimed made his blood run cold. It was not an atomizer, but a hypodermic needle, and although it was empty, it was not difficult to guess what it might have once contained.

This was the 'wonder drug' over which Vanessa had raved — the elixir that had brought her new life. This was why she never once mentioned her mysterious medication by name. Why he had never witnessed her take a single pill or dose of syrup. Now everything was clear, and yet, he felt more confused than ever.

Dropping the syringe to the floor, Creighton sat down upon the edge of the bed, put his head in his hands, and silently started to weep.

TWENTY-FIVE

Noonan held the paper bearing the chemical formula before Charles Cullen's nose. "You know what this is?"

The man adjusted his pince-nez and scanned the document. "It looks like a formula for some type of synthetic rubber."

"Any idea what a formula for synthetic rubber was doing in Alfred Nussbaum's pocket?" Jameson asked from behind his desk.

Charles, seated across the desk from him, merely shrugged, but his brother, positioned in a chair beside him, twitched nervously.

"Care to tell us something?" the detective addressed Kenneth.

"Y-yes, I do."

"Ken!" Charles warned.

"No, Charlie. I'm through listening to you. You're the one who got us into this mess, now I'm going to get us out." He turned to Jameson, "If we tell you everything we know, will you go easy on us?"

"I can try to put in a good word. It depends on what you tell us."

"Fair enough," Kenneth deemed. "That formula was intended for us — we were going to buy it from Nussbaum. That's the sort of work he did for us, you see. We told him what we wanted, and he got it for us. We didn't ask him questions, and he didn't ask us any."

"So the salesman thing was just a front," Marjorie opined from her position atop a nearby desk.

"No, Miss McClelland," Kenneth corrected. "Mr. Nussbaum was a salesman, all right. Only he didn't sell chemicals, he sold secrets. That's why my brother hired him." He made a face of disgust at Charles. "It started out as simple reconnaissance work — finding out what our competitors were doing — but we soon realized that it wasn't enough just to know what new products our rivals were developing. If we wanted to stay alive in this industry, we had to develop the same products and release them before anyone else did. That's where we ran into difficulty. We didn't have the resources to sink into the area of research and development, so Charles devised a plan. We would pretend to lay Nussbaum off from his job, due to a slowdown in the company — in reality it wasn't too far from the truth. He would then secure a position with one of our competitors and steal the formula for one of their up-and-coming products."

"And you sent him to Alchemy Enterprises," Marjorie filled in the blank.

"That's right," Kenneth confirmed. "However the choice was purely accidental. We hadn't even thought of Alchemy until we read their advertisement in the *Boston Globe,* stating that they were seeking to hire a new salesman. It fell together perfectly."

"What did Nussbaum get out of the deal?" Jameson inquired.

Kenneth deferred to his brother.

"Originally $7,000 up front," Charles grudgingly confessed, "then $7,000 upon delivery of the formula."

"You said 'originally'. Did that arrangement change?"

"Yes, a few months ago, Nussbaum contacted me and increased the final payment to $10,000."

"Why?"

"It was right around the time of the fire over at Alchemy labs — the one that killed Stewart Randolph. The police were poking around everywhere, making sure foul play wasn't involved. As it turned out, the fire was an accident, but Nussbaum felt he deserved more money in return for all his trouble."

"How did you react?"

"We consented."

"You were willing to pay $17,000 for this formula?" Marjorie asked. "Why didn't you take that money and invest it in developing your own?"

"Because, even after $17,000 worth of research and development, it's still possible to wind up with a product that fails. Or, worse yet, you could work months on a product, only to be scooped by a competitor. This plan was foolproof — it would have earned us millions. Well worth the investment."

"So you weren't at all upset at this change in your agreement," Jameson prodded, "even though Nussbaum substantially increased the amount of the last payment."

Charles smiled. "That's business."

"You call it business, others might call it extortion," Marjorie opined.

The elder Cullen shrugged.

"In your, um, 'business agreement'," Jameson cleared his throat, "where were you and Nussbaum scheduled to swap the formula for the cash?"

"At the Ferris wheel of the Ridgebury

fair," the younger brother replied. "According to Nussbaum's instructions, first thing Saturday morning, we were to place the money under the cushion of the green car. At approximately eleven o'clock, Nussbaum would ride that car, reach under the seat, take the money, and replace it with the formula. Charlie and I would then ride the car and retrieve the formula."

"So you were the two businessmen our witnesses described," Marjorie presumed. "And you were Nussbaum's eleven o'clock appointment."

"Did you know Nussbaum had put the formula in code?" Jameson quizzed.

"Yes," Charles replied. "Since Alchemy had been crawling with police, and the swap was to take place in a public area, we felt it would be best to encrypt the formula, just in case it were to fall into the wrong hands . . . which it apparently did."

"Hmm . . . incredible foresight on your part, Mr. Cullen. Tell me, just how did the formula happen to fall into the, um, 'wrong hands'?"

"You know how," Kenneth interjected. "Nussbaum was murdered."

"Yes, quite."

Charles' mood darkened. "What are you driving at, Detective?"

"Just this: you and your brother had a very good reason to want Nussbaum dead."

"You mean the money he tried to bilk from us?" Charles chuckled. "I admire your initiative, Detective, but I'm afraid killing Nussbaum would have been a cross-purpose, what with him having the formula and all."

"Ah," Robert replied, "but there was a way to have it all, wasn't there? You could have waited until Nussbaum made the swap to kill him, claimed the money found on his corpse, and then later, when things died down, retrieved the formula from the cushion of the green car."

"It would explain why the two of you were so keen on finding out whether we found any cash on the body," Marjorie interjected.

"Yes," Charles admitted, "but that's not what happened — otherwise you wouldn't be holding that formula right now, would you?"

"A miscalculation on your part," Jameson alleged. "Nussbaum probably leaned down, perhaps to tie a shoelace, but you and your brother, being more than a bit eager to get him out of the way, assumed he had made the trade and popped him."

Kenneth jumped out of his chair. "That's not what happened!" he exclaimed.

"Shh! Sit down!" his brother ordered.

"No, Charlie! They think we did it. They think we killed Nussbaum."

"Pull yourself together, Ken," the bespectacled man beseeched. "Detective Jameson has no proof that we were involved in Nussbaum's murder. He's simply theorizing."

"That's close enough to an accusation for my liking." Kenneth appealed to Robert: "Look, Charlie and I thought about killing Nussbaum, but it didn't happen that way — not the way you said."

"Ken!" the elder Cullen shouted.

"Sorry, Charlie, but it's time we came clean . . . with everything."

"Go on," Jameson urged.

Kenneth Cullen sat back in his chair. "You're right, my brother and I had planned to kill Nussbaum — we even brought a gun with us. The idea was to wait until Nussbaum made the switch and then follow him as he left the fairgrounds. When we were far enough from the crowd, we would shoot him, take the cash and then go back to the Ferris wheel for the formula. It was a perfect plan, and it would have worked, too, only . . . only Nussbaum never got off the Ferris wheel. He boarded the green car as planned, and we watched as he bent down to switch the formula for the cash, but, all of a sudden, he sat up and slapped his neck, as though a bug had bitten him. He didn't make a move after that. We assumed it was because he had successfully made the trade. We didn't think anything was wrong until the woman operating the Ferris wheel started to scream and we saw Nussbaum lying on the ground. Needless to say, we got out of there as soon as we could."

Jameson bit his lip. "Pretty story."

"It's true," Kenneth insisted. "If it weren't, you wouldn't have that formula right now."

"And the cash?"

"Still under the cushion of the green car. We came back for it last night, but some man must have heard us. He came out of the church to investigate."

"So you clobbered him with a tire iron," Marjorie surmised.

"Not a tire iron, a crow bar," Kenneth admitted. "We brought it with us in case we needed to pry open a crate or a lock. I tried not to hit the fellow too hard — just enough to stun him. Is he okay?"

"A concussion and an ugly bump to the head," Jameson answered. "But you took a chance. The gentleman you attacked is getting on in years; a blow to the head might have been fatal."

"I didn't know he was an old man until

after I hit him," Kenneth offered as defense.

"That 'old man' is also a minister," Noonan countered. "A man of the cloth."

"Terrific," Charles muttered. "Now not only do the police have it in for us, but God does too."

"You'll have plenty of time to apologize to the man upstairs while you're in prison," Jameson quipped. "Lock 'em up, boys."

Two burly officers grabbed the brothers by the arms and handcuffed them.

"Wait!" Kenneth screamed. "You can't do this! What are you locking us up for?"

"Assault and fraud for starters."

"But you said if I told you everything, you'd go easy on us."

"No, I said I'd think about it."

"Nice going, Ken," Charles griped as the policemen led them toward the door to the holding area. "You talked us right into the gallows."

"He gave me his word!"

"Oh, shut up."

Marjorie and Jameson stood among the crates and trailers on the fairgrounds, watching as Noonan, kneeling upon the grass, felt beneath the cushion of the green compartment. The Ferris wheel had been dismantled and all the passenger cars now rested upon the ground.

"I feel something," the officer declared as he thrust his arm, up to the elbow, into the narrow recess between the upholstery and the metal bench, "but I can't reach it. It's pretty far back. It must have slid back there when they took this thing apart."

"Let me try," Marjorie offered.

Noonan extricated himself from the padding and moved aside to allow the young woman a chance at the parcel. Marjorie pushed her slender, bare arm through the tight opening with little difficulty and felt around until the cool hardness of the metal bench was replaced with the supple resilience of cloth. "I got it!" With a deft motion, she grabbed the fabric in her fist and gave it a firm tug. Marjorie's hand emerged in the fading daylight. Clutched in it was a burlap bag.

Jameson grabbed the sack and turned it upside down. Two thin stacks of tightly bound one hundred dollar bills tumbled out onto the ground.

"Why, look at that," Marjorie commented as she rose from the kneeling position. "Bank night!"

"Is that $10,000?" Jameson asked his officer.

"How should I know what $10,000 looks like?"

"Count it."

Noonan set about the task and carefully counted out one hundred, one-hundred-dollar bills. "Yep, that's it. Looks like the brothers' story checks out."

Jameson pulled a face. "Still doesn't mean they didn't kill Nussbaum. They could have miscalculated."

"I admit they're no criminal masterminds," Marjorie argued, "but to kill Nussbaum before he even exited the Ferris wheel? It's difficult to conceive of anyone making that big a blunder."

Jameson sighed. "Then it's back to square one."

A faint voice crackled from the police radio in Jameson's squad car. The detective ran to the vehicle to retrieve it. When he returned a few moments later, his mood had darkened and a frown had fixed itself across his face. "That was headquarters. Logan just telephoned."

"What's wrong?" Marjorie asked.

"It's Natalie Nussbaum. She's been poisoned."

TWENTY-SIX

Bernice Nussbaum was seated in the emergency room waiting area of Massachusetts General Hospital. Detective Logan stood a few yards away from her, scribbling notes in a small memo pad. Jameson gave the detective a firm pat on the back.

He looked up from his notebook. "Hey, Bob. Didn't expect to see you here so soon."

"I left as soon as I heard," Robert explained. "Mike, this is Officer Noonan, my partner with the Hartford County Police Department. Noonan, this is Detective Logan. And you remember Marjorie, of course." The threesome exchanged greetings. "So, what have we got?"

Logan filled them in on the details. "Family came home from the wake and found a box of chocolates on their doorstep. Girl ate a couple of the chocolates. Half an hour later, she was as sick as a dog. Her mother called for the doctor, thinking it was food poisoning. The doctor recognized the symptoms immediately and ordered an ambulance. He also requested that the chocolates be analyzed. Good thing he did, too — they were laced with arsenic."

"Arsenic!" Marjorie gasped. "How is she?"

"It was close, but she'll be okay. Doctor says she's resting comfortably."

"Did any of your men happen to see who delivered them?" Jameson asked.

"No," Logan replied. "They were busy watching the mother and the two kids at the wake. And I was busy babysitting Josie Saporito — or Nussbaum as she insists on being called." He placed a hand on his lower back and shook his head in disbelief. "I tell ya, Bob, that was the most work I've ever done at a funeral. Minute I got back to the station, I called my wife and asked her to pick up some liniment. Do you know, she didn't believe me? Said I must have been up to no good to throw my back out again! Can you imagine?"

Marjorie and Noonan snickered to each other, while Robert patted his friend on the back again. "I'm sorry, Mike," he started. "I'll be sure to put in a good word with your wife when this whole thing is over."

Logan winced in pain. "Yeah, thanks, Bob. I'd appreciate it."

The group approached Bernice. Logan, walking gingerly, lagged behind the rest of the foursome, but eventually caught up.

"I'm sorry to hear about your daughter, Mrs. Nussbaum," Jameson apologized.

"Thank you" she sniffed as she dabbed at her moist eyes with the corner of a handkerchief. "The doctor says it was arsenic. Can you believe it? Arsenic! He said it was in those chocolates. First Alfred and now this! I don't know how much more I can take."

"If there's anything we can do . . ."

"There is something you can do." Her voice became scolding. "You can stop pestering me and my son and arrest that 'Josie' person."

"She's already in jail, Mrs. Nussbaum. What else do you want me to charge her with?"

"Murder, attempted murder . . . God only knows what else! She killed Alfred and now she's poisoned my Natalie. Herbert and I would never have done this! I love my daughter and Herbert loves his sister. It's obvious Josie is the one behind this whole thing."

"What reason could Josie have for poisoning your daughter?"

"Do I need to draw you a picture? The woman hates me! Why, she and I had a fight

334

just this afternoon — only a few hours before Natalie ate the chocolates. Coincidence? Not very likely!"

"As much as I'd like to charge someone in this case, Mrs. Nussbaum, I can't do so without evidence. Now, these chocolates that Natalie ate — I understand they were delivered to your house while you were at the wake."

"That's right. We came home and they were on our doorstep."

"Did they arrive in the mail or were they hand delivered?"

"I don't know," she sniffed. "I told you we were out when they arrived."

"Yes, I know, but did you happen to notice if the box was postmarked?"

"No," Bernice replied, "no, I don't think it was. The box was wrapped in plain brown paper and addressed to Natalie, but I don't think there was a postmark."

"I don't suppose there was a return address," Noonan said hopefully.

Mrs. Nussbaum shook her head. "Just a note inside, saying that they were from a secret admirer."

"Your daughter wasn't suspicious?"

"Natalie's a smart girl, Detective, but she's just that — a girl. She didn't give a second thought about the chocolates. She was swept away with the romantic notion that she might have a secret beau." She slid her eyes toward Marjorie. "You know how it is at her age. Boys are the most important things in the world."

Marjorie nodded sympathetically.

"Silly really," Bernice went on. "Especially when you come to realize what men are really like."

"What about you, Mrs. Nussbaum?" Jameson continued. "Didn't you think there was something odd about a box of chocolates appearing on your doorstep?"

"I had my misgivings initially, but Natalie was so happy. It was the first time in four months that I had seen her smile . . ." She added defensively, "I never dreamed they might be poisoned. If I had . . ." Her voice trailed off as she brought the hankie to her mouth. "Really, Detective, when will you arrest that woman?"

"I told you, she's already in jail."

"When will you charge her with murder?"

"When I have enough evidence to prove that she killed your husband and poisoned Natalie."

"Evidence! What more evidence do you need? Who else would have poisoned Natalie?"

"I don't know, Mrs. Nussbaum, but considering she's been in jail for the past twenty-four hours, I can't imagine it was Josie. Now, can you think of anyone else who might have done it?"

A strange chill took Marjorie. She looked up to see Herbert Nussbaum lurking in the doorway of the waiting room. He yielded a self-satisfied grin before retreating to whence he had come.

"Someone who wanted her out of the way," Marjorie suggested as she watched the figure of Herbert disappear down the corridor. "Tell me, what did Natalie know about her father's murder?"

"Nothing," Bernice answered sharply. "She didn't know anything."

"This afternoon, at the funeral parlor, when speaking with Mr. Ashcroft," Jameson pursued, "Natalie expressed guilt for something she had done. What did she feel guilty about, Mrs. Nussbaum?"

"I don't know."

Marjorie knelt before the woman. "Please, Bernice. There's already been one attempt on your daughter's life. If you know something, tell us!"

The dark-haired woman cleared her throat as though she were about to speak and then shook her head violently. "I don't know anything, I tell you! I don't know anything!"

337

Marjorie rose to her feet. "Then we'll speak to Natalie directly."

"You can't! She's sick. She was poisoned."

"Doctor says she's well enough to speak," Logan interjected.

"I won't let you! She's my daughter!"

"She's over eighteen," Jameson pointed out. "We don't need your permission. Besides, you have some explaining to do yourself."

"Me? What do you mean?"

"I mean that you were in Ridgebury the day of your husband's murder."

"What! That's ridiculous! How did — ?"

"The ticket agent at the bus depot remembers selling a round-trip fare to Ridgebury to a woman fitting your description. She was nervous, fidgety, and she asked if the bus would get her to Ridgebury before eleven in the morning."

"You have no proof that was me!"

"All I have to do is show him a photo," Jameson averred. "Hmmm . . . I wonder who'll be more surprised: your daughter, when I tell her that her mother was in Ridgebury that day, or you, when you find out that your daughter was in Ridgebury that day as well? Or, perhaps you both already know . . ."

"I-I," Mrs. Nussbaum's already pale face

went completely white, but she soon regained her steely composure. "I don't think I wish to speak with you any further, Detective Jameson. Not without a lawyer present."

Twenty-Seven

Marjorie, Jameson, Logan, and Noonan left the emergency room waiting area only to run headlong into Herbert Nussbaum.

"Going to see my sister?" he smirked.

"Yeah, now beat it, kid," Noonan replied brusquely.

"Oh, I won't get in your way. But, you do realize she won't tell you anything."

"How can you be so certain?" Marjorie challenged.

"Because, as insipid as my sister can be at times, she's not a complete fool. She works at a dispensary. She knows just as well as I do that if someone meant to kill her with those chocolates, she'd be dead right now. However, the person added only enough arsenic to make her sick. Not enough to be lethal, but enough to scare her into keeping quiet." He set his jaw and nodded his head slowly, matter-of-factly. "Which she will be, if she's as smart as I think."

"Are you trying to tell us something, Herbert?" Jameson urged.

Herbert shrugged. "You're the detective. What could I possibly know that you wouldn't?"

"You were at the fair that day. Maybe you saw something."

"I went for the rides and the cotton candy. Why else would a boy my age go to a fair?"

"You think you're somethin' don't ya, kid?" Noonan raised a beefy hand in the air. "Well, I have some lessons for ya that you can't get in any book —"

Marjorie and Jameson quickly grabbed Noonan's arm. Marjorie knew well enough that they shouldn't even be speaking to Herbert while his mother wasn't present, let alone using physical intimidation.

"He's not worth it," Jameson told his assistant. "He's just a know-it-all punk kid."

Noonan lowered his arm reluctantly. "I'd still like to wipe the smirk off his face."

The Nussbaum boy clicked his tongue. "That's the problem with our society — everyone tries to solve their problems with violence." He gave a quick smile and then retreated into the waiting area where his mother awaited his return.

Beneath the thin hospital blanket, Natalie

341

Nussbaum's slender frame looked even slighter than Marjorie had remembered. Her thick, dark hair formed a mass of snarls against the crisp white pillowcase, and her eyes, which had shown a spark of rebellion during their last interview, were now dull and cloudy. She looked up as they entered the room.

"Hi, Natalie," Marjorie spoke gently. "How are you feeling?"

"Okay." The girl searched among the faces of the men who had accompanied Marjorie. "Where's Mr. Ashcroft?"

Marjorie frowned slightly; every woman who met him — young or old, fat or thin — was bowled over by Creighton's wit and charm. Why would he choose her when he could have almost any female he wanted? "He doesn't know what happened yet. I'll call him tonight, after our visit with you, and perhaps he'll see you tomorrow."

Natalie showed a trace of a smile. "I'd like that."

Jameson approached her bedside. "Miss Nussbaum, we need to ask you some questions."

"Yes," she sighed. "I figured you would."

"The chocolates. Do you have any idea who may have sent them?"

Natalie cast her eyes downward. "No. No idea."

"Do you know why someone would want to poison you?"

"No."

It was Jameson's turn to sigh. "I'm going to be perfectly blunt with you, Miss Nussbaum. I don't believe you. We know you were in Ridgebury the day your father was murdered."

Natalie looked up, tears welling in her eyes.

"You took a bus from Boston to Hartford late Friday evening, stayed overnight at a friend's house, and then took a bus from Hartford to Ridgebury Saturday morning. We also know that your brother and mother were in Ridgebury on Saturday as well."

"So?"

"So, what were you doing there?"

"I wanted to speak with my father."

"Why?"

She blinked back her tears. "Because I hadn't spoken with him in months. I wanted to apologize."

Noonan stepped in. "Apologize for what?"

"For being . . ." the floodgates broke open and Natalie began to sob. "For being so angry with him."

Noonan pulled a wrinkled handkerchief

from his jacket pocket. "Here, kid." He handed it to the girl, who accepted it and blew her nose softly.

Jameson jumped back in once she had regained her composure. "When was the last time you spoke to your father?"

"Months ago. I don't know the date."

"So why now?"

Natalie pulled a face. "Huh?"

"Why did you want to speak to him now? Now, after all this time?"

"I told you I wanted to apologize."

"To apologize? Or to warn him?"

"To apologize," she stated emphatically.

"I don't believe you. I think you knew your father was in danger. I think you knew that your mother and brother were going to Ridgebury. I think you went to Hartford Friday night to tell your father and chickened out."

Natalie shook her head. "No."

"The next morning you decided again to tell him, but he was on his way to the fair, so you followed him and thought you'd tell him there, but it was too late."

Her protest became louder. "No."

"That's why you felt guilty, wasn't it, Natalie? Because you didn't warn him."

Her answer grew louder still. "No."

"You saw who killed your father, didn't

344

you, Natalie? That's why someone sent you those chocolates, isn't it? Because you saw who did it."

Natalie sat upright in bed and screamed with all her might. "No! That's not true! I didn't see anyone! I couldn't have! I couldn't have . . ." With that statement she buried her face in Noonan's handkerchief, her body convulsed in sobs.

TWENTY-EIGHT

After being evicted from Natalie Nussbaum's room by an irate nurse, the foursome sat in the hospital coffee shop, discussing the evening's events. Marjorie hurried to a pay telephone booth to apprise Creighton of the evening's happenings.

To her surprise, the Englishman answered the phone on the first ring. "Hello?"

"Creighton, it's Marjorie."

"Hullo, Marjorie," Creighton replied softly. There was a strained quality to his voice, a certain sadness she couldn't quite pinpoint.

"Are you all right? You sound . . . tired."

"I am a bit tired. It's been a long day. What did you call about?"

"Oh, things are really picking up speed, Creighton! First, we cracked the code on that piece of paper in Nussbaum's pocket."

His voice suddenly became animated. "How on earth did you do that?"

"The Bible!" she exclaimed. "I was visiting Reverend Price this afternoon when I realized that Matt isn't a person, but an apostle. And that so-called date at the bottom? It was a chapter and verse. Oddly enough, the verse is about murderers being punished. Talk about irony. But, the Bible was the key to the whole puzzle. Go figure!"

He laughed. "I suppose attending Catholic school as a girl did have its advantages, didn't it?"

"Yes. I'll have to write to the nuns at St. Brigid's to say 'thank you.' Of course, I'll omit the fact that I write about murder and other foul goings-on . . ." She punctuated the sentence with a giggle.

"There are worse things you could do for a living," he replied softly. "So what was the document in Nussbaum's pocket?"

"That's even more interesting. You may want to tell Vanessa about this one, or maybe not — she's bound to be upset by it. It's a formula for simulated rubber. It appears that Nussbaum was still on the Cullen brothers' payroll when he went to work for Alchemy. Only problem is he wasn't just a salesman. He was a spy. The formula belonged to Alchemy Industries and Alfred was selling it to the Cullens for $17,000 — $7,000 up front and $10,000 upon receipt of the formula."

"W— what?"

"I know. It's hard to believe someone could actually steal from someone as good as Vanessa. Just as it's hard to believe that the Cullens were so desperate, but they claim they would have spent more in research and development than in paying Alfred Nussbaum. However, now we know who held the eleven o'clock appointment with Nussbaum. We have a confession, the money, the whole shebang!"

"They confessed to the murder?"

"Oh no, just to industrial espionage, and hitting Reverend Price —"

A woman's voice interrupted. "To continue the call, please deposit five cents."

Marjorie did as instructed.

"Five cents?" Creighton repeated. "Where in earth are you?"

"Oh, that's right! I didn't get up to that part yet. I'm at the hospital."

"Good God! Are you all right? What happened to you?"

"Oh no! I haven't been admitted. I'm peachy. I'm just visiting Natalie Nussbaum — she's been poisoned."

There was a long pause.

Marjorie pushed excitedly at the disconnect buttons. "Hello? Hello? Are you there?

Creighton?"

"I'm still here," the voice on the other end of the line replied.

"Did you hear what I said?"

"Yes, Natalie was poisoned. Is she all right?"

"She'll be fine, but we're convinced she knows who murdered her father. What other reason could someone have to poison her?"

"Did you question her?"

"Yes. She wouldn't talk. Robert confronted her about being at the fair that day, but she denied having seen anyone. She just kept on yelling that 'she couldn't have seen who did it.' She said it a few times before the nurse came in and asked us to leave. I don't know what to think, Creighton. Between Josie, Saporito, and the Cullen brothers, most of our suspects are in jail. All that's left are Bernice, Herbert, and Natalie herself." She laughed. "If we continue on this path, we'll have no suspects left! They'll all be incarcerated in the Boston prison system."

There was a loud click. Once again, Marjorie pushed at the disconnect buttons, but it was to no avail. "Hello? Hello? Creighton? Creighton . . . ?"

Marjorie stirred at her cup of coffee pensively, the phone conversation with Creighton Ashcroft still looming in her mind. Her thoughts slipped momentarily to the thin, dark-haired Natalie and she thought she might burst into tears. "You needn't have been so rough on her, Robert. The poor girl's been through enough."

"And she'll be through even more if she doesn't tell us what she knows," Jameson argued.

Logan chimed in. "Miss McClelland, she has to realize she's playing with a murderer. The chocolates were just a scare tactic, but next time she may not be so lucky."

"Yes, the chocolates . . ." Marjorie mused.

Jameson rolled his eyes. "Once again, I can't know what you're thinking, honey."

"Well, it doesn't seem to fit, does it? Our murderer kills Alfred Nussbaum in broad daylight at a church fair, yet flinches at killing Natalie — the only person who can identify this person as the killer." She shook her head. "Letting Natalie live seems awfully risky. Why not get her out of the way once and for all?"

"It's psychological," Logan answered matter-of-factly. "Put the fear of God into 'em and they'll keep quiet."

"But it could have had the opposite effect," Marjorie pointed out. "Natalie could have been scared into telling everything. That's a huge chance to take, especially when the punishment for two murders isn't much different than the punishment for one. Unless . . ."

"Unless . . ." Noonan, who had until this moment been completely absorbed in consuming a large slice of apple pie, pointed his fork at Marjorie, his eyes wide in excitement. "Unless, Natalie poisoned herself to throw us off the track!"

His three tablemates stared at him incredulously.

"Hey, she works at a dispensary," he reasoned. "And c'mon, it's not like it hasn't happened to us before."

"Not this time, Noonan," Jameson replied in a patronizing tone.

The officer shrugged and went back to his apple pie.

"It's pretty obvious that Natalie's covering for someone," Logan stated confidently. "That's why she reacted the way she did when Jameson asked if she had seen the murderer."

"Mike's right," Jameson agreed. "Why else would she say she 'couldn't have' seen the murderer? She'd just say she didn't and leave it at that."

Logan nodded. "She witnessed either her

mother or brother murdering her father and she doesn't want to believe it."

"Mother is more likely," Jameson averred. "I don't think she'd be quite as upset if it were Herbert."

"So you fellows believe Bernice is our murderer," Marjorie declared.

Jameson and Logan glanced at each other and nodded in agreement.

Noonan looked up from his apple pie. "Hmph? Oh yeah, yeah. It's the only way it makes sense."

"And what about the box of chocolates?" she challenged.

"What about the box of chocolates?" Jameson repeated.

"Why would Bernice poison her own daughter?"

"Same reason anyone else would: to keep her quiet," Logan explained. "What's more, Bernice would know that her daughter would fall for the secret admirer ploy."

It was Marjorie's turn to roll her eyes. "Yes, because Natalie is very unique for a girl her age in that she enjoys receiving presents from male suitors," she stated facetiously. "That's a ridiculous statement. Besides, why would Bernice need to scare Natalie into silence anyway? Natalie loves her mother. They may not get along very well, but I truly doubt that she would want her to go to jail, or worse, the gallows."

"Yeah, Natalie also loved her father. Remember?" Jameson pointed out. "Then something happened and she didn't speak with him for how long?"

"The 'something' to which you refer happening, was Josie Saporito," Marjorie rebutted. "Which just proves that Natalie is loyal to her mother. She didn't speak with him for —"

She stopped mid-sentence. *How long had it been since Natalie had spoken to her father? Natalie never did answer that question. Why not?*

"She didn't speak with him for — ?" the men asked in unison.

She looked up to find that all eyes were upon her.

"Nothing," she dismissed. "I was just about to say that Natalie and Bernice live under the same roof. If Bernice were the murderer and Natalie knew about it, why wouldn't Bernice confront her in private? Why make a big scene out of it by poisoning a box of chocolates? It doesn't make sense."

"What about Herbert?" Logan suggested.

"I have to admit the idea has crossed my mind several times. But, again, why the box

353

of chocolates? He's a clever boy. He could have scared his sister in other, less conspicuous, ways." She shook her head. "No, if the murderer were in that house, the chocolates would only serve to call attention to him. But, on the other hand, I can't imagine our other suspects sparing Natalie's life."

"Well, someone had to do it, honey." Jameson chuckled. "We have a dead body on our hands."

"I know. There has to be something — something we're missing. Some piece of the puzzle we've yet to stumble upon."

"I don't know. I think Bernice did it," Logan opined.

Marjorie, however, was still lost in thought. "There's so much guilt involved — too much almost."

"What do you mean?" Jameson probed.

"Well, first, that Bible passage Alfred used to encode the formula. All that talk about murderers facing judgment — it's quite ominous. And, if I'm not mistaken, Nussbaum was Jewish."

"So?" Logan challenged.

"So, I would have thought him more likely to use a passage from the Old Testament, rather than the New Testament, but that's just my opinion, of course." She took a sip of coffee and resumed speaking. "Then, there's Natalie. Something isn't right there. You're assuming she knew about the murder plot and tried to warn her father, correct?"

"That's the only explanation I could think of," Jameson replied.

"But Creighton described her as expressing guilt at the wake today; remorse for something she had done. If she had gone to Ridgebury to warn her father about an intended murder plot and then backed out, she couldn't describe the situation that way, could she?"

Robert was totally confounded. "Huh?"

"I mean that Natalie was discussing something she had *done* that she felt sorry about, not something she *hadn't done.* If she were talking about her failure to warn her father, she couldn't say that she felt guilt over some wrongdoing. She could say that she was experiencing 'regret,' but guilt, as she described it, implies action — some kind of action for which she feels remorse."

"I see what you mean," Jameson concurred. "Kind of . . ."

"I don't," Logan said.

"I don't either," Noonan chimed in. "I think you're nuts."

Marjorie held her aching head and wished with all her might that Creighton were there; he always understood what she was trying to say. She sighed noisily. "The short version: Natalie is the key. She knows something that almost got her killed — most likely the identity of the killer — and she knows this because she did something that, intentionally or not, set the murder in motion."

"Like kill her father!" Noonan exclaimed, pie crust crumbs shooting all over the table.

"Umm, no, Noonan, I don't think Natalie killed her father," Jameson stated as he leaned back in his seat in an effort to avoid the crumbs.

"All the same," Marjorie interjected, "I'd like to speak with her or Bernice again."

Jameson shook his head. "I doubt either of them will see us."

"Oh they will," Marjorie stated self-assuredly, as she gathered her purse and gloves. "I'll make sure they speak with us. Don't you worry."

Jameson smiled. "That's my girl!"

"Now I know you're all nuts! Including you, Bob!" Logan exclaimed. "Noonan thinks the girl poisoned herself. Your girlfriend is giving us an English lesson: 'guilt is something you feel about an action.' And you're going along with the whole thing!" He raised his arm and summoned the waitress for the check. "You're all a load of crackpots!"

Marjorie wrinkled her nose and stuck her tongue in the detective's direction, just as the waitress presented him with the check.

Logan read it with surprise. "Four dollars? What do you mean, it's four dollars! We ordered coffee and a piece of pie, not four turkey dinners!"

Something instantly clicked inside Marjorie's brain. "Four!" she said aloud. "Four months! Bernice said Natalie hadn't smiled in four months. Oh, we need to catch her before she leaves!"

Twenty-Nine

Marjorie rushed into the emergency room waiting area to find Mrs. Nussbaum seated in the same chair, with Herbert's head upon her knee.

"Herbert," Marjorie commanded, "we need to speak with your mother."

Herbert lifted his head in defiance. "Anything you need to say to Mother, you can say to me."

Marjorie stared the boy straight in the eye. "Herbert, I won't tell you again. Go away!"

Bernice Nussbaum, sensing the tone of Marjorie's voice, urged her son to leave. "Go, Herbert. Mommy will be all right."

Herbert rose to his feet and sulked out of the room, his eyes focused on the young writer the entire time.

When he had gone, Bernice spoke up. "What is this about, Miss McClelland? Is it your wont in life to frighten young boys away from their mothers?"

"As if I could possibly frighten him," Marjorie scoffed. "I'm here about your other child. Your daughter."

Bernice took a cigarette from her well-polished cigarette case. "Oh, Natalie," she said, as if the subject were an affliction rather than a human being. "I thought we had finished discussing her."

"Not quite. I still have some questions regarding your daughter's relationship with her father."

Bernice lit the cigarette and took a long drag before answering. "I already told you I was finished answering your questions."

"Yes. And I'm here to say that you aren't. Are you so jealous of your daughter that you'd rather she were dead?"

The older woman dropped the cigarette from her hand. "What do you mean?"

"You know exactly what I mean! Your daughter is in danger. You know she is!"

Bernice rose from her seat and crushed the smoldering cigarette with the point of her shoe. "Natalie's always been melodramatic. Nothing she says ever means anything! She just — she just . . ." The woman fell back into her chair.

"This isn't some ploy to get your attention, Mrs. Nussbaum. She didn't poison herself." Marjorie knelt down. "Natalie is in danger. Unless you can answer some questions, she will die. The killer will succeed."

The woman nodded. "Yes. I'll tell you. I'll tell you anything."

"When was the last time Natalie spoke with her father?"

Bernice shook her head. "Oh, I don't know, she might have spoken with him and not have told me . . ."

"No, I mean the last time that you know of. Think, Bernice. Think!"

"A while ago."

"When exactly?" Jameson inquired.

"Oh, four months ago. Right before Alfred ran off with that floozy of his." Bernice ran her fingers through her dark hair and stared off into the distance, as though watching the entire exchange. "Alfred came home one night — it was very late and he was quite shaken. I asked him what was wrong, but he wouldn't tell me — at that point, relations between the two of us had already gone downhill. I didn't press the issue any further; I knew he had a girlfriend so I assumed he had a fight with her, and I went to bed. Natalie must have heard her father come home, and she went downstairs to greet him. She often did that; she and Alfred were close . . . very close. I used to imagine that Alfred cared more for Natalie than he did for me," she punctuated the thought with a small laugh. "What they discussed that night, I don't know, but from that night on, Natalie's attitude toward her father changed. There was a distance, a reserve, and a general distrust on Natalie's part."

Marjorie took the woman's hands in her own. "Now think, Bernice. Was there anything else occurring at that time. Anything you can remember?"

Mrs. Nussbaum took Marjorie's hands in her own and squeezed with all her might. "I don't want anything to happen to Natalie. You do know that, don't you, Miss McClelland. It would kill me if . . ."

Marjorie nodded her head solemnly. "I know it would. That's why you need to remember."

Bernice nodded and took a deep breath. "Oh, I don't know, it was . . . it was right around the time of that big fire at Alchemy. The one where that man died. Yes, that's it. I remember I was reading about it in the paper when Natalie came down for breakfast the next morning. She was in a terrible state."

Marjorie's eyes grew wide.

Mrs. Nussbaum continued her tale. "I thought she'd get over it, but a few weeks later, Alfred left town and moved to Hartford with Josie. I was quite distraught, as you could imagine, but Natalie was devastated. She hated her father, she said. Hated him for what he had done. I tried to comfort her. I explained that her father's actions weren't directed toward her but toward me, but she would hear nothing of it. She went on this way for months, until finally, the day before the murder, her mood changed dramatically. She was happy, cheerful even. She went out shopping, or so she said. She came back later than usual without making a single purchase. I asked her where she had been — she answered that she had gone to see someone in the hopes of righting her father's wrongs. I asked her what she meant and she just smiled and went upstairs to her room. Later that night, she went out again . . . I've tried! Honestly, I have, but I haven't been able to get anything else from her." She looked at Marjorie again. "Girls that age, you know, are very secretive."

Marjorie smiled sympathetically.

Bernice continued her story. "When she didn't come home that Friday night, I went into her room and saw that she had jotted some things down on her desk blotter. There was a time, 11 a.m., a location, the Ridgebury Fair, and the name of a hotel — the Hideaway Hotel. I didn't know what to think! I wondered if she had run off to meet some boy — she's done it before, you know! Or worse, I wondered if they had run off together. I don't want Natalie falling for the first boy who tells her that she's pretty or buys her a cheap twenty-cent pink carnation. I don't want her to end up like I did."

She cleared her throat and blinked back the tears that had welled up in her dark eyes. "I dialed directory assistance and found out that the Hideaway Hotel was in Hartford. So, the next morning I bought a bus ticket to Ridgebury, with a stopover in Hartford. Between buses, I wandered over to the Hideaway Hotel and spotted Alfred in the parking lot, getting into a cab." Her eyes slid to Jameson. "That's how I knew where he lived, Detective, because I saw him. I was stunned, but I immediately realized that Natalie was not meeting a boy — that this was something entirely different. I hurried back and caught the bus to Ridgebury, but it arrived a few minutes behind schedule. When I got to the fair, it was already too late. Alfred was dead. I can't tell you how shocked I was, but I was even more shocked to see Natalie standing in the crowd. And she was just as shocked to see me."

Bernice fumbled for another cigarette and

lit it. "And that's how it's been since. Natalie and I were never as close as she and her father were? I suppose all this time that I thought she was the murderer, she was suspecting me of the same thing."

"And what about Herbert?" Jameson prompted. "You forget he was there too."

She shook her head. "That's my fault, I'm afraid. I was so upset that Natalie might have run off with another boy, that I went into one of my tirades. I told Herbert everything — including how I planned to drag her back home by her ears. My son has always been extremely curious. He can't bear to think of being left out of things, especially when it involves his sister getting into trouble. I thought he was at home — that's what he had told me — but after that cab driver came forward, he confessed that he had taken a direct bus to Ridgebury and arrived just about the time of his father's murder."

"Perfect timing," Logan remarked.

"He didn't do it!" Bernice insisted. "I know what you all think of my son. You think he's 'strange,' 'creepy,' 'weird.' But he's harmless. He's a bright boy — an inquisitive boy. He's always been fascinated by rather morbid things. But when his father left, he really threw himself into his hobby.

And now, since his father's death, he's been trying to catch the murderer."

Logan and Noonan chuckled.

"No, I mean it, gentlemen," she maintained. "Those darts? He's been working all week trying to figure out what the killer could have used to make them. You see, he's convinced that the killer used a cigarette holder to fire the darts."

Marjorie leapt to her feet. "A cigarette holder? Why?"

"Because he saw the killer do it."

"Aw, c'mon!" Logan cried.

"Son of a —" Noonan threw his hat on the floor.

"What!" Marjorie shouted.

"Saw the killer?" Jameson exclaimed. "Why didn't he say anything before?"

"I told him not to," Bernice explained. "And it's a good thing too — look what happened to Natalie. Natalie had suspected the same person, but she hadn't actually seen them do it. After Herbert confirmed what she suspected, suddenly poisoned chocolates appear on our doorstep. Coincidence? I don't think so! Besides, it's not like the description he'd have given you would have been very helpful. He couldn't say anything about the woman except that she was dressed head to toe in white and that she wore a hat with a veil that covered her face."

The foursome stood in numb silence.

"I am sorry." Bernice grasped Marjorie's hand tightly. "I know I should have had Herbert tell you, but I've been afraid. You won't tell Natalie and Herbert that I told you, will you? Herbert wanted to present his findings personally — he'd be devastated if he couldn't. And Natalie . . . well, I'd hate to lose her trust. I do love her, Miss McClelland. I really do."

Marjorie gazed into the older woman's eyes and nodded before pulling her hand away.

"We won't say a thing," Jameson assured. "Thank you, Mrs. Nussbaum."

"Yes, thank you, Bernice," Marjorie smiled at the older woman. "And don't worry, your children shouldn't be in danger much longer."

Mrs. Nussbaum wept openly. "Thank God. Thank God!"

Jameson made his leave as quickly as possible. Shaking the Boston officer's hand, he excused himself: "Mike, I'll be in touch."

Marjorie and Noonan took off after him.

"In touch? Hey, where ya all going?" Logan shouted after them.

The trio did not reply.

366

THIRTY

Robert pulled the police car slowly out of the hospital parking lot and onto the streets of Boston. Marjorie, seated in the passenger seat, was lost in thought. Noonan, however, hadn't stopped talking since they left the hospital.

"Son of a gun," the officer remarked from his place in the back seat. "Those Nussbaum kids, I tell ya. Herbert saw the murderer and said nothin'. And Natalie? Here I was feelin' sorry for the kid, and it sounds like she might have known about her old man's work as a spy. The thing I don't get is, if she did know about his job with Cullen Chemicals, where did she go that Friday? Not that night, but the afternoon — what would have made her that happy?"

"I guess she could have hired someone to kill her father," Noonan continued. "But that would have required an awful lot of money. An awful lot of money that Natalie didn't have. And then who would have poisoned the chocolates?"

"Natalie didn't hire a killer, Noonan. She wanted her father to pay for leaving her family, but I don't believe she wanted him dead. I think she went to see someone — someone who had an axe to grind with her father — and things got terribly out of control," Marjorie speculated.

"Murphy seems to be doing all right for himself," Jameson ventured. "And he wanted Nussbaum dead. He may even have been willing to do it for free."

Marjorie shook her head. "I wasn't thinking of Murphy. I was thinking of what Natalie said earlier."

"About what?"

" 'I couldn't have seen the murder. I couldn't have.' Think about it. Think of the words she used. She 'couldn't.' "

"Yeah, it's like Mike said —" Noonan began.

Marjorie turned around to face the officer. "No, Noonan. No it isn't. She didn't say she 'couldn't have seen the murderer' because she doesn't want to believe she did. She's saying it because she honestly can't believe she did. She can't believe she saw the murderer because the person she saw shouldn't have been there — couldn't have been there!"

Jameson spoke up. "But Herbert claims that the murderer is the 'Lady in White.' "

"Yes, and he's right. Think about it. Natalie and Bernice saw each other at the fair immediately following the murder. If either of them had been in disguise, they wouldn't have recognized each other. Josie is another possibility, but the fact that her bags were packed and she had already checked out of her room when Noonan picked her up, doesn't give her a very large window of opportunity . . ."

"You think Saporito was wearing a dress?" Noonan ventured.

Jameson rolled his eyes.

Marjorie continued. "Creighton insisted the peashooter wasn't the weapon. How did he know? And that phone call from Creighton to Mrs. Hodgkin, there was no reason for it. Calling me would have been quicker. Unless . . ."

"Oh no," Jameson jumped in. "You're not thinking — no, you can't mean you suspect Vanessa Randolph!"

"You have to admit, Alfred's spying on Alchemy gives her a pretty strong motive."

"There's no way she could have done it," Jameson argued. "You saw for yourself how sick she is. She can't even walk."

"Herbert and Natalie couldn't have seen her," Noonan exclaimed.

"Yes . . ." Marjorie bit her lip in silent thought and smiled. "Exactly."

Jameson sighed noisily and then sent the police car barreling toward the neighborhood of Beacon Hill. "You're right. I don't believe she did it, but it might be worth our while to pay her another visit and find out if she knew about Nussbaum's double dealings." He asked excitedly, "Do you think that's where Natalie went that day? Do you think she told Vanessa what Alfred had been doing?"

Marjorie stared blankly into space.

"Marjorie? Have you been listening?"

Indeed, Marjorie had been listening, but she had also been ruminating over a certain fact in Bernice's story — something that made her wonder . . . Suddenly, she recalled the Bible passage that had helped them to decode the note: "You have heard it said to those of old, 'You shall not murder, and whoever murders will be in danger of the judgment'."

"I think," Marjorie averred, her green eyes flashing, "that the heart of this case has nothing to do with stolen formulas, jealous children, or secret lives. This is a case of murder for revenge. The only question left is . . . how?"

THIRTY-ONE

Creighton rushed into the dining room, where Martha, the young kitchen maid, was in the process of serving dinner.

"You're right on time," Vanessa announced from her place at the head of the table. "I had the cook prepare your favorite: fresh Dover sole." She noted her guest's sulky demeanor. "Creighton, what's wrong?"

Without a word, he stepped forward and placed the hypodermic needle on Vanessa's plate. The kitchen maid hastened from the room.

"Where did you get that?" Vanessa demanded.

"That's unimportant. What are you doing with it?"

"Why, it's for my medication. I told you the doctor prescribed something for my condition."

"What's the name of your medication?"

She grew flustered. "I can't remember. All

372

those medical names sound alike to me."

"No more lies, Vanessa!" Creighton roared, causing his friend to wince. "What is it? Morphine? Opium?"

"Heroin," she answered softly. "I don't expect you to understand, Creighton. That's why I tried to hide it from you . . ."

"You're right, I don't understand. I don't understand how my best friend could have succumbed to this poison. What were you thinking?"

"I wasn't thinking! I couldn't think. I couldn't eat. I couldn't sleep. That's how bad the pain was. Do you know what it's like, Creighton? Do you know what it's like to see your body deteriorate with each passing day? To feel your life slipping away from you?"

"Surely the doctors —" he began.

"Ha! The doctors? I saw every physician from Switzerland to the Mayo clinic. Each one said the same thing: multiple sclerosis — no cure. I bathed in hot springs, drank herbal potions, allowed myself to be covered with bees, all to no avail."

"Until the heroin," Creighton posed.

Vanessa nodded. "It doesn't stop the disease, of course — nothing will — but with it, there's no more pain, no more limitations. It sets me free," she explained, "all the while making me its prisoner."

"So is this the ghost you spoke about? The one that keeps you chained to the past?"

"Yes. And Stewart of course."

"Is that all? Or are there other ghosts that haunt you?"

Vanessa's blue eyes looked a question. "What do you mean?"

"I spoke with Detective Jameson this afternoon and it would appear that Alfred Nussbaum was still on the Cullen brothers' payroll when he started working at Alchemy. Actually, he was more than simply on the payroll. Cullen Chemicals cut him a check for $7,000."

"So? I don't know what arrangement the Cullen brothers had with Alfred Nussbaum. And frankly, I don't care."

"No? That's strange considering the check was cut just a week before Stewart died."

"What in heaven's name are you suggesting, Creighton?"

"I'm suggesting that $7,000 is a large sum to pay to an ordinary salesman."

Vanessa nodded. "Yes. Yes, it is. It's little wonder Cullen Chemicals had to close its doors."

"Is that all you think it was? Mismanagement? Poor business sense?"

"Well, what other explanation?"

"Oh, I don't know," Creighton rubbed his chin in an exaggerated gesture of deep thought. "Industrial espionage perhaps?"

"Industrial —" Vanessa started. "Don't be ridiculous!"

"I'm not. That was Marjorie on the phone earlier. The Cullen brothers gave a full confession."

"Confession! What — what are you talking about?"

"I'm talking about you having a very good motive for killing Alfred Nussbaum."

Vanessa stared incredulously at her guest and then began to laugh, quietly at first, and then louder. "Please, Creighton! Do you really think I'd kill some salesman for smuggling out Alchemy secrets?"

"No, you wouldn't. However, you would kill him for having murdered your husband."

The laughter ceased and the lines on Vanessa's face seemed to instantly deepen.

Creighton continued. "After I found the syringe, I went to the library to refresh my memory regarding the Alchemy fire. It wasn't too difficult, since all the major newspapers from here to as far north as Maine covered the story. All of them reported the same facts and the same final verdict: death by asphyxiation due to an accidental fire in the laboratory. But they also reported something else: the shock of those closest to Stewart, their inability to believe that a man as cautious as Stewart could be so careless and their inability to believe that a man as strong and resourceful as Stewart wouldn't have made an attempt to escape the blaze."

The Englishman shrugged. "But, despite their disbelief, the verdict remained — accidental death. Looking back now, I can't help but wonder if that verdict wasn't a bit too simplistic. However, the police didn't know about Alfred Nussbaum yet, did they? I got to thinking: What if he had been present in the laboratory that evening? What if Stewart found him, they struggled, and that's how the ashtray got knocked over?"

"The police didn't find any trace of a struggle," Vanessa pointed out.

"No, they didn't. And that would have been an accidental death as well. No reason for you to kill Alfred Nussbaum over that."

"Creighton," she scoffed. "You can't be serious! You know I didn't kill Alfred Nussbaum. Not only didn't I have a motive, but how could I have done it?"

Creighton wandered to the opposite end of the table and placed his hands upon the back of the chair. "The lady in white," he stated firmly.

"The lady in white?"

"Mm. Mrs. Hodgkin, a lovely elderly widow in Ridgebury, reported seeing a mysterious woman at the fair around the same time that Alfred Nussbaum was killed. The woman, a smoker by the way, was dressed in a long-sleeved white suit — hence the nickname — a wide-brimmed hat with a veil, and a pair of kidskin gloves. An elaborate costume for a church fair, particularly since the temperature that day rose to over 80 degrees."

"It would seem that she was trying to disguise herself," she offered.

"Yes, it would."

"And what does this woman have to do with me?"

"The lady in white is you."

"Creighton, don't be daft," Vanessa chortled. "You're really beginning to frighten me! Why, you know I can hardly get out of this chair, let alone traipse about a carnival!"

"Ah, but I think you can walk. The other night you made a slip of the tongue. You said that you 'marched straight into your doctor's office.' I grant that perhaps you can't walk for long distances, but I think that you're ambulatory enough to get around a fairground."

"Creighton, you're being ridiculous," she chided, her voice growing more shrill by the second. "What about the smoking? You said this woman smoked, and I, as you know, do not."

"Yes, I was just about to get to that. A poisoned dart killed Alfred Nussbaum, but the police have no idea as to how that dart made it into Nussbaum's neck. While I was talking to Natalie outside the funeral home, Herbert Nussbaum appeared on the scene with a peashooter. The combination of Natalie's cigarette and Herbert's toy blowgun got me thinking. When I came home, I called Mrs. Hodgkin and she confirmed what I had suspected. Namely, that even though this woman held a cigarette in her hand, she never actually smoked it. In fact, the cigarette wasn't even lit, but placed rather decoratively, in a cigarette holder." Creighton mused aloud, "An interesting thing, a cigarette holder. The hollow opening enables the user to draw in smoke, but if one were to exhale rather than inhale, the concentrated force of the air flowing through this tube could propel a small object, like, say a dart for instance, for several yards." He glared at Vanessa. "As I recall, you were a crack shot as a girl —

such a crack shot that neither the effects of disease nor opiates could cause you to miss a sitting target. And, I believe you possess a cigarette holder, don't you, dear?"

"Me and hundreds of other women."

"Yes, but hundreds of other women don't fit the profile of our mysterious woman in white. The hat and veil to mask a face which had been splashed across the newspapers." Creighton walked back to Vanessa and lifted her hand to his face. "The kidskin gloves to hide the gnarled, bony fingers." He rolled back the elbow-length sleeve of her dress. "The long sleeves to conceal the marks made by the hypodermic needle." He dropped her arm in disgust. "The motive to kill Alfred Nussbaum."

"What motive? All you've done is spew some wild theories about Stewart's death. You haven't proven anything!"

"I don't have to. Nussbaum's treachery gives you ample motive. There's not a court in the world that wouldn't convict you on it."

"If you're trying me for murder, Creighton, you'll have to come up with a better reason than that!" Vanessa's jaw set in indignation.

He stared her squarely in the eyes. "Then give me a reason."

The woman rose from her chair, slowly. "Revenge. Justice. Not for spying but for taking my life away. You've known me since we were children, and you're right. If I had killed Alfred Nussbaum, it would have been remuneration for an offense far worse than spying. Who cares if he stole company secrets? I have no emotional attachment to Alchemy Industries — I run the business because it was Stewart's business, and he loved it. And I . . . I loved Stewart. I loved him more than anything else on this earth, until Alfred Nussbaum took him away from me!" She walked slowly around the table, her eyes glazed over with grief.

"Weeks before he died, Stewart began to suspect that there was a leak somewhere in the company. Highly sensitive files kept disappearing from the lab only to reappear again a few days later in a place that had already been thoroughly searched. Likewise, on several occasions, Stewart would enter his office in the morning, only to find that the door was unlocked, after he was certain of locking it the night before. Guessing that the spy was working after hours, he decided to camp overnight at the Alchemy laboratory.

"He didn't need to wait very long, for around ten o'clock he caught Alfred Nussbaum picking the lock to the laboratory door. Stewart confronted the man and accused him of theft. Mr. Nussbaum assaulted Stewart and broke a heavy glass bottle over his head, thus rendering him unconscious. Realizing that he needed a more permanent answer to his problem, Mr. Nussbaum took the cigarette Stewart had been smoking from its spot in the ashtray, threw it into one of the beakers, and then left. The chemical solution inside the beaker ignited and the fire quickly spread throughout the laboratory." She turned and gazed at Creighton. "Stewart didn't have a chance to escape."

He stood, his mouth agape. "How do you know this? Stewart couldn't have told you, and Alfred Nussbaum wouldn't . . ."

"I learned it from Natalie Nussbaum. Her father had confided in her, in hopes that she would understand, but Natalie was quite disillusioned by her father's indiscretions, both business and domestic. She caught wind of her father's meeting with the Cullens to exchange the formula for the money — I don't know how, but she did — and she came here out of vengeance. 'My father must pay' she told me. And pay he did."

"With his life," Creighton presumed. "So

that explains Natalie's behavior today. She realized that by telling you about the fire, and the exchange, she had sealed her father's fate."

"She didn't know I was going to kill him. I didn't know myself at first. I told Natalie I would arrange for plainclothes police officers to be at the fair at eleven the next morning, to witness the exchange and give her father a chance to turn himself in. But jail didn't seem a harsh enough punishment — not for what he had done . . ."

"And the curare? Did you get that from the same source from which you get your heroin?"

"No, I got that from my ranch in Argentina. I spent a lot of time there when Stewart was alive and I was well. After Stewart's death, I bought some curare and kept it on hand in case I ever found the person responsible for his death. I remembered reading about South American natives using poisoned darts — from one of Marjorie's novels actually, but you'd best not tell her that — the poor dear will feel responsible.

"When I found out about Alfred Nussbaum I thought about how I would administer that curare. And then I realized 'a dart!' The dart allowed me to use Stewart's cigarette holder. It was an artistic touch, I thought. I put a call through to the caretakers of the ranch and they sent it along with some orchids for my bedroom. Quite simple," she stated matter-of-factly. "The next morning, I rented a car and drove to Nussbaum's address in Hartford, but he wasn't alone, so I followed him to the fair. The rest, as they say, is history, except . . . except Natalie was there. I don't know if she had a change of heart and wanted to warn her father or if she wanted to see the police put the cuffs on him, but whatever her intention, she watched him die instead."

"She knew you did it! That dirty look she gave at the funeral parlor — that was meant for you, not me. And that's why you were so eager to go outside and speak with her — you were afraid she'd spill the beans. You're lucky Herbert interrupted us when he did."

"Luck had nothing to do with it. I sent Herbert to look for you. The thing I didn't realize until then was that Herbert had actually seen the murderer and had mentioned it to his sister. Fortunately, Herbert didn't know enough about his father to put two and two together, but his description of the murderer would certainly confirm Natalie's suspicions about me." She shook her head.

"No, I couldn't allow her to speak with you."

"And to be sure she wouldn't try to contact me later, you sent her the poisoned chocolates," he filled in the blanks. "That's where you were this afternoon. Making a very special delivery."

"I had to do something," Vanessa replied.

Creighton's heart pounded so hard he thought it might leap out of his chest. "You . . . you . . ."

"Settle down, Creighton! I only put in enough poison to make her ill. What sort of monster do you think I am?"

"The kind capable of murder," he answered flippantly.

"Alfred Nussbaum was different. He was a traitor, a scoundrel, and a murderer. He got what he deserved. Natalie, on the other hand, is innocent. She's just a child. I could never bring myself to kill her. However, I'm not above frightening her into silence."

"Good lord!" Feeling dizzy, he sat down upon one of the side chairs. "I can't believe I'm hearing any of this."

"I'm sorry, Creighton. Did you hear from Marjorie or Jameson? How is Natalie? Is she okay?"

"What do you care?"

"I do care." She gazed at him beseechingly and made her way back to her spot at the head of the table. "I'm not an evil person, Creighton, despite the wicked things I've done. But now — now you know why I couldn't marry you . . . why I can't move on . . . why I'm trapped. But you, my dear, you can move on, and you shall."

She placed her hand on his, and once again, she was his old friend. "Go to her, Creighton. Go to Marjorie."

Creighton would not let himself be won that easily. "Why should I listen to you?"

"Because I, more than anyone, know what it's like to lose a love. Marjorie is to you what Stewart was to me — there will never be another. Go to her, Creighton, while you still have a chance."

"Hmph, a ghost of a chance."

"A ghost of a chance is still better than none! I, however, have taken all my chances — except for one." She was crying now, but despite the tears, her face seemed more serene than it ever had during the past few days. "I ask that you not notify the police of this matter. I'm already a prisoner to drugs, disease, and my own conscience. Is it necessary to make me a prisoner of the state as well? Besides, you know I'd rather die than leave this house and my memories of Stewart." She bowed her head. "I know I have no right to ask anything of you, not now. Nevertheless, this is my last chance."

Creighton rose from his seat and ran his fingers through his chestnut hair. He felt tired and old; his head, his knees, his whole body ached. He should never have come here. He was a fool — thinking he could recapture the past, chasing after some romantic boyhood dream. He had loved Vanessa as she was then, not as she was now. Years of disease had rotted her soul as well as her body. Yet, in those blue eyes, there remained a vestige of that indomitable spirit he so cherished. Everything had been taken from her — was he to take her dignity as well?

After a long pause, he turned to Vanessa. "Take it! Take your chance. I'll be gone in the morning and you'll never hear another word from me." With that, he stormed from the dining room.

THIRTY-TWO

Jameson's squad car approached Louisburg Square amid the blare of sirens and whistles.

"What the . . . ?" Noonan muttered.

On the other side of the park, flames licked the summer sky, illuminating the inky night with an eerie yellow glow. Jameson brought the car to a stop outside the square and the threesome proceeded on foot along a narrow path that bisected the park. It was the path where Marjorie and Creighton had argued just days before.

Marjorie hurried along the trail, her anxiety growing with each step until, finally, near the exit of the grounds, she saw what she had been dreading. It was the Randolph house, completely engulfed in flames.

Marjorie pushed her way through the crowd of onlookers until a large police officer in a dark blue uniform held out a restraining arm. "Stay back, Miss."

"But I —" she began to argue, before

Jameson came to her aid.

He flashed his badge. "Detective Jameson, Hartford County Police. The lady's with me."

Noonan showed his badge as well, and the officer ushered them inside the cordon. "Little out of your jurisdiction, isn't it?"

"I know the woman who lives here," Jameson explained. "What happened? Where is she?"

"Best ask the fire chief." He directed them to a short, heavyset man with a rubicund complexion, who was barking orders to men in full firefighting regalia.

Jameson approached and flashed his badge. "Detective Jameson. Hartford County Police. What happened?"

"Fire started after dinner," he reported with telegram-like brevity. "Neighbor saw the smoke and called it in. By then, it had spread through the house. Moving quickly. These old homes are tinderboxes. Have to move fast if we don't want it to spread to the others." Spotting a group of firefighters who had arrived on the scene, he shouted, "Hurry! Hurry, men! Get the larger hoses! Quickly! No time for lollygagging!"

"The woman who owns this house, where is she?" Jameson continued his inquiry.

The chief shook his head. "No one's seen

her. Best we can figure she's still inside. Invalid, isn't she?"

"Yes, yes she is," Marjorie replied hastily. "There was a man staying with her — a tall Englishman with light brown hair. Have you seen him?"

"Haven't seen anyone come out of the house. Not surprised. Between the heat and the smoke, a person would lose consciousness within a minute or two."

Lose consciousness . . . that meant Creighton was still inside! Marjorie felt her knees buckle. Jameson and Noonan grabbed her before she could collapse to the ground. "No!" she shrieked. "Creighton! No!"

A shot of adrenaline pulsed through her veins. She could not, would not, let him die! She rushed forward toward the burning structure, but the three men wrestled her back. "Creighton!" she screamed, breaking into tears.

Jameson put a comforting arm around her shoulders and pulled her closer to him. Marjorie buried her head in his chest, her body convulsing in loud, violent sobs. It wasn't possible! Creighton dead . . . and after she had learned that he loved her . . . after she had been so cruel to him. Had she known earlier, how different things would have been! He may never have come to

Boston, never have been with Vanessa tonight. If only . . .

She looked up at Robert and his sanguine countenance. How could he remain so calm when Creighton was trapped inside that burning house? She pushed him away and all the emotions that had been pent up inside of her came rushing forth in a torrent.

"You! You wanted Creighton to stay here with Vanessa . . . suggested that he keep an eye on things here. You hoped something like this would happen, didn't you? You were jealous of Creighton! You even forced him to resign as my editor! Well, now he's out of the way — permanently. Are you happy now? Are you happy?" Her voice cracked as rage gave way to another onslaught of tears.

Jameson watched mutely as Noonan placed a soothing hand on Marjorie's arm and passed her a blue plaid handkerchief. Just then, a young woman approached them. Marjorie recognized her as Vanessa Randolph's kitchen maid, Martha. "Oh, heavens! Mrs. Randolph! Is she hurt?"

"Don't know yet," the fire chief replied. "Think she's still in the house."

"Heavens, no! I shouldn't have gone out tonight! I shouldn't have left her — not in the state she was in!"

"What state was that?" Jameson asked.

"Oh, she was awfully depressed, sir. She and Mr. Ashcroft had a terrible fight during dinner."

"What was the fight about?"

The maid blushed crimson. "I'm sure I don't know, sir. I don't listen through doors, but there was an awful lot of yelling. Then it got kind of quiet-like, and Mr. Ashcroft stormed out of the room and said he was leaving in the morning. Only he didn't wait. He left a few minutes later."

Marjorie pricked up her ears. "He left? Then he isn't in the house!"

"That's right, ma'am. I went into the dining room to clear away the dishes. Mrs. Randolph was still at the table, but she told me to clean around her. While I was cleaning up, Mr. Ashcroft came back with his hat and his things and said he was leaving. Said he couldn't stand being in the house with her another minute, not after what she had done."

Marjorie and Jameson exchanged glances. "What did Mrs. Randolph say?" the detective queried.

"Nothing. She was awful upset, but she let him go. Then she told me to stop my cleaning and take the rest of the night off."

"Did she do that often?"

The servant shook her head. "No, but I guessed she wanted to be alone, so I didn't argue and went to the movies. That's where I just came back from."

"Young lady," the fire chief addressed, "before you left, did you ensure that you had shut the gas off in the oven?"

"Oh yes, I even triple checked."

"And the other appliances?"

"Yes. I always do before going out."

Someone shouted to the chief and the group turned to see two firefighters carrying a stretcher covered with a white cotton sheet — the remains of Vanessa Randolph.

Tears welled in the kitchen maid's eyes. "Oh, no!"

Marjorie patted the young woman comfortingly on the back, while blinking back her own tears. Vanessa's life, so full of sadness, had come to an equally tragic, and untimely end.

A third fireman approached the chief with an item in a clear cellophane bag. "Looks like that's your fire starter. We found it near the body along with what looks like a can of lighter fluid."

In the flickering light of the dwindling flames, they were able to distinguish the form of a cigarette holder, now blackened and distorted by the fire.

The maid gasped. "That belonged to the Missus," she identified the ownership of the object. "Means she did it to herself, then. That's why she sent me out. Oh, I shouldn't have left her! I should have known she might have done this! Poor Mrs. Randolph! She always said she should have burned along with her husband."

Swallowing her tears, Marjorie said, "She's gotten her wish."

With the fire at the Randolph home under control and the death of Vanessa Randolph deemed a suicide, Marjorie, Jameson, and Noonan made the journey back to Ridgebury without a single word to each other. Only after Noonan had been deposited at the station and Marjorie and Jameson were on the front stoop of Marjorie's cottage was the silence finally broken.

"I'm sorry, Robert," she apologized. "I'm sorry for all the things I said to you tonight."

Jameson flashed a weary smile. "That's all right. You were worried. I might have reacted the same way if a friend of mine was in danger."

Marjorie shook her head. "You and I both know that there's more to it than that."

"You were tired. It's been a long day . . ."

"No, Robert."

He sighed. "You're in love with him, aren't you?"

She nodded, her eyes moist with tears. "I never wanted to hurt you."

"When did you discover this?"

"Tonight. At the fire, when I thought Creighton was dead. It was as if a part of me had died, too. I couldn't imagine my life without him. Just like Mrs. Patterson had said . . . I couldn't imagine my life without him." She slid the engagement ring from her finger and placed it in Jameson's hand.

"No, you keep it, for now," he argued. "Think it over. You've been through a lot today —"

"I'm not going to change my mind." She took his hand and closed his fingers around the gold band with the diamond chip. "I know what I have to do, Robert. I know what I need. I know what you need, and it's not me."

"As they say, it's for the best," the smile on his face belied the hurt in his eyes.

"I think so. Eventually you'll see it too."

"If he —" he started. "If it doesn't work out, I'll be here."

She smiled. "It will work out. It has to. But thank you." She wrapped her arms around his neck and hugged him. "Thank you for being you."

"I hope Creighton knows how lucky he is." The detective embraced her tightly. "He was right about one thing — it's terrible losing you." He kissed her softly on the cheek and bid her adieu.

Marjorie watched as Robert walked away, and a gentle rain began to fall.

Thirty-Three

Detective Jameson entered Schutt's Book Nook on his lunch break, seeking a specific tome as well as a brief respite from the blazing summer sun.

Walter Schutt appeared from the back room. "What can I do for you?"

"I'm looking for a cookbook."

Schutt's beady eyes narrowed. "This for a case?"

Jameson smiled. "No, it's for me."

"Hmmph. Would have thought you'd have better things to do on a Tuesday afternoon — being paid with our tax money and all."

Robert recalled all the stories Marjorie had told him about Mr. Schutt and decided that an argument over money — particularly Schutt's perceived waste of money — was futile. "I do. It's my lunch break and I happened to be in town."

"Hmph. What did you say you were looking for again? A cookbook?"

"That's right. Since I'm going to be a bachelor a while longer, I figured I'd better work on my cooking skills."

"Why, that's ridiculous, son! Cooking is women's work. You have more important things to do. Business. Men's business. You need to find a nice girl to do all the cooking and cleaning for you."

"I had," Jameson frowned. "Marjorie and Mrs. Patterson used to cook dinner for me all the time."

Schutt waved his hand dismissively. "Marjorie! Not that one! Not with her flibbertigibbet ways."

"She sure is clever and exciting, though," Robert argued.

"Clever and exciting. Bah! You're a policeman, aren't you? A man's man. You need a wife whose idea of excitement is a good game of canasta. Someone who is content staying home, ironing your shirts and darning your socks. A homebody."

Jameson shrugged. "I guess I am used to that. My mother took care of the house, my father, and raised us kids."

"Of course. That's what a real woman does. That's what my Louise does. Has that house of ours in tip-top shape." A gleam entered his eye. "Say, why don't you come over for dinner tomorrow night? I'll show you that a man's home really can be his castle."

The detective was about to accept when he recalled that Sharon still resided with her parents. "No, thanks, I don't want to impose. Mrs. Schutt has her work cut out cooking for the three of you, she doesn't need another mouth to feed."

"Bah! Besides, Sharon has choir practice on Wednesdays. She'll be gone all evening, so you'll be keeping an old couple company."

Jameson pulled a face. He was none too keen on the Schutts, but if he had to dine at their home, it would be best to do so on an evening when Sharon wasn't present. "All right. What time?"

"Louise always serves supper at six. And she hates it when guests are late."

"I'll be there a few minutes early."

As Schutt nodded his approval, the shop door opened to admit the corpulent figure of Sharon Schutt. She was carrying a picnic basket and humming a melancholy and off-key rendition of "Ghost of a Chance."

"Sharon!" Schutt greeted.

"Hi, Daddy. I brought you lunch. I didn't want to, but Mother —" she spotted Jameson standing at the counter.

"You remember Detective Jameson, don't

you, Sharon?"

"Yes," Sharon blushed and tittered idiotically.

Jameson tipped his hat in her direction and smiled politely. Sharon cackled and snorted.

"The detective is having dinner with your mother and I tomorrow night. We'll save your dessert for when you get back from choir practice."

Sharon knitted her bushy eyebrows. "Choir practice? But tomorrow's Wednesday, Daddy. I have choir practice on Thursdays."

Schutt snapped his fingers together. "Oh, that's right! I forgot. It's horrible getting older. You forget everything," he explained, to Jameson, with a sly twinkle in his eye. "But you won't hold that against an old man, will you, Detective?"

Jameson watched as Sharon waltzed into the back room with her picnic basket, this time grinning from ear to ear and humming what sounded like "I'm in the Mood for Love." The detective swallowed hard and leveled a glance at Schutt. "No, I don't hold it against you. But I'm not certain about dinner. I have a lot of paperwork piling up."

Schutt ignored Jameson's attempt to extricate himself from the invitation. "It's so good to see her smiling again. She hasn't smiled since that Ashcroft fellow ran out on her. Dreadfully worried, Louise and I have been."

"I imagine you would be." The younger man cleared his throat. "Listen, about tomorrow night —"

"Oh yes, tomorrow night is just what Sharon needs. Her mother and I love her, but we're not young folks anymore. She needs to be around people her own age."

"Yes, she does. But I'm not sure —"

"Oh I know you're not sure about going out either. Broken hearts are terrible things, but you have to keep your chin up, son, and it will get better. You need to get out and meet new people."

"Yes, I do, but I —"

"Why, just look at Sharon, she's simply beaming about having you over tomorrow. She's been so disappointed lately. I don't think she can handle any more disappointment." He glanced at the detective. "Were you going to say something?"

Jameson sighed wearily. "Yes. What are we having for dinner?"

Thirty-Four

"Honestly, Marjorie! For a smart young woman, sometimes you don't have enough sense to come in out of the rain!"

Marjorie, once again seated at Mrs. Patterson's kitchen table, took umbrage at the elderly woman's remark. "Well, what do you suggest then?"

Emily Patterson placed her teacup back on its saucer. "You should contact Creighton, tell him you love him, and ask him to come back home."

Marjorie rolled her eyes. "You're forgetting something — I don't know where he is."

"Ask that butler of his. What's his name? Oh, yes, Arthur. Ask Arthur. Or Agnes, his cook. I'm sure they must have some idea of how to reach him."

Marjorie propped her head in her hand. "What if . . ." she started despondently. "What if he no longer loves me? What if I've driven him away? After all, I already did drive him to propose to Vanessa. What if he's proposed to someone else since he's been gone?"

"There's only one way to find out — ask him!" The elderly woman rose from her seat and began shooing Marjorie out of the kitchen. "Now stop your moping! Go talk to Arthur and Agnes and see if they know Creighton's whereabouts."

Marjorie, chased out of Mrs. Patterson's back door, trudged along Ridgebury Road until she reached the gates of Kensington House. Agnes, almost unrecognizable without her starched white apron, greeted her. "Miss McClelland, what a nice surprise. I was just heading out to market to get some ingredients for supper. Mr. Ashcroft called — he's coming home today."

"Oh? When today?" Marjorie strained to remain aloof.

"Late this afternoon. He's taking the train to Hartford. He'll be hungry I expect. The food they serve on trains is never very good. All packaged."

"Mm," she replied distractedly.

"I'm sorry, Miss. Was there something you wanted?"

"Hmm? Me? Oh no, I just came to do some research. There are a few books in Mr.

Ashcroft's library I'd like to take a look at."

"Well, help yourself. The front door's open and there's lemonade in the icebox." The cook took off down the road toward town.

Marjorie wandered up the long, tree-lined drive and to the front door. Stepping inside, she noticed how desolate the house seemed without the presence of its primary occupant. After a brief conversation with Arthur, she went into the library, grabbed a weighty tome from one of the shelves, plopped onto a brown leather sofa, and made a half-hearted endeavor at reading it.

It was hours later, in the midst of a summer thunderstorm, when she heard a car pull up outside and the familiar sound of Creighton's footsteps passing the threshold.

"Miss McClelland is waiting for you in the library," Arthur announced.

Marjorie gave her hair a quick combing with her fingers and stood facing the doorway.

"Marjorie!" Creighton greeted. He strode over and gave her a kiss on the cheek. "You must excuse Arthur. He's not yet accustomed to calling you Mrs. Jameson. I apologize for the error."

She gazed up at him with hopeful eyes. "No need. Arthur's right to call me Miss

McClelland. I didn't marry Robert."

"Oh, I thought in the three weeks I was gone, the two of you would have tied the knot. Decided to take your time?"

"No. We're not getting married."

Creighton's eyes grew big. "You're not? What happened? Finally push him over the edge with your antics?"

"No. I called off the engagement."

"Oh. Oh, that's too bad. Nice chap, Jameson." He leaned against a bookshelf and pulled a face. "Well, I guess you'll find someone else eventually."

She grinned. "Yes, eventually."

He didn't match her smile, but instead went into the hallway where he retrieved a small valise. "Here, let me show you what I brought back for Mrs. Patterson."

"Brought back from where?"

"Oh, here, there, everywhere," he replied vaguely as he opened the clasps of the suitcase and extracted a floral printed silk scarf.

"Lovely," she commented.

"Yes, I think she'll like it. I brought gifts for everyone. One of those automobile model kits for Freddie, a detective novel for Noonan, a chess set for Reverend Price, and for Jameson — a box of cigars to celebrate his recent nuptials."

"Poor Robert," Marjorie clicked her tongue. "I don't think he's going to be celebrating for a while."

"Because you — as the Americans say — jilted him?" he chuckled. "You never know. He may be rejoicing over his escape from the confines of matrimony."

Marjorie grimaced but did her best to keep her temper in check. "Did you bring anything for me?"

"A wedding gift — but I can't give you that now, can I?"

"Nothing else?"

"No. It would hardly be fitting for me to bring back gifts for another man's wife, now would it?"

"But I'm not another man's wife."

"Yes, but I didn't know that until now. Besides, I'm not sure you deserve a gift. First, you practically leave poor Jameson standing at the altar and now you're begging for gifts. I think I should have a discussion with Mrs. Patterson about your manners."

This last comment was too much for Marjorie to bear. She had expected Creighton to be relieved over the news of her broken engagement, to proclaim his long hidden feelings and embrace her with open arms. Instead, all he had done was cast his usual sarcastic remarks.

In tears, she sprinted out of the house and down the driveway, oblivious of the rain that pelted her face and body.

Before she reached the end of the drive she heard the sounds of footsteps on the gravel behind her. Someone grabbed her by her wrist, stopping her dead in her tracks. She whirled around and saw that it was Creighton, struggling to pull her beneath the shelter of the large, black umbrella that he carried.

"Come back in the house," he commanded. "It's pouring. You'll catch your death."

"Why should you care?" she spat back.

"Why? I'll show you why!" He grasped her around the waist and pressed his lips on hers.

Marjorie's anger quickly subsided. Robert had never kissed her like this! Had anyone ever kissed her like this? She slid her arms about his neck.

When he had finished, Creighton smiled. "Honestly, Marjorie. For a smart young woman, sometimes you don't have enough sense to come in out of the rain."

The young woman pulled away from him. "You've been talking to Mrs. Patterson!"

"She called me two weeks ago," he confirmed. "She got the number from Arthur."

"Then, you've known all along that I broke up with Robert!"

"All the time. From the beginning."

"Yet you strung me along!"

"Ah! Revenge is sweet."

"I'm sorry, Creighton," she said remorsefully. "I'm sorry for treating you the way I did — for hurting you. Do you think you could forgive me?"

"Already done." He kissed her again.

A thought occurred to her. "If you knew I had called off the wedding, why didn't you come back sooner?"

He sighed. "I needed some time to myself, to collect my thoughts. So much had happened . . ."

"Vanessa," she stated solemnly. "She's dead, you know."

He nodded. "I read about it. Suicide."

"Did you know when you left?"

Again, he nodded. "After I confronted her about Nussbaum, I thought she might kill herself. Even if I had stayed I wouldn't have been able to stop her. You understand why I didn't call the police, don't you? Her spirit was the only thing left that was free. I couldn't let that be imprisoned as well."

She hugged him. "I understand and I'm sorry, Creighton. I know you loved her."

"I cared for her, but I didn't love her. Not like I love you," he smiled.

"But, you were going to marry her," Marjorie countered.

"No, I wasn't. In hindsight, my proposal was only a way for me to avoid being alone. Vanessa realized that and turned it down. But I lied about it that day in the park. I wanted to hurt you, the way I was hurting when you announced you were engaged to Robert. I lied about all the other things too. It has been fun being with you. In fact the past few months have been the happiest in my life." His eyes twinkled. "Especially the gurney in Dr. Heller's lab. Perhaps we can relive that for old time's sake — only not in a morgue. I'll ask the good doctor if he has a gurney or two to spare. We'll bring it back here, climb underneath and . . ."

Marjorie put a finger to his lips and laughed.

"I missed you, Marjorie."

"You missed me so much that you stayed away for three weeks," she teased. "Traveling to . . . say, where did you go?"

"Oh, New York for a spell. Then Chicago, Miami, and finally New Orleans. I can happily report that they don't eat opossum or squirrel."

"Mm. Chicago, Miami, and New Orleans," she repeated. "Quite a colorful itinerary for a man supposedly pining for the woman he loves."

" 'I cried for madder music and for stronger wine,' " he declaimed, " 'But when the feast is finished and the lamps expire, then falls thy shadow, Cynara, the night is thine, and I am desolate and sick of an old passion, Yea, hungry for the lips of my desire: I have been faithful to thee, Cynara . . .' "

"In your fashion," Marjorie grinned. "Speaking of faithfulness, have you spoken to Sharon recently?"

Creighton brought a hand to his forehead. "Oh no! I knew I had forgotten something."

"You'd better talk to her and explain your feelings. I saw her in the dressmaker's shop the other day, looking at a bolt of white satin."

He blanched. "White satin?"

"She seems to have some definite plans for you."

"For me?"

Marjorie watched as his face went from white to red, and back to white again. She could no longer suppress her laughter.

"Oh, I see. Very funny."

"You're right," she laughed, "revenge is sweet. In truthfulness, I wouldn't worry about Sharon. She's found someone to replace you."

"You're kidding. Who?"

"Robert."

"Robert?" He tilted his head back and chuckled. "Poor guy. Talk about going from the frying pan into the fire!"

Marjorie took a step back and placed her hands on her hips. "What do you mean 'frying pan'?"

Creighton blushed, "Oh, that's — that's just a jazz term I picked up in New Orleans. It means you're so hot, you're sizzling."

"Nice save. I'll let it go this time," she said coolly, "but only because your explanation was so creative. Although, why I should be so nice to you is beyond me. After all, you brought a gift back for everyone but me."

"Mmm . . . I kind of lied about that, too. I did bring something back for you, but it is rather small." He reached into his jacket pocket, pulled out a small velvet box, and with one deft motion, popped it open, revealing a marquis-cut diamond ring.

Marjorie gasped.

"This is why I stopped in New York," Creighton explained. "I hope you like it. It's two carats, flawless, and the setting is platinum."

"Does this mean what I think it means?"

"It means 'Will you marry me?' "

"I — I don't know. It's so sudden. I've only just broken my engagement with Robert. What will people say?"

"Do you care?"

"Yes . . . I mean no . . . I don't know what I mean. I wasn't expecting this. I need some time to think it over."

"You can have all the time in the world, my darling," he closed the box with the ring still inside. "I'll be waiting."

Marjorie frowned. "Why are you putting the ring away? Can't I wear it while I'm deliberating?" she asked sheepishly.

"I don't know. What will people think?" He quipped while he took the ring out of the box and slipped it on her finger.

She held her hand out admiringly. "Then again, maybe I should take more time. Why, I don't even know your birthday."

"October 18, 1901."

"Or your middle name."

"Yes you do. It was on the card I gave you when I met you. Not that you gave it a second thought."

"Or your favorite color."

He gazed into her eyes. "Green. Emerald green."

She pressed her nose to his and smiled. "Or your childhood nickname."

"You know that too, you stinker. You

guessed it."

Marjorie burst out laughing. "Wart! That really was your name?"

"Yes, it was. I told you, you're too smart for your own good." He started laughing too. "Now that that's over with, and you know everything you could possibly want to know, would you care to join me for dinner?"

"I'd love to."

"Very well." The rain having ended, Creighton collapsed his umbrella and scooped Marjorie into his arms. "This way, Mrs. Ashcroft," he declared as he carried her off toward the house.

She slid an arm around his shoulders and giggled despite herself. "I accepted your proposal for dinner. I didn't say I accepted your proposal for marriage."

"No, but you will," Creighton answered confidently. "You will."

ABOUT THE AUTHOR

Amy Patricia Meade graduated cum laude from New York Institute of Technology, and currently works as a freelance technical writer. Amy lives with her husband, Steve, his daughter, Carrie, and their two cats, Scout and Boo. She enjoys travel, cooking, needlepoint, and entertaining friends and family, and is a member of Sisters in Crime. She has also written *Million Dollar Baby* and is currently working on *Shadow Waltz*.